DEE

"We're going to be its parents."

Ben spoke with authority, as if everything was already worked out. "Of course I'm going to be part of its life."

"Right. We'll need to work out the details of how that happens." Even if she and Ben were finished, Anna had no intention of keeping father and child apart.

He let her hand go and stood. "Anna, I don't think you get it. I'm not talking about some bargain where we split this child's time between us."

Not letting him intimidate her, she stood, too, and got in his face. "If you think for one second I'm going to let you take my child—"

"Calm down." He put his hands on her shoulders. "Your face is turning red. I'm not taking the child. You're not keeping the child. We're raising the child. Together. Anna, you're going to marry me."

The words hit her in the face like a slap. He wanted her to marry him. How completely and totally awful. She had only one response to his proposal.

"No way."

Dear Reader,

For any readers who read my October 2012 book *One Final Step,* you probably saw Anna and Ben's story coming. Actually when I thought of the stories for the characters associated with the Tyler Group, I always imagined doing Anna and Ben's story last. But I just couldn't wait to write their happily ever after.

I have always loved boss/secretary stories, and in some ways this fits that bill. What's different about Anna and Ben's story is that they have to make their relationship work after the ties of business are behind them.

They had the easy camaraderie between two people who knew how to get along inside the confines of the office. But now they have to see if they can take that working relationship and turn it into something more personal. I can promise you it isn't the easiest transition, but hopefully well worth the ride.

I always fall a little in love with my characters. In this case I've gotten to know Anna and Ben over two stories, which makes their journey and their happily ever after that much more satisfying for me. I hope you enjoy them, as well.

I love to hear from readers, so if you want to talk about the book you can reach me at www.stephaniedoyle.net.

Happy reading!

Stephanie Doyle

An Act of Persuasion

STEPHANIE DOYLE

HARLEQUIN® SUPER ROMANCE®

ISBN-13: 978-0-373-60762-4

AN ACT OF PERSUASION

Copyright © 2013 by Stephanie Doyle

Printed in U.S.A.

ABOUT THE AUTHOR

Stephanie Doyle, a dedicated romance reader, began to pen her own romantic adventures at age sixteen. She began submitting to Harlequin Books at age eighteen and by twenty-six her first book was published. Fifteen years later she still loves what she does, as each book is a new adventure. She lives in South Jersey with her cat, Lex, and her two kittens, who have taken over everything. When she isn't thinking about escaping to the beach, she's working on her next idea.

Books by Stephanie Doyle

HARLEQUIN SUPERROMANCE

1773—THE WAY BACK
1810—ONE FINAL STEP

SILHOUETTE ROMANTIC SUSPENSE

1554—SUSPECT LOVER
1650—THE DOCTOR'S DEADLY AFFAIR

SILHOUETTE BOMBSHELL

36—CALCULATED RISK
52—THE CONTESTANT
116—POSSESSED

Other titles by this author available in ebook format.

As promised, Christy, you're last but never least.

To a bright future!

CHAPTER ONE

Twelve weeks, 3 days ago

DEATH SUCKED. Ben Tyler leaned his head against his office chair and closed his eyes while he considered his fate. The leukemia was winning and it pissed him the hell off. As a man who had control over his thoughts and emotions—typically two difficult things to rein in—losing control over his body wasn't sitting particularly well with him.

He was angry, he was irritated and, worse...he was scared.

He'd spent four days and nights in a cave halfway up the side of a rock cliff in Afghanistan being ruthlessly hunted by Taliban forces.

Cakewalk compared to this.

Because there he had some control. He could hide his tracks, he could shoot his attackers, he could plan his silent escape. *He* controlled whether he lived or died, not some damn disease.

That's why he made this decision. His doctor agreed.

Anna wasn't going to like it. Of course, he had no intention of telling his executive assistant—the title she preferred to be called rather than a mere assistant—anything until it was too late.

Anna would get emotional. Anna would look up studies then quote medical research and statistics. Anna would call the people who worked for him and tell them to change his mind. But his mind was set. Since she was living in his house now, seeing to both his personal and professional needs, it would be hard to avoid her finding out. However, for a few days he could manage to keep this secret.

He was particularly good at keeping secrets. His CIA training and his ability to endure water boarding proof of that.

At this point, nothing would change his mind. He was done with this disease. Done with letting it control him. It was time for him to take charge. Once that happened, the fear went away.

The sliding wood door opened and a familiar redhead popped in. Anna's hair was always messy and moving about her face. He couldn't say why that bothered him but it did. Especially when she told him her hair stylist cut it that way with intent.

"Hey, you want to watch a movie or something tonight?"

"No."

He'd made a life or death decision. Something as silly as watching a movie didn't make the cut on the list of things he wanted to do right now.

Of course it wasn't her fault. She thought he was only gearing up for a second round of chemotherapy in the coming weeks. She didn't know that he was ready to bypass that step and go directly…to the end.

Cure it or die. That seemed much simpler to him.

The stem cell transplantation was his secret to hold on to. He knew it was a risk without a genetic match. Anna had already diligently searched for potential matches, finding no one closer than a second cousin who lived in Boston. And while Ben was listed in the donor-matching program, so far there had been no hits close enough.

Turns out his particular DNA was rather unique.

That's where the risk came in. Without a genetic match the threat of Graft-Versus-Host disease was very high. If contracted, the GVHD could kill him before the cancer had a chance to.

Only, science was always evolving and making new discoveries. An alternative to a match was to use stem cells from a newborn's umbilical cord. The theory was the host body was less likely to reject the new cells.

After a severe round of chemotherapy to kill all remaining leukemic cells, the stem cells would be injected to help stimulate new cell growth. If his body accepted the foreign cells, it could cure him of the leukemia.

If his body didn't, it could kill him.

"Okay, no movie. We know how you love the TV shows I like to watch so that's out. How about I read to you? You like that."

He did like it when she read to him. The last thing he felt like doing when he was nauseated was reading, and something about the sound of her voice soothed him. But he didn't feel sick now. Instead he felt edgy.

He rose and walked over to his fireplace. It was early spring and still mostly chilly in Philadelphia. Although it could be a hundred degrees outside and he doubted he would feel warm. His internal thermostat was always off now and he found himself constantly cold. Except when a flash of heat would come over his whole body leaving him drenched in sweat.

Seriously, how did women live with this for years?

"How about Nelson DeMille?" Anna was browsing the bookshelves that encompassed one full wall of his office. "You like him."

Ben watched as she bent to one of the lower shelves to search for the book she had in mind. The *M* row was second from the bottom toward the left. It wasn't like she was being intentionally provocative, he knew that, but it seemed as though her ass was just there dancing in front of his face. She was wearing a pair of yoga pants as she normally did around the house. Yoga was something she was forever trying to talk him into doing.

As if he had any desire to stand on his head.

She claimed it was relaxing and would be good for his mental state. She also believed staying physically active in any way he could while he went through treatment would be beneficial. Truthfully, he thought she was full of it and the only reason she cared for the activity at all was because it gave her the opportunity to wear pajamas all day and still call them active gear.

Whatever the hell that meant.

Even now he could see very clearly the demarcation line of her panties beneath the stretchy material. He had a sudden image of himself standing behind her and putting his hand on her ass and holding her hips while pulling the stretchy material down and away…

"…okay?"

He blinked. She'd said something and he hadn't heard it. Instead he'd been lost in a sexual fantasy involving Anna.

Anna. It was inconceivable. She worked for him. He paid her salary. He had strict rules about any romantic fraternization between employees, let alone employer and employee. To him she was the most off-limits woman on the planet.

Not that he was going to be so self-righteous or so self-deceiving to say he'd never once thought about her sexually in all the time she'd been working for him. Of course he had. He was a man and she was an attractive woman.

There was something wild about her. The way her hair moved and the way she laughed out loud. The way she practically folded her legs into her lap every time she sat on a couch. It was like she had no restraint. And so yes, from time to time, he'd thought about what she might be like in bed. Unrestrained entirely. Unrestrained except by him. On top of her. Inside her.

But his self-imposed mental discipline would never let him think about that for too long. Those thoughts were dangerous. Those thoughts, if allowed to linger, could make a man lose control, which Ben swore he would not let himself do.

This time, however, the thought of ruthlessly shutting down his fantasy the way he'd done all those times in the past didn't appeal to him. After all, he knew what the next week would bring. The chemo would be stronger, his symptoms more violent. He would feel like shit for weeks, and after that he could suffer an even more debilitating reaction if he contracted GVHD.

If the transplant didn't work, or the GVHD couldn't be controlled…there was only death.

Tonight, though, he was still alive.

Ben coughed into his fist to cover his lack of attention. "I'm sorry, what did you say?"

"I asked if you wanted me to read this book. Are you okay? You look a little funny."

"I'm fine." He walked to the couch and sat. He was wearing loose pajama pants and the flannel robe Anna had purchased for him during his first round of chemotherapy.

He hadn't had a robe since he was a child. He'd forgotten how comforting the garment could be.

And practical. When he got sick it was easier to lose the robe and vomit over the toilet without worrying about getting splatter on his T-shirt.

Now, however, the robe served as cover for his growing erection. God, he thought. How long had it been since he'd been hard. Really hard. Sex had never been a priority in his life. Nothing ever trumped his work. In his previous life working for the government, opportunities to get laid were few and far between, especially given his rule about not comingling with his coworkers. Most of the other women he knew then were his enemy.

After he left the agency his focus had been about establishing his business, finding a qualified staff and building a reputation as a troubleshooter/consultant of all trades. Finding time to date while he'd been getting the business up and running hadn't been possible. Then once he had it established and he'd tried to get himself back into the world of women, dating and sex he'd found it unsatisfying.

No one was exactly what he wanted. Meaningless sex with strangers for the sake of a few minutes of pleasure was not worth the trade-off in his mind. He had to deal with either the awkward next morning when he knew he had no plans to ever see the person again, or the game of trying to leave immediately after the sex was over without sending the woman into a fury…or, worse, tears.

Then he'd gotten sick and any thought of sex had been relegated to the furthest reaches of his mind.

Only now his death was a specter standing in front of him and the idea of doing something so completely life affirming had appeal. Doing it with someone so completely alive as Anna had even more appeal.

You could do it. You could have her.

He wasn't exactly sure where the certainty came from. But it made his dick swell even more. He watched her as she moved to the couch to sit next to him. Watched as she folded her legs across one another Indian style and opened the book to the first page. Watched her lick her lips before starting to read.

Ben tried to imagine how she might react to a sexual advance from him. If he tossed the book aside, tugged on her hand and brought it down on his lap, would she pull away? If he let her see his erection, let her know what he wanted from her, would she reciprocate?

He could see it so clearly. He would pull her onto his lap, he would cup her face in his hands and lower her mouth to his so he could finally, finally know what she tasted like.

"What?"

Again, he blinked. "Huh?"

Anna closed the book and carefully set it on the edge of the couch. She looked at him as if somehow she knew what he'd been thinking. Like she could read his wicked sexual thoughts. She licked her bottom lip again and he almost groaned against the near painful swelling of his penis. He adjusted the robe over his lap hoping it didn't draw her attention down there.

Or hoping it did.

"You're staring at me," she accused him.

"Don't be ridiculous. I was looking at you. You always exaggerate."

Her eyes dropped for a second to where his hand was trying to casually bunch the material in his lap.

She met his gaze and he knew he was caught. He thought about leaving, going to bed. They would ignore this awkward incident as if it never happened and she would continue to be nothing more than his assistant. As it should be, his rational brain tried to convey.

Instead he sat there and said nothing.

He watched her swallow and wondered why she hadn't gotten up and pretended to need something from the kitchen.

You know why. You've seen the way she looks at you.

It was an insidious thought. One he'd stifled for months as Anna extended her duties from being his employee to his primary caregiver. Or maybe she had been looking at him like that for years. He didn't want to think about that.

She unfolded her legs and he thought that was a

good thing. She would leave now and end this uncomfortable moment so he didn't have to. Because,
in truth, he didn't want to. Instead she shifted so
she was on her knees on the couch directly facing him.

"Ben."

He stared straight ahead. He couldn't answer
her. He was too conflicted. If he looked at her, he
might act on these impulses and he knew intellectually that doing so could only end in disaster.
There was no future in this. Hell, there was possibly no future in him.

"Look at me."

Typical of Anna. She made everything so damn
messy. Not at work. No, in that arena everything
was neat and efficient. But everywhere else around
her there was clutter. The way her hair swept
across her eyes. The way she was always smiling.
She made him feel...not like himself. He didn't
care for it.

He turned his head to look at her but still he
said nothing.

She was the one, the bold one, the courageous
one, to cup his face in her hand. She leaned over
him and pressed her lips against his.

On a sigh his mouth opened and he felt her
tongue slide inside and rub against his. It was such
an awful pleasure. His whole body lurched at the
unfamiliar contact and then his decision was made.

He would never say he allowed his body to dictate his actions. The idea that sexual need could overcome good sense was preposterous to him. What he was making right now was a rational choice.

In this moment, he needed what she was offering. Because the reality was this might be the last time he ever had a woman. In an odd way it seemed fitting that the woman would be Anna. Reaching behind her neck to hold her still he took control of the kiss, thrusting his tongue against hers and relishing in the feeling.

When she started to pull away he almost didn't let her. It was as though she was his very own oxygen mask, and he wanted to inhale her inside his body. But then she stepped off the couch and moved to stand between his legs. Legs he opened to make room for her there.

Brazenly she pulled off her T-shirt, then the tank top she wore in lieu of a bra. He was looking at her pert breasts with large brown nipples.

I always wondered what color they would be.

Pulling her forward he dipped his head so his mouth was even with one nipple. He teased it with his tongue before pulling it into his mouth to suck. At first he was gentle, but the feeling of Anna's hands on his shoulders squeezing his muscles urged him on until he was sucking on her with deep pulls. He released her to move to her other breast—such a divine thing that women had two to play with—but she pulled away again, this time to pull off the yoga pants and panties.

Slim but soft, with a smattering of freckles over her body, she looked like some dream he'd imagined once. His eyes were pulled to the small thatch of curls between her legs and he had this idea that she would taste like strawberries and cream.

Proudly naked in front of him, she sank to her knees between his legs. She pushed away the material of his robe he'd been unsuccessfully hiding his erection with. Then her hands went to work on the drawstring of his pajama bottoms. At one point her palm lay flat against his stomach and it was as though she warmed him all over with only her touch.

Knowing what she was about, he helped her by lifting his hips so she could pull the cotton pants out of her way. They slid off easily over his too-thin frame. It was one of the things he'd had to get used to during his illness. His body was changing before his eyes, getting leaner, thinner and weaker despite his efforts and wishes to the contrary.

Fortunately one part of his body hadn't lost anything to the disease. His cock sprang up looking much like he remembered it. The first touch of her hand on him had his body shifting on the couch. He wasn't sure about this. She was too close, too up-front. It would be better, he thought, if they were less intimate in this act. If she would turn around and maybe he could take her from behind, then he wouldn't have to acknowledge that he was actually doing this.

Screwing Anna.

But as difficult as she was to handle in all other areas of their life together, sexual intimacy wasn't any different. She simply acted without guidance or direction. First stroking him with her hand then taking him into her mouth where his body tightened out of sheer unadulterated pleasure.

"It feels so good. I feel so good. I haven't felt… I couldn't feel…"

The sucking continued. Deep and wet with her tongue teasing him in a way that made the top of his head want to explode. The word *explosion* brought the urge to do exactly that to mind, and he had to work to gain control of himself. It was time to end this, but he would end it his way.

"Anna, enough. I need…now."

She lifted her head and looked at him with a smile that said she knew him better than anyone else in the world. He wanted to refute that, but he knew he couldn't. Tugging her up from the floor she shifted to straddle him, her knees on either side of his hips.

She bent to kiss his neck, her hands rubbing along his chest. The sensation was nice, but he didn't want nice. He wanted to come. He wanted that mind-numbing pleasure that would make him forget that he was sick, that he wasn't getting better, and that the choices he made could end his life in a matter of weeks.

With one hand on her hip guiding her, the other wrapped around his cock, he pushed her down on him. His first thrust only got him halfway there as he registered her tightness and considered maybe it had been as long for her as it had been for him. Undaunted he used both hands on her hips now and pushed her down while he thrust up.

There. He was inside her deep, all the way to his balls and she was panting a little in his ear.

"Okay?" He nearly choked the word out.

"Hmm."

That simple response was enough. He leaned against the couch, planted his feet solidly on the floor and began a steady pump of his hips. Anna kept her balance by holding on to his shoulders as she found his rhythm and moved with him, coming down on him while he was pushing up into her.

Yes. There it was, the liquid heat moving through his body and his brain making him feel strong and warm. Like a king. While his woman was on top of him, riding him, taking his cock deep as if she lived to do so.

Her pleasure. He hadn't thought enough about it. He slid one hand up her stomach until he was cupping her breast again. Toying with the nipple that was as hard and as delicious as a raspberry. His other hand slipped to where their bodies were connected. He could feel the wet silky heat of her folds and he stroked her there on the outside of her body as he continued to stroke her on the inside.

Her orgasm came over her suddenly and her whole body twisted on his like she was caught up in a tornado and helpless against its power.

"Again," he said, wanting her to do that all over. He wanted to feel the way she tightened around him; he wanted to watch the way her breasts jiggled. And next time he wanted to hear her. Because while her body told him what she'd felt, she hadn't made a sound.

At his command, she only whimpered.

"Tell me," he murmured, moving his hand from one breast to the other. "I want to hear you."

He pinched her nipple between his fingers until she gasped. There. *That* was the sound he wanted. Then his thumb found the perfect spot between her legs and pressed.

"Ben," she moaned.

"Yes, Anna. That's my girl. Come now."

He saw her body start to move again but then he was lost to the rest of it as his body took over and started demanding its own conclusion. He thrust hard and heavy, nearly lifting them both off the couch with his need.

It came crashing down on him, that perfect rush of ecstasy. He hugged her to his chest as his body poured himself deep inside her.

Alive. Still alive.

When it was over he collapsed against the couch.

His arms felt too heavy to lift anymore and his legs were like big blocks of useless bone. Anna was still pressed against him, her now sweat-slick body stuck to his stomach and chest, while her head rested on his shoulder.

The loose mess of her hair tickled under his chin as together they struggled to get their heartbeats regulated.

He closed his eyes and, without being able to stop it, he felt himself drifting to sleep.

Surely, she would want to talk. All women wanted to talk.

And Anna would want to talk more than most.

When he woke up he was disoriented as he tried to place where he was. He hated the sensation.

In his life before going private, he'd trained himself so that, upon waking, he was fully cognizant of his surroundings and ready for action. For a man who rarely fell asleep in the same place two nights in a row this was an important skill.

Now his body determined when he fell asleep and sometimes it didn't give him the benefit of foreknowledge. Traitorous machine.

He was in his office. On his couch. His pajama pants had been fully removed and were folded next to him, his robe had been wrapped securely around him and a throw blanket covered him from shoulders to feet.

Anna.

Maybe this was a good sign, he thought. Maybe

falling asleep postcoital spared him a nasty scene. It was completely conceivable she also realized what a mistake they had made. It was possible she was as embarrassed as he was.

They could simply ignore that the sex had happened, or shrug it off as a temporary lapse in judgment. Between his illness and the stress she was under as both his assistant and live-in nurse, maybe she, too, needed a momentary outlet.

Some mindless, harmless pleasure. Enjoyed for a time, then it was over and forgotten.

He recalled the way she had felt in his arms, the way she sighed his name when she came. The way she had smiled at him as if she knew...

No, he wasn't sure who he was attempting to delude with the hope that this incident was nothing more than an aberration. He didn't buy it for a second.

Everything would change between them and it was his damn fault.

Brought down by a pair of skintight yoga pants. Who would have believed it?

CHAPTER TWO

Twelve weeks ago

ANNA STOPPED WHEN she entered Ben's office and saw that he was dozing behind his desk. His color wasn't good and the lines around his mouth had grown deeper. She could only hope his decline wasn't a result of what they did on the couch a few days ago. She hated to think that maybe she had robbed him of the last ounce of energy he had left in his body.

She shook off the ridiculous idea and thought about how incredibly odd these past few days had been between them. She was still caring for him, cooking for him, handling his business for him. And he was still letting her. All without saying a word about...*that night.*

At first she had this crazy idea that maybe they didn't have to talk about it. Maybe things had changed, and they could accept that change without having to rehash the obvious. They were lovers now. End of story. Anna was sure Ben would appreciate the least messy approach to making that transition.

Except she didn't feel like his lover. She felt like…a ghost. An apparition without any real substance walking around his home.

Unless they were arguing—something they rarely did, but they seemed to be on the verge of it now. Because she was certain that, beyond what had happened between them that night, something else had shifted. She sensed he was hiding something from her and as much as she pressed him on it, he wouldn't budge. There were moments when she feared that the doctors had told him something about his condition. A prognosis so horrible he wouldn't share it with her.

That, too, seemed ridiculous. If his condition was worsening, the medical team would be giving him more aggressive treatment. It wasn't as though Ben would simply surrender. No, he'd fight his enemy—in this case his body—to the bitter end before ever conceding defeat.

Ben Tyler would live. It was the only outcome she could, or would, accept.

And since he was going to live, and since they hadn't done a very good job of simply making the switch from coworkers to lovers, it meant they would have to talk.

Anna had promised herself that she would wait until he initiated the subject. Since he had made the first move, it was his responsibility to step up and explain himself. All she needed to spark that conversation was a reference, a vague mention of what they did on that couch not five feet away from her, and it would open the discussion.

She was about ready to break that promise.

Three days and nothing.

The entire incident could have been a dream she had, if she hadn't woken the next day with a faint soreness between her legs letting her know that what had happened had been entirely real.

She allowed him every excuse in the book. He was sick and didn't have the energy to focus on how their relationship might have changed. Until his prognosis improved, he couldn't commit to anything in the future. Her personal favorite explanation for his avoidance was that he was shy about admitting how he felt about her because before *that night* he'd never given her any indication he was attracted to her.

No, any sexual or romantic thoughts, she had been sure—almost sure—were entirely one-sided. *Her* side.

Looking at him now, thin and exhausted, the portrait of a man who appeared to be wasting away, it was hard to imagine the man as he had been when she first fell in love with him.

Ben Tyler then equaled power. Ben Tyler now equaled frailty.

The crazy thing was she didn't feel any differently about him. And he certainly hadn't been frail when he thrust himself deep inside her. So why didn't he want to talk about it? She understood most guys didn't like to do postmortems the day after, but this was slightly different.

What happened had been incredibly unexpected.

They hadn't flirted. They hadn't teased each other with sexual innuendos. There hadn't been any buildup of tension that had finally demanded release. She had loved him from afar, keeping her feelings completely to herself thinking he would find them inappropriate, and he...

He what? Had done the same? Had been feeling an attraction to her all this time? If so, the man was the best actor she'd ever known.

Or maybe it was the circumstance of his condition that finally brought home to him the realization that life was fleeting. A person needed to act on what he felt because he might not get a second chance. Maybe Ben had let his instincts take over his ruthless control.

Or maybe Ben had just wanted to get laid.

Either way, together they had made a big fat elephant and sat it in the middle of the room with them. It was getting to the point where not addressing that elephant was making it uncomfortable to be around each other.

The phone rang and it startled her out of her thoughts. It also woke Ben, which annoyed her. She'd told him on more than one occasion to turn the ringer off on his office phone while he was napping.

Except the great and almighty Ben Tyler didn't

acknowledge that he took naps. Rushing forward she attempted to snatch the phone off the hook, but he beat her to it.

"Ben Tyler," he answered.

She noticed he didn't look at her while he talked and it occurred to her that he hadn't looked at her, *really* looked at her, in the past three days. Her strategy of not talking about *that night* hadn't worked, and her strategy of letting him initiate the conversation was obviously not working, either. It was definitely time to forget about playing games. The elephant would not go away on its own.

"Yes. I understand. Yes, I'll be there first thing tomorrow. Thank you." He hung up the phone. "Yes?"

"Who was that?"

"The doctor's office. Confirming an appointment. I need to be at the hospital by 7:00 a.m. Can you take me?"

"Of course," she answered instantly. Then it occurred to her—something wasn't adding up. The canceled appointment of a few days ago he wouldn't discuss, the sudden hospital trip tomorrow. "Why do you need to be at the hospital tomorrow?"

"Anna, I'm sorry. I'm really tired. Can we talk about this later?"

It was her cue to leave. What person wouldn't? The man was sick, he needed rest. Leaving now would give him what he needed.

Only leaving now would make her crazy. For the past few months—hell, since the day she started working for him six years ago—she'd put his needs first. It made sense, he was the boss. Only he wasn't the boss anymore. Now, whether he was going to admit it or not, he was her lover. Kind of.

"No."

He raised his eyebrows. Recognition of the fact that she'd never said *no* to him before.

"I want to know why I'm taking you to the hospital. In fact, I would like to know why you haven't mentioned anything about what's happening next regarding your treatment. It's not like this is news you have to hide from me, Ben. I get it. The chemo isn't working like you or the doctors hoped. Okay. We knew this might happen. There are other steps. Many other steps to go before this is over. I thought the plan was to go for the consultation regarding those next steps, but suddenly you're expected at the hospital in the morning."

"My doctor and I are making decisions regarding my future health that I would prefer to remain private between me and her. Is that really too much to ask?"

Anna could feel her anger bubble over. She'd been walking around his house like a shaken-up can of soda with the lid firmly in place for too long. She couldn't contain it any longer.

"Yes. It is too much to ask when three days ago I was on my knees in front of you."

He flinched, then paused as if collecting himself before he spoke. Or maybe he was trying to recall the speech he'd already had prepared.

"Anna, about that night…"

"I don't want to talk about that night." She could feel the panic creeping in and she had to force herself to calm down. "I want to know why I'm taking you to the hospital."

"Look, if it's too much of an inconvenience—"

"Don't play the guilt card with me. You know I would take you anywhere. Just tell me the truth. What. Is. Happening. Tomorrow."

He brought his hands together on the desk and leaned back in his chair. "I've decided to move forward with the stem cell transplant."

"You can't. You don't have a direct biological match and so far nothing has hit in the donor pool. You know this."

"They're going to use embryonic cells. The research—"

"Don't talk to me about research. I know the research. What the hell do you think I've been doing these past months? Every medical journal, article, anything I could find regarding the cure for this disease I've studied. What you're doing is taking a major risk when you don't have to."

"It's my life. It's my risk to take. I'm done playing with this disease."

That was the thing about emotional pain. It wasn't sharp. It wasn't stinging. It wasn't even dull. It just moved all over the body like one big blow that you didn't see coming until you felt it everywhere.

"So that's it. You weren't going to tell me."

"I was going to tell you in the morning. Frankly, I didn't want to have the argument we're having now. I knew you wouldn't be happy. But really this isn't your concern."

"What the hell are you talking about? What do you mean it's none of my *concern?*"

His words actually made it worse. He knew what he was doing to her, but he chose to do it anyway. What he was doing...this *treatment* could kill him. Faster than the leukemia. She was standing in this room with this man who she'd worshiped for six years, and in months, possibly even weeks, he could leave her. Forever.

His life. His risk. What about her life?

"And you made this decision when?" Then she held up a finger to stop him. "Wait, let me guess. Three days ago."

"Anna—"

"No, I don't want to hear your excuse."

"I'm not making any excuses. What I did was... unforgiveable. I let myself...lose control and for that I'm sorry. But what happened wasn't completely one-sided."

Of course it wasn't. Yes, she had willingly participated. Hell, she'd practically jumped him when she realized what he was thinking. Six years she'd waited for Ben to make a move, give her some sign that what they had between them was more than business. When he'd looked at her that night and she'd seen the desire in his eyes it was as though her whole body imploded with one simple, single answer: yes.

Only what she thought was a realization of his feelings for her was simply an opportunity for one final bang. He'd used her, and she didn't know if she could stomach that.

"I was nothing more than a convenience for you," she muttered.

"No, that isn't true. It wasn't like I made this decision and then decided to...to—"

"Screw me?"

Again, he flinched, but she was tired of walking on eggshells around him, tired of taking all her cues from him about what they could and could not talk about.

They had sex. And within that act there had been intimacy. He couldn't lie about that. He couldn't say it was a mistake he made. What she'd seen in his eyes when he came into her...that was real.

"Look, Anna, I'm sorry for what I did. It just happened. But it doesn't change anything between us."

It just happened. The most significant moment of her life to date and he'd dismissed it as an impulse.

"I am sorry you're upset. I'm sorry my actions have made you feel this way."

Messy and emotional. Everything Ben Tyler rejected in his life, she knew. It pissed her off all over again, especially since she couldn't control it. Blindly, she reached out to the shelves that covered most of the walls of his office. A snow globe she'd bought him on a vacation to Vegas was within range. He'd laughed when she had given it to him, telling her it was the tackiest thing he'd ever seen. But he kept it in his office, where he could see it every day.

She threw it as hard as she could and listened as it shattered against the bookshelves on the other side of the room.

"That was childish," he said calmly.

Anna crossed her arms over her chest knowing she needed to get away. First, she needed to leave the room before the tears came. That would be step one. The second step would be infinitely harder. But as she looked at him, his face now expressionless, she knew she couldn't stay with him. Not like this. It didn't matter what happened anymore. It didn't matter that she knew now how he truly felt.

The truth was the treatment he chose for himself might kill him. Was she supposed to stay and watch that?

Was she supposed to sit like a good girl while she was abandoned? Again.

No. She wouldn't do it.

She needed to leave him before her heart bled out into her chest after being crushed so thoroughly. And she died alongside him. That's the thought she had to cling to.

She wasn't leaving Ben, she was saving herself.

"Fine," she said, calling on every ounce of strength she had to do what needed to be done. "It just happened. You need to be dropped off at the hospital. I understand perfectly. I'll make sure the glass gets cleaned up. Stay away from it in the meantime."

"Anna—"

"No," she said, holding her hand up. "I control what we get to talk about from now on and I don't want to discuss this any longer."

He didn't like that, she could see it in his expression.

He sneered then, not content to let her have the last say on the matter. "I was only going to say… you throw like a girl."

"Screw you," she fired back. "Oh, wait. I already did."

CHAPTER THREE

Present day

SHE WAS HERE. The deep satisfaction he felt as he watched her walk through the country club room where they were hosting the party was intense. Ben stood on the balcony talking to one of his clients. And without turning his head, he knew the instant she'd arrived.

He wouldn't suggest anything so melodramatic as to say he could intuit her presence. But he wouldn't discount his body's response to her arrival. His muscles tightened, his heart rate accelerated.

It had been twelve weeks since he'd last seen her. Three months since he'd heard her voice. The fact that he knew down to the minute when she'd last spoken to him—shouted at him actually—was appalling. It was a sign he wasn't busy enough. He would think about resuming a more normal working schedule now that he was finally back on his feet.

"I heard it was a close thing."

Ben stared at the short balding man he'd invited

to the party, which was in part a celebration as well as a goodbye. Madeleine Kane, one of his employees and dearest friends, was leaving Philadelphia to join her fiancé, Michael Langdon, in Detroit. While she would still work for the Tyler Group as a political consultant, she would no longer be in the office on a regular basis. Ben thought it fitting to send her off with the well-wishes of her colleagues and a few high-profile clients.

Stan Butterman was one of those clients.

"I mean, word was you were on death's door."

Ben despised euphemisms. They trivialized what was never trivial. "I was sick, but I'm doing much better now."

And he was. Where the first round of induction chemo had failed to put his cancer in remission, the second round of treatment killed off the cancer cells completely. The stem cell transplantation, while risky, had worked to rebuild his immune system. His red and white blood cell counts were normal, and there were no signs of his body rejecting the foreign cells.

He still fought fatigue like it was a mortal enemy, but in the past twelve weeks since undergoing the treatment, he'd put on weight and had managed a limited strength-building exercise routine. It was starting to make a difference. Now he could go hours without needing to rest.

"Well, you're looking good. Even see your hair coming back. Not like mine, huh? Maybe I need some chemo to go the other way." Stan rubbed his bald head and laughed while Ben smiled politely.

Yes, of course, let's laugh about chemo together.

But Stan was right, there was hair on Ben's head where there hadn't been before, even if it was just a buzz of it. He'd lost most of his hair after the first round of treatment, but the second round had left him completely bald. Everywhere, including his chest and other areas of his body where he'd never really concerned himself with not having hair before.

It had pleased him to see all the hairy parts of his body returning to normal. He considered it a sign of regrowth. A return to normalcy.

"When do you plan to be back in the office full time?"

"Soon. After weeks of quarantine I'm a little stir crazy. I'm ready for something more challenging than a trip to the drugstore."

"I bet. I mean a guy like you, former CIA agent turned into an invalid. You must have taken it especially hard."

It didn't surprise Ben to hear Stan mention his government background. In fact, he believed it was what made the Tyler Group attractive to potential clients. There was something badass about having been in the CIA that clients liked to think they shared simply by contracting with Ben for particular jobs. Their very own spymaster.

What kept bringing them back were the results

they got. Ben was a man who solved problems. He'd done so for his country for fifteen years before moving into the private arena. He found talent in a wide range of areas and then hired that talent out to clients looking to utilize his team's special skills. Currently the Tyler Group employed over twenty employees.

"I couldn't say. I don't know anyone else with leukemia," Ben muttered. His eyes followed Anna as she made her way to Madeleine. The two women had always been pleasant to each other as colleagues but they seemed to have bonded over Ben's illness. Madeleine was the one Anna had chosen to watch over Ben after she quit. Now the two women were smiling at each other. Laughing.

It bothered him that Anna should be so at ease while he was…not. Then he saw Madeleine lift her chin in the direction of the balcony and knew he was the topic of their conversation. It was time to be the bigger person. To go to her, like the adult he was, and confront her.

Instead his feet remained rooted where they were.

"Another drink?" Stan asked, raising his empty glass to indicate he was going in for another round.

"No, thank you. But don't let me hold you up. Enjoy the party."

Ben was drinking club soda, and while it had gone flat he couldn't be bothered with a refill. Beyond that, he didn't want to give Stan a reason to return. Alone now, he set the glass on one of the tables and waited.

The sticky heat of summer was starting to get to him. He could feel the perspiration gathering under his arms and soaking his shirt. But while it was cooler inside, it was also crowded with more people. Yes, his doctor deemed it safe for Ben to reenter society, however he still felt a lingering reluctance to be around crowds and their germs. There was no point in taking any chances.

"Hello, Ben."

Anna stepped onto the balcony and smiled. No, this wasn't how it was supposed to be. He was supposed to be the bigger person. He was supposed to go to her. It would have given him control over the moment.

Now he could feel his heart bracing and the sweat that had been only irritating before was now spreading down his arms. It was embarrassing.

But then this woman had seen him at his worst already. It seemed silly to be worried over sweat stains when she'd spent so much time holding his head up while he vomited.

She looked different to him. Softer maybe. Her red hair still shifted about her face, and her freckles were still scattered across her face, but there was a change. Or maybe he'd just missed seeing her.

"Hi."

She nodded and took a deep breath. "How are you?"

"Better." He couldn't remember a time when he'd struggled to communicate his thoughts, but she was making him crazy. Partly because he thought he needed to apologize to her but mostly because he was waiting for her to apologize to him.

She'd quit. When he needed her the most, she'd quit and left him. How could she do that?

"I'm glad."

"And you?"

She shrugged. "I'm fine."

"Working?" It felt like he had to pull the word out of his mouth.

"Yeah, I'm working. Listen…"

"Where?" He wanted to know. Suddenly he was furious with her all over again for leaving what had been a high-paying, intellectually challenging job with tremendous benefits.

Benefits like helping you up from a chair you were too weak to get out of on your own and cleaning up after you each time you got sick. Great benefits. But don't forget the sex you used her for. There was that.

She shook her head. "I wasn't going to tell you, but that was stupid. You're going to find out anyway. I'm actually working with someone you know. You worked with him while you were with the CIA. He said you were together for a time in Afghanistan."

Ben hadn't worked *with* anyone during those days. He did his job, he ordered people to do theirs.

"Mark Sharpe."

The name felt like a punch to the chest as the facts quickly bombarded him. Sharpe was out of the game. Sharpe was somewhere in the Philadelphia area and Sharpe had Anna. This was unacceptable.

"You're working for him. Doing what?"

"Basically, I'm helping him set up his new business. He's left the government and settled here. He's opened a private investigation firm specializing mostly in cold cases others won't take."

"And it's a coincidence he hired you."

She gave him a look as if to suggest that was a silly statement. Which it was. "No, it's not a coincidence. He knew I worked for you, knew I had left my job and approached me directly to work for him."

Of course he had. Sharpe had always considered Ben a rival. Younger, more ambitious maybe, Sharpe had targeted Ben as the man to beat on his way up the government ladder. He'd shown up in Afghanistan while Ben was serving as section chief and announced to anyone listening that Ben was just keeping his job warm. Backing up his ego, Sharpe had quickly made a name for himself by taking chances no one else would. Ben considered him a talent, but also reckless.

If he'd left the CIA, it was because he'd either

taken one too many chances and Uncle Sam had given him the boot, or maybe without having his rival on hand to actively pursue, he'd simply gotten bored with the game. Whatever the reason, it didn't matter.

Anna was under his control, albeit in a limited way, and that was unacceptable.

"You need to quit."

She snorted. "Not going to happen."

"You don't know him like I do. He can be dangerous."

"And you can't be? Look, I figured Mark out in five seconds. He's an information junky just like you. It's what makes it so easy to work with him. After six years with you, I'm pro in handling his type."

Ben didn't want Anna to handle *anything* of Sharpe's.

"He's not safe. He takes unnecessary risks—"

"Maybe back then. But all he does now is dig up old information. It's a decent job and it's cool."

"Cool," Ben sneered. "You sound like a child."

"Not so much anymore. Look, I didn't come out here to fight with you."

"I didn't, either." This conversation wasn't going how he planned it. He'd assumed she would offer an apology for leaving. He'd planned to be graciously forgiving as he offered her the job again. Once she came back, then he would feel as though things were finally returning to normal.

He was going to apologize to her, too. For that night. For what he did. And yes, for how he treated her after it happened. He'd shut her down. He'd hid his treatment decision from her which angered her so much she left. Or was it because he brushed off the sex between them like it didn't mean anything? He wasn't sure. It didn't matter.

None of it had been her fault and he supposed she'd been right to be angry that he hadn't even considered her feelings with regard to his treatment. But he had never thought she would be so angry as to walk away. Not once had he even considered Anna would leave him.

"I came to this party because I knew you would be here and we need to talk."

Ben smiled. "That's funny. I held this party because I knew you would come and I, too, think we need to talk."

"Don't tell Madeleine her party is a sham."

"Who do you think gave me the idea?"

Anna nodded. "She thinks she's helping me by getting us in the same room together."

Ben didn't think so. He thought Madeleine was trying to help him.

"Party or not, I would have come to see you anyway. I mean, we worked together for six years. Hell, you were my first job out of college. Yes, I quit. And yes, I was mad, but I'm not going to hold a grudge. I really can't anymore."

"You changed your cell phone number," he accused her. The first time he'd gotten the message stating the number was no longer in use he'd been so angry he wanted to break something. Lucky for him, he'd been too weak to do anything of the sort at the time.

"I guess I didn't want talk then."

"But you do now?"

"Now I have no choice."

She was confusing him. She was here because she needed to talk to him. Because she didn't have a choice. "Are you in some kind of trouble?"

"You could say."

"What is it? I'll fix it," he said before she could answer his question.

She shook her head. "Oh, you're going to fix it? Just like that? Snap and it's done? Sorry, forgot who I was dealing with."

Ben sighed. He could feel his strength waning. He'd purposefully slept for a time before the party. But talking with so many people, being on his feet for the past hour, was starting to take its toll. Not to mention the heat was draining him, as well.

"Can we go some place? Some place cool where I can sit down."

Instantly, he watched her face change. Concern, sympathy and...caring. It poured out of her like she was a pitcher of water. Then he watched her deliberately shut it down, as if she was reminding herself that he wasn't hers to care for any longer. It made him strangely sad.

"We don't have to do this today. We can pick another time."

She wouldn't meet his eyes when she said it and he had an awful feeling that if he let her walk out on him tonight, he might never get another chance to talk with her.

"No. I'm okay. I don't want us to be disturbed," he said.

"My car's outside. I can drive you home."

"That will work. I took a car service here."

Again, accounting for his condition. He knew driving himself to the party wouldn't be an issue. But it was how exhausted he would be driving home that concerned him. Not comfortable with cabs and the multitude of germs that could compile in a backseat over the course of any one day, he'd hired a private car service to be on call whenever he needed to go some place.

With the briefest of waves, he acknowledged Madeleine and a few of his other colleagues as he followed Anna through the room and outside where the valet attendant took her ticket. If he thought he saw a satisfied smile on Madeleine's face as he left, he ignored it. The woman was blissfully in love with her fiancé and it obviously distorted her thinking.

Once Ben and Anna were alone in the car the tension between them increased. He watched her fiddle with the temperature controls and turn off the radio, but she didn't immediately open up with whatever her problem was.

Ben found himself glad for her trouble, because she obviously had no plans to apologize for quitting. And given that she'd already found a new job, she apparently had no intention of returning. That would change though once he talked to Sharpe. Ben would explain that there were rules against poaching another man's woman...*assistant.*

"So what did you want to talk to me about?"

"Huh?" Ben asked, lost in his own thoughts.

"You said you planned the party so I would come and you could talk to me. What did you want to say to me?"

He'd been hoping she would have forgotten that part. Once they started talking about her and why she needed him, he hoped that would overshadow everything, including why she was mad at him.

But that smacked a little bit of cowardice to him. He was a grown man who fully accepted his actions. Hiding from them wasn't the best way to proceed if he and Anna were to move forward... in business.

"I wanted to apologize."

She turned to him and then quickly turned back as if she forgot she was the one driving. "Seriously? You are apologizing to me?"

"Yes. I didn't really account for your opinion when making my decision. In hindsight I can see why that might have...hurt you. Also, I was probably more defensive than I should have been. We both said some things in the heat of the moment. I'm sorry."

He could see her eyes narrow but she kept them focused on the road. "Exactly what are you sorry for, though?"

"I told you. I'm sorry I upset you."

They approached a red light and once the car stopped, she faced him again. "Do you know why I reacted the way I did?"

"You mean why you quit?"

"Yes."

"You weren't happy with my decision to have the stem cell transplantation. You were less happy that I deliberately kept it from you. I understand that. Up until that point you had shared much of my treatment and recovery. But the decision was mine to make and I didn't want it up for discussion. I didn't expect you to leave because of it."

She opened her mouth and then closed it. The light turned green and she resumed driving.

"So you're apologizing for lying to me and that's it?"

That irritated him. "I didn't lie. I simply didn't tell you my plans. Do you think you were entitled to know everything?"

"Yes."

Her answer surprised him. Ben didn't believe he had a person in his life who was entitled to know everything about him. He was purposefully insular and preferred to live his life that way. Then he realized he'd been dancing around the elephant in the car and not very successfully.

"Because we had sex," he said.

"No, because I thought we were... It doesn't matter. I was upset about your decision, yes. But also because you shut me out of your life when you made it. After we'd been together. Once you did that, I knew the sex meant nothing to you. I was only a convenience for you that night."

"I told you, that's not true."

"You said it yourself. *It just happened*. Remember?"

As if he would forget anything he said to her that day. Immediately after they had sex, he thought he had escaped unscathed. She hadn't needed a postgame breakdown of the event. Amazing. And he assumed that nothing had to change because of one night.

It wasn't until he finally told her about the stem cell transplant that everything exploded. She'd been furious, angrier than he'd ever seen her.

Hell, she threw a snow globe.

She didn't say anything to him after that fight, but he'd seen something in her eyes had died. Something he was certain he'd killed.

She was there for him the next morning to take him to the hospital, although they didn't speak a word to each other. It wasn't until later, when he was in recovery after chemo and he saw Madeleine at the hospital that he knew.

Anna was gone.

Madeleine never said anything and Ben didn't ask. It was implied that Madeleine would handle the business end of things and she would hire a nurse to help him when he returned home after his quarantine period in the hospital.

Reflecting on that fight he entertained the possibility he'd been lying then. Maybe he wanted to believe that what they had done that night was nothing more than time-out for both of them. A temporary reprieve from the sickness, done and then forgotten. But if that were true, he wouldn't still be thinking about it months later.

If Anna was nothing more than a convenience, then he wouldn't be in this car right now. And if she had felt it was only a harmless night of sex, she wouldn't have needed to quit.

And that put an entirely different light on this negotiation to get her under his employ.

"We're here." She stopped at the top of his driveway and he blinked, thinking he'd been so intent on watching her face that he hadn't even recognized they were on his street.

"Come in."

She shook her head. "I don't think so. I'm kind of drained."

He could see it, too. Her face was pale, which made the freckles stand out. It wasn't like Anna.

Anna was always alive, always on, as if she was constantly filled with energy. This paleness worried him.

"We're not done talking."

"I can say what I need to. You're going to need time to process it anyway."

Now he was really worried. He reached over and grabbed her hand. It was damp. She pulled it away and wouldn't look at him.

"Tell me you're not sick." She had to tell him that she wasn't sick. The words had to come out of her mouth now. Panic started to bubble up in his stomach, a feeling he'd never felt before.

"I'm not sick."

Relief washed through him. "You're scaring the crap out of me, Anna."

She looked over and smiled. "Yeah? Well, my news isn't going to be any less scary."

"Tell me."

"I'm pregnant. Three months, to be exact."

CHAPTER FOUR

ANNA LOOKED AT the clock on her kitchen wall. It was one minute to noon and she held her breath waiting for the minute hand to move. As soon as it did, her doorbell rang. Ever punctual Ben.

After she'd dropped her bombshell on him, he'd insisted she come inside so they could talk about it, but she hadn't lied when she'd said she wasn't up for it. Even starting her second trimester, nausea and exhaustion could still sneak up to overwhelm her. And given how pale he'd gotten after the words left her mouth she knew he wasn't up for a discussion, either. They both had needed some space and time.

He agreed to let her leave on the condition he would come over today at noon when they could have a calm and rational conversation after both of them had time to rest. Anna had gone to her apartment and had crashed hard, falling into a dreamless sleep. In truth, she didn't know if that was from the baby or from the relief at finally having told him.

Rising, she walked to the tiny foyer, undid the chain on the door and opened it.

Ben was on the other side already frowning. "You didn't ask who I was."

"Oh, here we go." She knew to expect this. Ben was overprotective and paranoid in normal circumstances. She usually gave him a pass because she figured a man who spent over fifteen years with the CIA had a right to always be watching over his shoulder for bad guys. Now that she was carrying his child, she could foresee those protective instincts leaping into overdrive.

Because of the baby, of course. Not her.

"Don't roll your eyes at me, it's childish. When someone knocks on your door you need to ask who it is before you open it. It's a basic precaution."

"It's twelve o'clock. I knew you were coming. You're punctual as all hell. I didn't need to ask who was on the other side of the door."

"You're pregnant," he said, marching into her apartment. He filled the living room instantly. It was amazing to her. Ben wasn't especially tall, or particularly buff. But he had this presence that made everyone in the vicinity around him take notice. At least she always did.

"I told you that, remember?" She closed the door and waited for the interrogation to begin. She'd had weeks to prep her answers and felt fairly confident she was going to pass this test.

"How long have you known?"

"Since I took the test maybe two weeks after I realized I was late."

"So at least six weeks ago, but you waited to tell me?"

Taking a deep breath she mentally ticked through all her very sound, very logical reasons. "One, miscarriages happen most commonly in the first trimester. I wanted to be certain everything was fine and the baby was healthy before telling you anything. Two, you sort of had your hands full with the cancer. I wanted to wait and make sure you weren't dealing with any type of rejection from the stem cells. Three—"

"No three. No one or two." He was clearly angry. "I am the father of the child you are carrying and I should have been told!"

Anna jumped. In the six years she'd worked with him she'd never heard him raise his voice. Not even when she had been shouting at him for leaving her out of his life-and-death decision had he ever shouted back.

Instantly contrite, he bent his head and pushed his hands into his pants pockets. "I'm sorry. I shouldn't have yelled. I'm upset."

Obviously. Anna wasn't sure how his admission made her feel. She didn't know she had that kind of power over him. She didn't think anything could rattle Ben Tyler. Then again, he'd never been confronted with fatherhood before. It was definitely a game changer.

"Why don't you sit? I'll make us some tea."

"Can you have tea in your condition?"

This time she turned her back on him before rolling her eyes. "I have decaffeinated."

He sat on the couch as she made her way to the kitchen. She watched him as she filled the teapot with boiling water. He was touching her stuff. The throw blanket she kept on her couch. The decorative pillows she'd picked out. He should have looked silly—someone so incredibly masculine sitting on her deep purple couch surrounded by the electric blue and yellow pillows—but he didn't. He owned the couch, bright colors or not, the way he owned the room.

She thought about what her life would be like if the kid inside her turned out to be anything like its father. The world would have to watch out having two like him in it.

"It's not as messy as I thought it would be."

Anna wasn't sure how to take that statement. Her office was always neat and orderly—everything in her place. Of course she kept her home the same way. Not that it was hard to keep a one-bedroom apartment neat, but still, all of her possessions meant something to her. Each purchase had meaning and she would never treat her things so carelessly. He should have known that about her. There was no reason for him to assume she would live like a slob. Still, she cut him some slack because she could see he was out of sorts simply being here.

"Okay."

"You have no pictures."

Anna carried the two steaming mugs to the living room and handed him one carefully. Glancing around, she pointed at some of the pictures she had hanging on the walls. "What are you talking about? Last time I checked those were pictures."

"I mean personal pictures. Of you and friends."

"Neither do you."

"That's different."

"Is it? Neither of us have parents or siblings. We're both dedicated to our work. It's not like either one of us spends time at places where we would be snapping photos of ourselves."

"I guess I just imagined your place differently."

"Messy and with pictures apparently. Sorry to disappoint you, but this is it. Although not for much longer."

"What do you mean?"

"My lease is up early next year. They're converting to condos but the price is a little out of my reach. Not that I want a condo anyway. I'll need to rent something else for a while. Definitely a two bedroom. From what I understand babies require a lot of stuff."

He nodded, but looked away from her as he spoke. "I thought you wanted to buy a house."

"Sure, that's the dream. And I'm almost there

with my savings fund. Luckily for me, Mark pays as well as you do. But I don't want to simply settle for something. When I buy my house it's going to be perfect and mine."

A place no one could ever take her away from. Anna shook her head and tried not to think about what that would be like when that day finally arrived. That would make her too anxious about the money she still had to save and the length of time that would take her to do so. She would worry about possible renovations and furnishings for this future, unknown house. She didn't want to do any of that until she was ready to buy.

He seemed as though he wanted to respond, but hesitated. Eventually he shrugged. "Makes sense."

"Do you know I've worked with you for six years and this is the first time you've ever been in my home?"

"You've never invited me before."

Anna considered that. "True. But then why would an assistant invite her boss over?"

"You were more than an assistant," he said. "And maybe I'll get luckier with your next place."

He put the mug on the coffee table and stood as if he needed to move. Another thing Anna had never seen him do. He wasn't fidgety. Ever. In fact there was usually a stillness about him that implied his absolute control over everything—including his thoughts, his words, his emotions, hell, even the air around him.

"So you were planning on telling me. About the baby. It wasn't just because you saw me last night."

"Yes, I was going to tell you. It's why I went last night. Do you really think I would hide something like that from you? Beyond any personal considerations, you're half responsible for this, which means you're going to help support it."

"Of course I'm going to support it!"

Again with the shouting. And now he was pacing. Based on his behavior now, Anna wasn't sure she even knew this man. "Relax. I know. You wouldn't walk away from your responsibilities. You're not that guy. I truly only waited to make sure everything was fine. With you and the baby."

"You never said anything…about not being on birth control."

It was true. Like every other woman who got knocked up unintentionally, Anna had let the moment take over and had stopped thinking. She wanted to regret her actions. She really did. But she couldn't. Not the sex and, strangely, not the baby. Realistically, she should be way more freaked out by the whole single-mother thing. But when the indicator on that stick had turned pink she suddenly felt as if this were meant to happen.

"We didn't exactly do a lot of talking that night."

He seemed at a loss. "I should have protected you."

"I should have protected myself. It happened."

He stared at his feet, avoiding her eyes for his next question. "Did you ever consider having an—"

"Nope," she said quickly, not even wanting to hear him say the word. She didn't imagine he was happy about this pregnancy, but she couldn't stand the thought that he might have wanted her to end it. "My body. My decision. Not your call."

"No, no…I mean, I'm glad. I wouldn't have wanted that. It's not something I could ever see you doing. Hell, you got emotionally attached to the spiders living in my house."

She smiled and couldn't stop the rush of warmth that went to her heart knowing even if she had given him the choice, he wouldn't have wanted to end the pregnancy. Then she crushed that warm, gooey feeling. She needed to remind herself constantly that this would not end with some happily ever after moment.

"And for me… While I never considered being a father, this is my only chance."

"I don't know what you mean."

He crossed his arms over his chest. "I'm sterile. The doctors told me it was a possibility with the heavier dosage of chemo I was subjected to. Before I left the hospital I had them test to be sure and they confirmed it."

Oh.

She hadn't thought of that. Naturally she had talked with her OB/GYN about the fact that Ben had gone through chemo prior to them having sex and what, if any, repercussions that might have on her child. While there are some concerns on the impact to the sperm and the possible structural change of the chromosomes, the data so far had not shown any increase in defects normally associated with pregnancy. Which meant her risks were the same as any other woman's.

However, thinking back on that appointment, the doctor had mentioned how lucky she was. Anna now knew what the doctor had meant. Chemo could not only potentially alter sperm, it could also kill it. Ben's swimmers had apparently survived his first round of treatment, but no such luck the second time. Talk about timing.

"Wow." The weight of the responsibility she carried was suddenly much heavier.

He sat next to her on the couch, close but not touching. "At the time it didn't bother me. I mean, I was convinced I wasn't going to marry or be a parent. That wasn't my plan for my life. But now I'm thinking what happened might have been a miracle. That's selfish, I know."

It was, but it was understandable. She'd been his last shot. Literally. In a way, it thrilled her to know she'd given him something no other woman would ever be able to give him. It meant she would always be important to him, always be connected to him. At least in that way.

"So you're…happy about this?"

He took her hand and held it. "Anna, I'm not

just happy, I'm ecstatic. I'm worried and nervous about my abilities to parent a child, but I—I don't know how to say it really. I've never felt this way. Like suddenly I'm completely and totally attached to that baby growing inside you."

His words should have made her happy. It was a good thing he was excited for this baby. *She* was excited for this baby. But all she could think about was how he had never once felt that way about her. They were attached to the growing life inside of her, but not to each other. There was something tragic about that.

She swallowed her self-pity and nodded. She needed to put aside her feelings and think only about the baby. It was good he felt attached. This meant he would be involved with the baby and that was important for the child. A child needed parents who loved and wanted it. Nobody understood that more than Anna. After being abandoned by her mother at age six, she'd spent the rest of her life not really mattering to anyone.

Until she met Ben. As his assistant, she had mattered. Then as his caregiver, she had mattered. Now as the mother of his only child, she really mattered.

Too bad she didn't matter to him in the way she wanted to.

"Okay. So I guess you'll want to do a visitation thing. We can talk about that. I mean, maybe not in the first few months because I'll be breast feeding, but after—"

"Stop," he said squeezing her hand. "What do you mean?"

"I mean if you're happy about this, I'm assuming you're going to want to see the baby, be part of his or her life." She could see he was genuinely confused.

"Of course I'm going to be part of its life. We're its parents."

"Right. We'll need to work out the details of how that happens."

He released her hand and stood again. This time not to pace but to tower over her. "Anna, I don't think you get it. I'm not talking about some arrangement where we split this child's time between us."

Not letting him intimidate her, she stood, too, and got in his face. "If you think for one second I'm going to let you take my child—"

He put his hands on her shoulders. "Calm down. Your face is turning is red. I'm not taking the child. You're not keeping the child. We're raising the child. Together. Anna, you're going to marry me."

The words hit her in the face like a slap. He wanted her to marry him.

How completely and totally awful.

"Oh, hell no."

BEN WAS FURIOUS. When he finally pulled into his driveway he turned off the ignition and allowed himself a moment to express his fury by slamming his hand against the steering wheel.

He'd succeeded only in hurting his hand.

Her face. The completely and totally horrified look she had on her face when he told her they would marry. He didn't think he would ever forget it.

It's not like he was an ogre. Yes, he'd been sick, but the cancer was in remission and he was getting stronger every day. He still had a very successful business and all the money they could ever need and then some. The Tyler Group was proving to be an infinitely more profitable source of income than the United States government.

Yet, given her reaction, a person might have concluded that he'd asked her to go to the pits of hell instead.

"Oh, hell no."

The words rattled around in his head. What kind of answer was that? She was carrying his child. Since the moment she'd told him about the baby he'd been unable to think of anything else. Anna and his child. His child. Anna. His.

Maybe that wasn't entirely true. He'd also thought about how they created that child. Memories of *that night* came flooding back. Where once he'd ruthlessly suppressed them, now he didn't see the point. There was no pretending it hadn't happened. In six months there would be undeniable proof.

That night when he'd felt as if his grip on life was slipping, she'd given him a taste of why it was so important to hold on. God, she'd been so sweet. Hot and wet and welcoming. Soft all around him.

Yet another reason why he would make a suitable husband. Good sex.

Because it had been good for her. She couldn't deny that. As clumsy and as urgent as he'd been, he'd still felt her orgasm. Now that he was healthy, he could make it even better for her.

Moaning, he leaned his head back against the seat and felt his body react to the images in his mind. It wasn't the first time he'd gotten hard since his recovery. No, he'd had a few morning erections, which he considered a good sign that his body was healing.

Each damn one had been brought on by the memory of *that night*.

When he'd thought about seeing her today, when he'd thought about what might happen after he proposed—because his plan had been to *propose* rather than *announce* that they were going to marry—he'd thought that maybe *that night* might happen again.

The image he'd created was very different from what had actually happened. In his fantasy she was thrilled with the idea of having him as a husband. They would kiss to seal the deal and then she would have taken him to her bedroom where they could formally solidify their status as a couple.

Ben snorted. *Formally solidify their status as a couple?*

Truth was he wanted to screw her brains out.

He wanted another chance to see her breasts with her soft brown nipples and he wanted to slide into her body knowing that the act that they were doing had created life. Life, when he'd been so close to death.

It occurred to him that maybe he should have led with that. Maybe he should have told her how special that night was to him. How much he thought about it. How much he thought about repeating it.

It would shock her, he knew. The way he'd acted after it happened probably made it seem as if it had all been a big mistake he wanted to forget. Not something that impacted their relationship at all.

He had his reasons certainly. The biggest and most undeniable one was that, at the time, he'd made a decision he knew could cost him his life. He hadn't wanted her to dispute that decision and he didn't want her to think of him in any long-term capacity. On the off-chance he actually did die.

He'd been an ass. And Anna being Anna wasn't going to tolerate such behavior. No wonder she quit.

He thought about the weeks he'd spent in quarantine at the hospital. Weeks lying in a sterile room waiting for her to get over what he'd done to her and come see him.

Only she never came. Not even after she found out she was pregnant.

Ben considered hitting something again, but he knew it was pointless. Instead he got out of the car and stood still for a moment as a wave of fatigue washed over him. He'd simply gone to Anna's house and back, but suddenly he felt as if he'd climbed a mountain.

Focusing, he pooled his energy and concentrated on getting through the front door. That he could manage. He would not be reduced to crawling there on his hands and knees. Feeling shaky but determined, he took small, even steps until he was at the door, then through it.

Climbing the steps to his bedroom was beyond him, but the couch in his office was waiting for him. Making his way down the hall, he thought only of the end result. Himself lying prone. The couch was like a beacon calling him to it. He slid the door to his office open and with only a few final steps, collapsed onto the comfortable cushions.

Toeing off his shoes he lay down and accepted the fact that his body required regular rest. To this day he would not refer to the process of restoring his energy as a *nap*. Instead he referred to it merely as recovery time. And today, after facing Anna and the certain knowledge that last night hadn't been a dream and she really was going to have his baby, he figured he was entitled to a longer recovery time.

Yes, he thought as his eyes closed and he could feel his body relax, he certainly would need to be at full strength before their next encounter. Anna was no pushover. And given her obvious reluctance to his idea that they should be married, he would have to try another stratagem.

Because before this was all over she was going to be his wife.

CHAPTER FIVE

MARK SHARPE GLANCED up at the sound of the office door opening. He'd taken a small but expensive two-room office in Liberty One, Philadelphia's second-tallest building since the completion of the Comcast building. With the glass wall between his office and his assistant's desk, he could see and hear everything in the space he occupied, which soothed his always alert senses.

As a former CIA agent, there were some habits he knew he would never be able to break and being completely aware of his surroundings at all times was one of them.

Anna walked in and set her purse on her desk. Her shoulders were slumped, her face was pale and there were circles under her eyes. She wore a particularly cheerful sundress that did nothing to alter the impression that she wasn't a happy person.

Damn Ben. Mark had expected more from him.

Pushing away from his desk he walked out to greet her.

"So how did the big reveal go?" he asked.

She'd told him on Friday about the party for her

former coworker, and her intention to come clean with Ben. Looking at her face, Mark was pretty certain he knew the answer. Ben might have been a brilliant spy, but when it came to interpersonal relationships, the guy was a wash.

Mark had known Anna now for only eight weeks, and known about the pregnancy that whole time. She was probably the only woman alive who would announce during an interview that she was pregnant—it wouldn't occur to her to keep that fact a secret until *after* she landed the job. Not that it mattered. His goal was to have Anna working for him, pregnant or not.

In those eight weeks he'd never once seen her look so…depleted. Even with the morning sickness there was always a vibrancy about her that never waned.

At least not until today.

"He wants to marry me."

Huh. Okay, maybe Ben had come up to snuff. That proposal wasn't completely unexpected. Ben had always been a do-the-right-thing kind of a guy and when you knocked up a girl, the right thing was to propose.

It's what Mark had done all those years ago. He would always be thankful Helen had the foresight to not take him up on his offer.

Helen. It was an ache that still hurt when he thought of her. The girl he'd known was now dead and, although she never would have believed he was capable of it, he grieved for her. Deeply.

With a huff, Anna slumped in her chair. "Can you believe he did that?"

"Yes. You know Ben. What did you think he was going to do?"

"The right thing by the kid."

"But not the right thing by you?"

She scowled at him. "What is this? The nineteen hundreds? Do I look like I can't handle this on my own?"

Immediately, he backed off. After all, it wasn't exactly like he was on Ben's side in this situation. The man had been Mark's rival for more years than he cared to admit. The aggravating part of the rivalry was that he didn't think Ben reciprocated it.

And why should he? The man had always been one step ahead of him. Mark used Ben as a benchmark as he made his climb up the ladder within the ranks of the agency. Mark pushed himself as hard as he could to catch up to the man who had beaten him into the service by three years.

Only, he never did. Somehow Ben was always a grade higher and always a step ahead on the job. So like any man embittered with constant defeat at the hands of a self-appointed rival, Mark competed in the one area where he knew he could get even—seduction.

If Ben was interested in a woman, that woman became Mark's next conquest. And he was sure to beat Ben every time. The man was atrocious at the art of seducing a woman. The concept of flirting was no doubt alien to him.

Yet, while Ben's interest in a particular member of the fairer might have been piqued from time to time—enough for him to even pursue a sexual relationship—it never held for long.

So, really, what did it matter that Mark repeatedly got the girl when he knew Ben never really cared one way or the other.

Except not this girl, Mark thought, looking at Anna. She meant something to Ben. Strange, because he would have thought she was way too young for Ben. He had to be nearing forty-five and Anna was only twenty-eight. But Mark could see she was older than her years—no doubt the effect of having been abandoned then spending most of her childhood in various foster homes. She would probably be annoyed that he knew her history since it wasn't something she'd offered up during her interview, but collecting information on people was simply his nature.

He hadn't yet managed to discover exactly what had happened between her and Ben. Something obviously had—the woman was pregnant, after all. But that *something* should have been an absolute showstopper for Ben. The guy had always avoided any personal connection with people who worked for him.

Mark spent years in various assignments reporting to Ben and watching female agent after female agent try to engage him in a sexual relationship. Some, Mark imagined, did so because they were actually attracted to Ben. More did so because they thought sleeping with a spymaster was a pretty cool notch to have in their belt. And every single one of them did so because Ben was a big fat walking challenge.

But he didn't mess around with agents assigned to him. Period. It was a rule he'd never broken, as far as Mark knew.

Only he'd broken it with Anna in a hell of a big way. Maybe it had to do with the whole almost-dying thing. But it was hard to imagine Ben reacting to death that way. Not when Mark had seen Ben, on more than one occasion, confront it head-on. The man was fearless. Mark didn't see cancer changing that.

Someday he would get the story from Anna. Ferreting information from reluctant sources was a particular gift of his. Given that she was his employee, he had all the time in the world to work on her. Eventually she would cave.

Of course, as soon as Ben found out that Mark was in Philadelphia and that she was working for him things were going to get a lot more interesting.

Ben might suspect Mark was up to his old tricks and had moved here solely for the purpose of continuing the competition. My business against yours, let's see who can make the most money kind of a thing.

Maybe that was true to a certain extent. Mark still liked to needle Ben any time he had a chance. Plus aspiring to Ben's level of success was great professional motivation. Mark had done his due diligence as soon as he arrived. He knew what the Tyler Group was, knew Ben's reputation around town and had pretty extensive background information on every single person working for the Group. It was only natural. Two former clandestine operators living in the same city, hell yes they were going to know what the other was up to. It was simply how they were programmed.

And when Mark's routine searches into Ben's employees turned up a résumé on a job search site from one Anna Summers, he knew he'd hit pay dirt. The ultimate steal. Anna wasn't just some woman Ben showed interest in, she had been his trusted assistant for six years. *Six years.* As far as Mark knew this was the most committed and long-term relationship Ben had ever had with a woman besides his mother.

But as intriguing as competing with Ben in the private sector might be, the reality was Mark had much more personal reasons for making Philadelphia his home.

Helen's death had decided everything.

"He knows I'm working for you." Anna's announcement brought Mark back to the present.

He grimaced, recognizing how futile the hope to keep his presence in the city under wraps awhile longer had been. "How did he find out?"

"I told him." She said it as if she didn't understand why he might care.

It figured Anna would confess. She was too bone-deep loyal to not be up front with the fact that she was working for the man who confessed to be Ben's competition. Mark had liked having the upper hand for a time, had liked being in the city covertly, but now that was over.

Since hanging up his private investigator shingle, Mark had solved a few small-profile cases, but nothing that would have registered enough attention to attract Ben's notice. Now that notice would be notched up to full-alert mode. "I'll go out on a limb and say he wasn't happy to learn you're working for me."

One didn't need to be a good detective to know how Ben would react to the news that Anna was now in Mark's clutches...*employment.*

"Correct. He insisted I quit and said you were dangerous."

"Dangerous?" It was silly, but the idea that Ben considered him enough of a threat to call him *dangerous* was flattering. Someday, Mark would really need to let Ben know what their rivalry was all about. Then he would see that Mark wasn't the enemy. Mark actually respected the hell out of his old section chief. Ben was the guy Mark wanted to be when he grew up. If he ever did.

But he didn't plan on sharing that information anytime soon. At least not until after he'd watched Ben go crazy with the idea that Anna worked for Mark.

"This was yesterday?" he asked.

"No, the night before at the party."

Surprising, he hadn't already heard from Ben. Maybe because he had a few other things on his mind right now. Like being told he was about to become a daddy. It was enough to shake any man up.

Which meant he'd seek out Mark today.

Home or workplace?

Workplace, Mark concluded. Kept things less personal.

During the day or after work?

After work. After Anna had left because Ben wouldn't want her to see him confronting Mark directly. Hell, Ben was probably scouting the building now.

First he would figure out where Mark had rented office space. Child's play for a professional of Ben's caliber. Then he would locate the building and determine the layout of the parking garage. Posing as someone interested in renting an office, he would ask at the security desk in the lobby if parking spaces were reserved for leaseholders or open to the general public.

He would learn that only a few select spots were

marked for the executives in some of the higher-rent offices. Which meant he would spend some time finding Anna's car amongst the five parking levels beneath the building. Once he found it, he would tag it with an electronic device to monitor her movements and alert him when she'd left the building. Or, if performing such an act as a civilian left him feeling squeamish with guilt, Ben would simply locate a discreet place from which he could watch her car unseen and wait for her to drive away.

He would—correctly—assume that Mark would remain in his office after normal business hours, because he knew the only thing Mark ever cared about was his job and he dedicated nearly every waking moment to it. Starting a new business would only make his work ethic even more stringent.

None of this Mark would share with Anna, of course. No, this was just a little game between former spies. Still, he wondered…how well did she know Ben? She had been with him for six years, after all.

"He'll come for you, you know. Probably tonight after I leave," she said matter-of-factly.

Yeah, his Anna was no fool. "Yep, he will. Worried he might sway me and I'll fire you?"

"You would fire a poor pregnant woman who needs a salary so she can raise a child on her own?"

"In a heartbeat. Didn't Ben tell you? I'm ruthless as well as dangerous."

She smiled, knowing he was teasing and he was glad to see it. Glad that he'd made it happen. Anna was a good woman. He'd known it the first time he met her. She was grounded and level-headed and would be cool in a high-pressure situation. There was a steadiness about her that probably should have been washed away by the years she'd spent in uncertain situations as a child. It hadn't been. She was rock solid and would have made a good operative or soldier. For his sake and Ben's, Mark was glad she was neither.

No, he imagined it wouldn't be hard at all to spend a lifetime trying to make her smile. But, as was his pattern, Ben had gotten there first. This was Mark's bad luck.

"So what are you going to do?" he asked.

"Uh...I was thinking of working for the rest of the day with periodic time-outs to eat saltines and drink ginger ale."

"I meant about Ben. He proposed, remember?"

"And I said no. Actually I said hell no. He was pissed but he'll get over it. When he calms down we can discuss our situation like rational people. Marriage isn't the answer."

If Mark's gut was right, he didn't think that rational discussion would happen. Not because Ben wasn't rational, but because he'd broken his number-one rule and slept with his employee. For a man like him that was like a tectonic shift in his principles. And he would be immovable until he got the results he wanted. In this case, Mark suspected the results were marriage.

And that came back to Mark's original assessment. Something about Anna was different for Ben. Given how sad she looked when she came into the office after having been proposed to, it didn't take a professional observer to know how she felt about Ben in return.

Mark shrugged. None of it should be his concern. He'd hired Anna simply to piss off Ben, but he'd quickly grown to like her. Now, because of that, it seemed terribly important to him how all this worked out. Which, he realized, was nothing more than a stall tactic on his part from having to make the most important decision of his life.

Yes, Ben had beaten him to the punch in a lot of different areas in his life. But the one thing Mark had done first was father a child.

BEN WATCHED as Anna drove out of the parking garage into downtown Philadelphia traffic. He waited until she'd turned right at the first corner and was out of sight before he exited his car.

He entered the building he'd been in earlier that day gathering information. He stopped at the security desk briefly and flashed the badge he'd spent the afternoon forging before making his way to the elevators. He hit the button for the appropriate floor and felt a surge in his stomach as the sleek elevator climbed the distance so fast he could actually feel pressure against his eardrums.

Leave it to Mark to pick a flashy office. By contrast, Ben and his staff used a small, serviceable office in the Northern Liberties section of the city. Results were what mattered, not a slick image.

Once the elevator stopped, he made his way down the hall and wasn't surprised to see Mark lounging in the doorway that opened to his office. So casually as if to suggest he could predict Ben's actions and knew he would be arriving.

"Sharpe," Ben said, acknowledging him.

"Tyler," Mark replied, sporting his legendary smile.

Women went crazy for that smile. Hardened female foreign agents revealed secret information because of that smile. All Ben ever wanted to do was punch it.

Mark stepped back and allowed Ben to enter. He passed Anna's desk—had to be hers because there was a small potted plant on the corner of it. She hated planting and hated having to remember to water them even more, yet held firmly to the belief that an office needed real life in it. Not plastic decorations.

He made his way past the glass partition to the larger space and sat in one of the two guest chairs available and waited for Mark to take his seat behind the desk. He would like the position of authority it gave him, Ben knew.

Mark sat in his high-back leather chair, knotted his fingers together and waited. It was a power play, keeping silent so Ben would speak first and state his purpose for showing up. Silence was better than asking a question that could potentially deliver an answer you weren't prepared for. He couldn't necessarily blame the man for the ploy. After all they both knew why he was here. And this *was* Ben's move.

"You're going to let her go."

"Let her go?" Mark affected a confused expression. "If you mean as my employee, then, no, I'm not. If you mean it in another way…"

Ben knew Mark was toying with him. Using the one advantage he'd always had over him—his ability to seduce women. The interesting thing was Mark was hardly a Casanova. He was much too focused on his work to ever devote a lot of time to seducing women.

But when he did want a woman he made that a priority. The fact that he always seemed to want the women Ben showed interest in was no coincidence.

This situation, however, was different. Ben was confident Mark's attention to Anna wasn't sexual. Or if it was, there hadn't been time for him to act on it. Not with all Anna had going on recently with Ben's weeks of quarantine, finding another job and coming to terms with being pregnant.

At least he hoped so.

"Bullshit."

Mark shrugged and obviously wasn't willing to lie beyond what he'd already alluded to.

"What the hell are you doing here anyway?" Ben asked. "Shouldn't you be the new section chief in Afghanistan?"

Initially he'd been annoyed he hadn't been aware of Mark's presence in the city—it wasn't until Anna had announced who she was working for that Ben had known. A former agent, moving into his territory. It should have shown up somewhere on his radar. No allowances for the fact that he'd been quarantined in a sterile room at the hospital while Mark set up shop.

"I quit. Just like you did."

Ben had left the agency when the politics started to matter more than the results. There were days he'd felt the entire agency was a tool being used solely for the administration's end game. Instead of uncovering information, they were manufacturing it—something he was not willing to be a part of. Unfortunately, the higher up in the ranks he was promoted, the closer he got to the bullshit that was D.C. It was either leave or have his career stall at the same level, watching less talented but more politically savvy agents advance ahead of him.

"Like I did?" He thought Mark would have been one of those more politically savvy agents.

"Stevens got promoted to section chief."

Then again, obviously not. Stevens's quality of work left a lot to be desired—a fact overlooked by the key decision-makers he networked with. "You were better than him."

"Yes, I was. But you know that doesn't always matter."

"No, it doesn't."

"After you left the fun of trying to one-up you was gone and my ambition seemed to tank with it. I couldn't deal with the politics any more than you could. Watching men and women who cared more about furthering their careers than getting the job done was driving me mad. I discovered I wasn't willing to play and so I got skipped over. Then some other things in my life changed and that was a sign that it was time to get out of the game. The fact that I made the transition so easily tells me I already had one foot out the door."

"Really, you're finding the…transition…easy?" Ben hadn't. It had taken him nearly a full year to stop looking over his shoulder every other second. Now, he did it only every other minute. So far in the six years he'd been out no one had ever been behind him.

"I'm…adjusting."

"Why here? Why Philadelphia?"

"I have my reasons," Mark said. His attention seemed to wander momentarily before he refocused on Ben. "They weren't all about you."

Ben believed him. In a strange way, as much as

Mark had always annoyed him with his antics, it felt right to be sitting here with someone who had lived the same life he had, who had seen the same things and knew the same information. Like he was finally connected to someone again.

He hadn't felt like this since…Anna.

The reason he was here.

"She's pregnant with my child."

Mark didn't flinch from the sudden shift in the conversation. "I know. She told me when I interviewed her. You want to talk about how you let that happen with an employee?"

"You knew she was pregnant and you still hired her?" Ben asked, ignoring the other comment.

"I'll take that as a no, you don't want to talk about how it happened. Okay, fine. Why did I hire her? Ben, you know it would be discrimination if I held her pregnancy against her. Besides, she could have come to me and said she had two months to live and I still would have hired her. She was your trusted assistant for six years. Which means she's completely and utterly capable. You wouldn't have kept her around for so long if she wasn't."

"What do you have her doing?"

"Right now setting up the office. Placing ads in appropriate print media and online, setting up a computer system for billing and a fair amount of researching on the cases I currently have."

"She said you specialize in cold cases."

"I do. I have no intention of spending my days

photographing cheating spouses. I'm fortunate enough to have saved quite a bit of money during my years abroad so I can select only the cases I want. Which means criminal cases most likely. And I like challenges, so the older the case, the bigger the challenge."

"You said *right now.* What are your plans for her in the future, if she chooses to stay with you?"

"You mean, if she doesn't return to work for you? Do you really see that as a possibility?"

No, Ben didn't. Regardless of what happened regarding her job here, he doubted she would ever agree to work for him again. They were beyond that now. Trying to blend their relationship as both parents and coworkers would be too complicated. In one area they had to be equals, in the other area they wouldn't be.

Besides, that's not what he wanted. His thoughts on having sex with his employees hadn't changed. His thoughts on having sex with Anna had. He wanted her. So he had to let her go professionally. If she had to leave his company and work for someone else, he could think of worse things than it being someone he knew and ultimately trusted. As long as he knew what her responsibilities would be.

"What are your plans going forward for her?" Ben asked, again refusing to answer Mark's question.

"She has aspirations to be an investigator. I'm

going to train her, help her get her license and give her cases to work."

Ben crossed his right leg over his left and smoothed out the material of his pants. "The hell you are."

"She's got a knack for research."

"She will not be investigating criminal cases. Cold or hot."

Mark smiled. That blasted smile that had Ben's knuckles itching to remove it from his face. "You really don't have any say over that, do you?"

"Maybe not, but I can make sure she knows the type of man she's working for. A man who doesn't see a problem putting other people at risk for his own ends."

"You're never going to get over that, are you? No one forced you out of that helicopter. That was your choice."

There had been an assault on a suspected al Qaeda leader's home. Mark had done most of the work gathering the intel and wanted to be with the SEAL team when they raided the property despite Ben's protestations. The agency's job was to collect the information, pass it over and let the military do the work. However, in this instance, the team hadn't been opposed to having Mark with them in the helicopter to provide specific detail about the small complex before they attacked. Ben had accompanied them to oversee his operative.

A good thing he had, too, because not a minute

after the team deployed, Mark broke protocol and followed the SEALs onto the ground.

"It wasn't a choice. You were being fired upon."

"Yeah, good old Ben to the rescue. Because there was no chance I would have made it out of the situation on my own like I had countless times before."

As far as Ben was concerned, he wouldn't have. "I'm not here to rehash the past. I'm here to tell you how it's going to be with Anna. Beyond any history you and I have, she's carrying my child. I will not let you put her in harm's way."

"*I'm* putting her in harm's way? *You* knocked her up. You didn't even know about it until a few days ago. Tell me, Ben, which one of us is the bigger jerk in this scenario."

The accusation hit Ben directly in the gut. What was worse, he couldn't refute it. "My relationship with Anna is none of your concern."

"And *my* relationship with her and her future career here is none of your concern. I can tell you this, she's one stubborn girl. That's easy enough to see. Push her to quit this job and you'll only be playing into my hands."

Ben waited a beat until the rush of anger he felt subsided. "You've known her eight weeks. I've known her six years."

"But you know I'm right."

He did. He also knew that Mark Sharpe was a risk taker and, as he said, the bigger the challenge the bigger the high for him. She would be taking on cases that involved potentially dangerous people and the idea of her out there alone, unprotected by Ben, sent a chill through him he wasn't totally willing to acknowledge.

"We're done with this conversation. Stay out of my way."

It was an old command. One he'd used with many operators working under him when he was on a particular mission. He didn't want their help, he didn't want their input, he wanted them out of his way so he could do what he did best.

Before that meant hunting down known terrorists.

Today it meant hunting down Anna.

CHAPTER SIX

ANNA LEANED AGAINST the passenger door of Ben's car waiting for him to exit the building. Not much past six o'clock and the afternoon rush was nearly finished in the city. Everybody was already heading home to the burbs in Pennsylvania and New Jersey. Only a few cars passed by occasionally and Anna had no doubt Ben would see her immediately upon leaving the building.

She was right. He was looking at his phone, then stopped in his tracks. Glancing around, he spotted her quickly. The yellow sundress helped. She lifted her hand and waved, happier than she would admit at having gotten the better of him.

He jogged across the street in a blatant act of jaywalking.

"I guess I didn't fool anybody," he said, frowning.

She knew he hated when he was predictable. She imagined when he'd been working for the government nothing about him had ever been predictable. But being in the states, starting his own business and settling into a normal life, he'd grown com-

pletely banal. She thought it suited him. She hadn't
known him in his old life, but she imagined there
would have been an intensity about him, a bar-
rier that no one could penetrate. Given he'd never
married or never mentioned any other significant
relationship he'd had back then, she suspected she
was right.

"What are you doing here, Ben?"

"Sharpe and I were getting reacquainted."

"I'll bet. Look, I knew you would pull this move.
Mark told me enough about your past together for
me to know you wouldn't be happy with me working for him. I get that it sucks for you. But it's a
good job. I like it. And I'm not leaving. So can we
get that out of the way and move on."

"I'm supposed to be okay with the idea that you
might be in danger?"

She had to struggle not to roll her eyes. "The
only thing I'm in danger of right now is getting
carpel tunnel syndrome. Am I stupid?"

"No."

"Do I look like someone who would take unnecessary risks, especially in my condition?"

"No."

"No," she repeated. "For the next six months,
and probably well after that, the closest I'm going
to get to any of Mark's cases is via my computer.
I'm going to be a single mom. I respect the responsibility of that."

He ducked his head and she could see she'd made her point. She could also see she'd annoyed him.

"He used to take extreme risks. Unnecessary ones. I worried about you being in that environment."

"But you're conceding I can make my own decisions in this."

It took a moment, but eventually he nodded.

"And you won't give Mark any more trouble?"

"As long as he stays out of my way…no."

Since Anna couldn't imagine a scenario where Mark would need to get in Ben's way, she figured that provisional agreement had to be good enough.

"Okay. Then that's settled." She pushed her bottom against the car, using the momentum to set her in motion. She was stopped by his hand circling her wrist. "So close to a clean getaway."

"Not really. I tagged your car. I knew you had returned and parked in the building. I was hoping we could talk."

"Ben." She sighed.

"Back left bumper. You can remove it, but please give it back. It's a rather expensive one."

"Fine. Are we finished?"

"Not even remotely. Come have dinner with me."

The invitation took her by surprise. It almost sounded like a date request, but she knew it wasn't. Instead her meal would include a side lecture on the merits of marriage and the benefits a child had being raised in a two-parent home. By now he would no doubt have statistics and hard-core facts at his fingertips.

"I don't know that we have anything to talk about."

"Well, how about...our child?" His jaw clenched and she could see she was making him angry again. It was so strange to watch his emotions like this when he'd never shown any emotion at all.

Except *that night*. That night when everything had changed. When she'd looked into his face and seen—

But she hadn't. She had only thought she'd seen his affection. Because a man who truly cared about a woman didn't shut her out of his life after sex. Instead he let her in.

"That's my point. Is there anything new to discuss now? Biology demands the kid's living with me for at least the next six months. When it's out, we can talk again."

She watched the incredulousness in his expression and wondered if she'd looked the same way when he said they would get married.

"To quote you, oh, hell no."

Okay, maybe she'd been foolish to think he would cool his heels until after the baby was born. But the truth was she was struggling with seeing him again. Apparently, three months hadn't been long enough to get him out of her system. If she were honest with herself, three lifetimes probably wouldn't be enough.

Looking at him now, she thought about how happy she was to see the color in his cheeks, even knowing she'd put it there by pissing him off. She was struck by the desire to cup his face in her hand and tell him how glad she was that he was still alive.

God, she'd missed him. Missed him like nothing she'd ever known in her life. More than she'd missed her own mother after she'd left. It had been pure hell waiting day to day to find out from the hospital if his status had changed. Spitefully, he'd removed her from the list of people allowed access to his health information. The only thing the hospital could confirm was his status.

Every day she called, every day the same answer. Stable. Until finally she knew that he wasn't getting worse and his body wasn't going to reject the new cells.

He'd won his battle. But she still had lost everything.

Until that little white stick turned bright pink.

"What do you want, then?"

"I want to have dinner with you. I've missed… eating with you."

"That was a nice thing to say."

"I didn't say it to be nice. I said it because it's the truth. We were together for six years and you just… You were gone. Was it easy for you? Was it easy to walk away?"

The intensity in his expression startled her. He

was closer to her now, nearly pressing her against the car door until she felt the handle dig into her spine.

"How can you ask that?" she said, her heart suddenly beating in her throat. "How can you—" She put her hand against his chest. His heart was beating fast, too. "Oh, no, you don't get to play the guilt game with me."

"Don't I? I was in the hospital and you didn't come to see me. Not once."

Because she couldn't. She couldn't pretend anymore that he cared about her. And being there as some disinterested employee/part-time nurse…it was just too painful.

Still, she hadn't known that he would miss… eating with her.

"If you want to take me to dinner, we can talk. But it's got to be about the future and this child and that's it. I'm not talking about the past."

He smirked. "The past? It was only three months ago. But fine, I'll take it. We'll leave your car in the garage and take mine."

He pulled out his key fob and pressed a button unlocking the doors and Anna got in. Their only conversation was about where to eat and, ultimately, he drove them the few blocks to Market where he'd heard of a French BYOB restaurant that was supposed to be amazing. Since she couldn't drink and he drank infrequently, they didn't bother picking up wine to take with them.

When they were seated Anna eyed the menu in front of her with some reservations. French cuisine and pregnancy apparently didn't mix, because most of the items—food that she would have fawned over a few months ago—were now making her queasy.

Snails were so not going to happen.

She ordered a ginger ale and dug into the bread when it came.

"I would like to go to your next doctor's visit."

She considered his request. She'd had her last appointment only a few days ago. She'd heard the heartbeat for the first time and had made her decision that it was time to tell him. "That's fine. They are pretty routine."

"When do I get to see the picture? You know, the grainy thing that no can really tell what it is but people make a big deal out of it anyway."

She smiled. "That's at eighteen weeks, I think."

"Are you going to find out the gender?"

Hmm. She hadn't thought about that. She hadn't really thought about anything other than finally getting over the hurdle of telling him. Now she realized she would have to let him share in all these decisions. In a way it was like working with him again.

They had always worked together very well.

"Do you want to?" she asked him.

"I'm willing to compromise on that issue."

"So noted. Let's table it until we actually have the sonogram."

They ordered. Just some pasta in a French cream sauce for her, while he'd opted for the rabbit.

"You're normally more daring in your food selection."

She rubbed her belly while she sipped on the ginger ale. "Yeah, well, junior has other ideas. I've been a nonstop vomit mobile for the past three months. It's easing up a little but I don't want to push it."

"I can sympathize." He looked at her a little sadly. "I would have held your head. With a damp washcloth on the back of your neck."

It's what she had done for him. She wasn't even sure why the washcloth was necessary or what it accomplished. She just remembered it as something her mother did when she'd been a little girl and had been sick. It was one of the few nicer memories she had of her mother.

Their meal came and Anna picked at hers while she watched Ben eat. Before the cancer, he'd enjoyed his food. But once he'd gotten sick, the weight fell off him quickly as his appetite had fled. It had been a struggle every day to keep pushing the calories into him. During that first round of chemo, she'd basically pumped him full of fruit smoothies and milkshakes which were the only things he seemed able to tolerate.

It was ridiculous, and if asked, she would totally blame it on the hormone thing, but she could feel the tears coming as she watched him steadily clean his plate. He wasn't going to die. Ben Tyler was going to live and now, seeing him devour his rabbit, she finally let herself believe it.

"You're not touching your meal," he said when he finally looked at her plate. "You should order something else. Something more palatable."

"You see how ironic this is, don't you?"

He leaned back. "The shoe is on the other foot."

"I'm not potentially dying. At least, I hope not."

"Yes, but you need taking care of. You're going to be tired and you're obviously still dealing with nausea. I understand your concerns about rushing into marriage. It seemed like a natural conclusion, but maybe you're right. We're not there yet and I pushed too fast. But come home and live with me. At least for the duration of the pregnancy. Let me take care of you at least."

Home. Come home with him. Anna put her face in her hands and fought to control her breathing if not the tears.

"Anna, what the hell…"

He was out of his chair and crouching next to her, his hand rubbing her back and that only made her weep harder.

"Damn hormones," she blubbered.

He handed her the napkin off her lap and she used it to dab her eyes. When she lifted her head she imagined her face would be blotchy and red and her eyes swollen. Just the image she wanted to portray in front of him. He was right about her. In some ways she was very messy.

He resumed his seat across from her, setting his elbows on the table and leaning in intently. "What did I say?"

She shook her head not even willing to think the word again. He wouldn't understand. Sadly, she didn't think he could ever understand what those six years with him meant. Maybe it was time to tell him. Maybe if she came clean with him, he would finally get what her problem was and back off.

"You don't get it." She hiccupped.

"Obviously not."

"All these years— Oh, crap."

It rushed up on her like a wave. Instantly, she stood and darted around the other tables. She covered her mouth just in case and managed, with scant seconds to spare, to find the ladies' room in the rear of the restaurant and kick open a stall.

Leaning over the toilet bowl, every traitorous bit of food she'd consumed came spewing out of her mouth. She fell to her knees and braced herself, trying not to think how disgusting it was to do this in a public bathroom.

Her only salvation was that it appeared to be spotlessly clean.

She heard the door behind her squeak open and thought about trying to gather herself up to explain. Surely another woman would understand her plight. Especially if the woman was a mother.

Only it wasn't a woman who'd entered. She knew it when the stall opened and a cold, wet towel was placed on the back of her neck, while he handed her another one so she could wipe her mouth.

That's right. A cold towel on the back of the neck *did* make her feel better.

"It's okay. I'm here, Anna."

She closed her eyes. He was here.

BEN INSISTED on seeing her home. He'd paid the check and escorted her out of the restaurant, but instead of taking her to her car he drove her directly home.

"I need to get to work tomorrow," she protested. But he could see the objection was only mildly stated. After heaving up the contents of her stomach she looked decidedly weak. She leaned her head on the seat and he watched her eyes close for a prolonged count before she struggled to open them again.

"I'll pick you up in the morning."

"Or I can take the bus. I'm not an invalid, you know. It's just morning sickness. All day morning sickness."

"I want to be helpful. Besides, it's not like I have anything better to do."

She tilted her head in his direction. "You're still not working."

"In spurts. But certainly not full time. The replacement you found—well done, by the way—has kept everything moving. Everyone is booked with a consulting assignment of some sort. It seems the business can run without me."

Ben had struggled to digest that fact once he'd started to feel better again. He'd told himself he wasn't going to the office because of his concerns about being around people. The truth was he was afraid that once he got to the office there wouldn't be much for him to do.

To her he could admit that. Only to her. "It's a hard lesson to learn that you're completely and totally dispensable."

"Don't be ridiculous. They'll need you. When something goes wrong, they always need you."

He found a parking spot on the street in front of her building then got out of the car to walk with her to her apartment. He had this absurd urge to lift her off her feet and carry her, but considering his strength was only nicely returning he could see himself dropping her halfway up the stairs.

That wouldn't be very Rhett Butler of him.

Once inside her apartment, she immediately went into her bedroom—no doubt to change out of the sundress, which had suffered from her time spent kneeling on the bathroom floor. He could hear the water running and imagined she was standing under the shower, cleaning herself off.

He imagined her naked.

Her breasts covered with hot running water that would trickle over her skin and down her belly to…

Ben groaned and cut off that line of thinking. Not twenty minutes earlier she'd been head down in a toilet bowl. It wasn't fair to be thinking of her and sex when she obviously felt so poorly.

But when she came out of the bedroom, dressed in a pair of yoga pants and a tank top—an outfit he remembered fondly—with her hair pulled back and her face washed clean she looked better.

She looked beautiful. The freckles that dotted her face and arms and body stood out against her white creamy skin and he found himself wanting to connect the dots. With his tongue.

"I am flipping hungry."

"Seriously?" He recalled never being hungry after vomiting. In fact, the sensation of hunger altogether had been stripped away by the drugs until very recently. Now he was hungry for food and… other things.

"I know. But it's not like chemo. It hits me like a truck but then it's gone and I want a gallon of ice cream."

Ben wandered into the kitchen, which was merely an extension of the living room but with ceramic tiles on the floor instead of carpet. In the freezer he found a pint of triple chocolate fudge. He held it out to her. "Will this do?"

With a spoon already in hand she practically bounced on her feet. "Gimme, gimme."

Given her enthusiastic pouncing on the container he was surprised to see his hand still attached when he brought it back empty.

It was so quintessentially Anna. No half measures for her. Ever. She was the kind of woman who bounced up and down for ice cream and ate it directly out of the carton.

That lack of middle ground was why he knew when they were working together that, despite his attraction to her, she would always be wrong for him in any type of relationship outside of their professional one. Of all the women to choose from for marriage and parenting, he never would have considered Anna. Not that he had thought much about marriage or a long-term relationship, but when he had, he conceded he would need something distinctly different from Anna. Someone more sedate, more practical. Someone like him, who would understand him.

She understands you better than anyone.

The thought came and went. It didn't matter what he thought he wanted in a relationship anymore. He and Anna were in one. They'd had sex. They'd made a baby. While he had to concede he didn't see her letting him drag her to the altar any time soon, he did want to solidify and define them as…something. A couple. Expecting parents. Something.

In the living room Anna sat on the couch, her

legs crossed Indian style, and her mouth puffy around an oversize spoon of ice cream.

"Are you feeling better?"

"Hmm… *Good.*"

"Then can we get back to our conversation earlier? I asked you to come live with me. So I can take care of you."

She swallowed and set down the container. "You did."

"Then you burst into tears."

"I told you—"

"I know. Hormones. But why did the idea of living with me bring on said hormones? We've done it before, Anna. I'm not asking you to share my bed. I just want to go back to the way things were."

Suddenly an image of her in his bed popped to mind and forced him to turn his back to her slightly so she wouldn't see his thickening erection. He needed to get control of this. It was embarrassing. He was a walking hard-on around this woman.

She unfolded her legs and stood. He could see she was gathering up courage for some big proclamation.

"I can't go back to the way things were, Ben."

"Why not? Just a simple answer."

"Because it will hurt too much," she said sadly. She walked up to him and rubbed his arm like she was soothing a child. "It's not your fault. It's mine."

"What are you saying? Speak coherently."

"Since I was six years old I lived in three dif-

ferent foster homes. The longest I had stayed anywhere since my mother abandoned me, was with
you. In your office, then in your home when you
got sick. Don't you get it?"

"No. What am I supposed to get?"

"You became my home. You became my family. I fell in love with you."

He jerked at the words. "Please don't be melodramatic."

She smiled and rubbed his arm again. "I know.
You don't like the messy stuff. But it's true."

"I don't know what to say." His chest felt hollow
and he had to concentrate to breathe.

"Let me get it all out. Now, once and for all, and
then you'll see why I'm not going to marry you or
live with you or anything like that. You were my
life, my reason for getting up. You made me happy
and angry and sad. That night we had sex was the
most amazing night of my life because I thought
you finally understood what I felt. And I thought…
I thought maybe you felt…something, too."

I did. Only he couldn't seem to get the words
out.

"But then you shut me out completely. You made
this decision that could have ended your life."

"It didn't. It worked. I'm alive because of it."

She shook her head and pressed her lips together.
"Maybe. It doesn't matter. To me it was like having my mother walk away all over again. You were
willing to leave me. To take that risk, without even

considering how I might feel about it. Any chance we had, any hope I had…it was done then. I had to face the truth. You didn't care for me like I cared about you and that night was only about some last-chance sex for you."

Her conclusions were ridiculous. "Anna, I was fighting for my life. Not abandoning you."

"See, that's just it. I thought *we* were fighting for your life."

"I'm sorry. But I still don't understand. You say all these things. About how you feel. I'm offering to marry you. I'm giving you a chance to come back to the place you said was your home."

Anna shrugged. "I know. Crazy, right? But it's gone now. The delusion, or the hope, or whatever. I can't pretend you love me and I can't love someone who doesn't love me back. I mean, how pathetic would that be? So we're done. We've got to figure out the right thing to do for this kid, but the you-and-me part of it is over."

No. He wouldn't accept it. Simply hearing her say the words felt as though this heavy weight dropped on his body.

He remembered being trapped in a foreign embassy where he was planting a listening device. He remembered hearing footsteps getting closer to the room where he was working. He remembered seeing the bars on the window and knowing that the only exit was through the door where the enemy was about to walk through and capture him.

He'd felt this same sensation then. A sense of hopelessness.

No way out.

Except he'd managed to find a loose panel in the dropped ceiling. He'd been able to lift himself up into the crawl space and replace the panel just as the door to the room had opened.

He'd stayed in that space for hours until the diplomat who had returned to the office to work late had finally left.

It taught him a valuable lesson.

There was *always* a way out.

"Over?" He shook his head. "Hell, Anna, we're just getting started."

CHAPTER SEVEN

"Hey." Anna waved at Mark through the glass partition. He was on the phone, but he lifted his hand in acknowledgment.

She'd avoided Ben this morning by getting a ridiculously early start to the day and taking the bus into the city. She imagined he was parked outside her apartment building right now waiting for her. She told herself that only served him right for being so high-handed and presumptuous as to ignore her insistence that she would be taking the bus.

She would not feel guilty.

Anna settled into her office chair and booted up her computer. As the machine went through its processes, she thought about last night.

"Over?" she said out loud in bad imitation of Ben. *"We're just getting started."*

Why did he have to be like that? Why couldn't he let it go? She thought her confession would have freaked him out. She knew him well enough to know that he was not comfortable with difficult things like emotions and feelings. The very idea that she'd been suffering from unrequited love should have sent him running for the hills.

Ben didn't do romance. He certainly didn't do romantic tragedy. As far she could tell, Ben didn't do love, either.

Instead of bolting out the door, he'd made his proclamation. They weren't over. They were just beginning.

It was enough to give a pathetic girl hope. Anna wasn't sure she wanted it. She didn't need another six years of suspended animation. What she needed was to move on from him. All those years of loving him and waiting for him to love her back was enough. If something was meant to happen between them, surely it would have already happened.

Although getting angry at him because she had fallen in love didn't exactly seem fair. It wasn't exactly his problem, it was hers. But who cared about fairness when you were knocked up and alone?

"Hey," Mark said, popping his head around the glass wall. "Ben said I have to fire you."

"What did you say?"

"To shove it. Also, I implied you're my girlfriend now."

Anna sighed. "I wish you wouldn't do that."

Mark wiggled his eyebrows. "I have to have my fun. Come to my office and bring your notepad. I'm going to need you to take some dictation."

"Hardeehar."

Mark loved to use secretary references from the 1950s because he thought it made him sound cool. Occasionally he shouted from his office that he needed coffee or martinis. Every once in a while she brought him a cup of tea, just to be difficult.

Anna sat in the chair in front of his desk while he took his seat.

"So what do you need?"

"A case," he said. "We don't have one."

"You solved the Monroe case already?" Anna was stunned. The case had been cold for more than eight years.

"Child's play. Turns out Caroline Monroe had run away with a boyfriend and hadn't been kidnapped at all."

"That's awful! All those years she was alive and wouldn't let her parents know."

Mark shook his head. "She wasn't alive. A couple of months after she ran away she overdosed on whatever her drug of choice was. The boyfriend then promptly took off. Once I found him, I was able to track down the record of the Jane Doe who had been left at a hospital in Boston in a coma where she died a couple of days later."

Anna slumped in her chair. "Her mother was right, then. She knew her daughter was dead. She just wanted to know how and where."

"Parent intuition. Get ready for it. You'll sprout some the minute the kid makes his or her arrival. Anyway, while I think the boyfriend was more than culpable at least in not calling for an ambulance when the girl was obviously in trouble, there are no real criminal charges that can be proven against him. His story is he came back to the motel room with food and she was out cold. He called the police anonymously from a pay phone."

"Sounds too easy."

"It does. But there's no evidence to refute his claim so there's no way for me to go after him. Anyway the Monroes will get to bury their daughter after all these years. So there is that."

"Yeah, swell." Anna thought about Mark's words. Would she be blessed with parent intuition? Could a girl who hadn't been given good parents actually become a better parent? Her mother, and even her father, had been looming large in her mind lately.

Actually, they'd taken up occupancy ever since Anna had decided she couldn't stay with Ben any longer. When they had their fight over his decision to do the stem cell transplantation, she remembered what it had felt like to be left alone that day. A crowded room, people walking around her, bumping into her, but no one paying attention to her. Her mother missing.

In the dark days after she'd left Ben, while she waited to hear if he would live or die, she spent the time trying to recall details of that day her mother was gone so she could let the pain sink in deeper and take root, ensuring she wouldn't forget. Like an immunization, she hoped the memory of losing her mother would serve to keep her protected from ever falling in love again. Because the pain of it, of not having that love reciprocated, had felt too heavy to bear. She'd decided then she wasn't ever going to have her happily ever after like other people did.

Because she wasn't other people. She was someone who had been left by her father. Left by her mother. And she'd done a very good job of causing enough strife in some of the foster homes where she'd lived to make them want to get rid of her, too.

Focusing on those memories wasn't easy. They were vague at best. A six-year-old's memory could hardly be trustworthy. She remembered the busy room. The people bumping into her as they walked by. She remembered the scalding fear she had when she could no longer see her mother. There hadn't been any awareness of the separation happening. It was just suddenly her mother was there and then she was gone.

Vanished. And inherently Anna knew from that moment on she was alone. Eventually a woman in a dark blue uniform had knelt in front of her to ask her what her name was. Anna had been wearing a pair of jeans, sneakers with holes in the toes and a Disney princess T-shirt.

She wanted to remember if she'd said anything to her mother. If her mother had said anything to her. But Anna didn't. She didn't remember her even saying goodbye.

Anna wished she could go back and tell that woman her abandonment was going to really screw Anna over.

Not just because she would be put into the foster-care system, but because by leaving, her mother was going to turn Anna into someone else. Someone who didn't trust people. Someone who didn't need people. Someone who didn't put up a fight for the people she loved.

Ben had been the only person in her life to crack through that well-constructed wall of caution. And when she considered it, how messed up was that? The man was an emotional ice block. Maybe she'd subconsciously chosen to love him out of all other people because she knew she would never really have to deal with being loved back. Ben: the safest crush on the planet.

"Totally messed up," she muttered.

"What's messed up? I solved the case. But now I need another one. I know we talked about doing discreet ads to start, but maybe we need something a little flashier out of the gate. Or maybe we should look at the major newspapers. People have to actually want me before I can be exclusive."

"I have a case."

Mark's eyes widened. "Don't keep me in suspense."

"I'm pregnant."

"Not news. You turn green and run for the bathroom at regular intervals."

"Well, I was thinking, I've never really tried to find my birth parents. I should probably do that… to get their health information and stuff. Any genetic conditions. Things like that."

Mark nodded. "Anna, you know how to track down personal information on the internet as well as anyone I know. You've never done that on your parents? Do you not know their names?"

Elizabeth Rochester and Luis Summers. Those were the names on the copy of her birth certificate she had. Her first foster family had encouraged her to have a copy of it. Thinking someday she might want to try to find her parents. Under the father's name was printed Luis Summers. Under the mother's maiden name was Elizabeth Rochester. She didn't know if they were married or not, but she did know her mother had said her name was Anna. Anna had been what she'd been called. She took Summers because it seemed logical. He was her father. And because she liked summer. No school during summer. A perfectly sound reason to adopt a last name.

"Their names were fake." Anna had been eighteen when she did her first internet search for some record of them. She hadn't expected to find much, but wanted to see if anything popped. When nothing did, she dug deeper until ultimately she had to accept the truth.

Anna Summers wasn't really her name.

"You're sure?"

"I've never been able to find any records of an Elizabeth Rochester or Luis Summers that fit the description or age of my parents in the states of New York, New Jersey, Delaware or Pennsylvania. The only thing that makes sense is either my father or mother gave the hospital fake names when filling out the paperwork for my birth certificate."

"They could be real names, but not from anywhere around here. Maybe they made their way across the country to the East Coast."

"Maybe. It's a possibility. But I was born here. They were drug users here. I can remember that much. You might think they had a criminal record, but there was nothing in the system for either of those two names. Two fake names on a certificate, not easy to track down."

"What are you thinking?"

Anna shrugged. "I'm thinking you can do your magic. There were two people in this world. They lived and breathed. They conceived me. They lived together with me for a time at least. And left me. I would like you to find them. I would like to know if there is any family history I can trace."

Mark hesitated. "This could open up a big can of worms for you. Emotionally."

She'd finally confessed she'd been in love with Ben for six years. She would become a mother in the next six months. And she had no idea what the hell Ben meant when he said they were just beginning.

Can open. Worms out.

Besides, after all these years, finding her parents felt like the right thing to do. She was going to be a *mom*. She was going to have to, by moral obligation, give a shit about another human being who, for the first time in her adult life, wasn't Ben Tyler.

It wasn't right to hold on to her past like some kind of armor shield. She needed to let it go if she intended to give her child her full self. But before she could do that she needed answers.

"I'm ready for it. Whatever you find."

"Okay."

"I get an employee discount, right?"

"Absolutely," Mark said, holding out his hand so they could shake on it. "Is, like, two percent off okay? Or hey, I know, I'll write up a coupon and you can use that."

"I can't believe you decided to work for the government so long ago when clearly comedy has always been your calling."

"I'm multi-talented. You still have that birth certificate?"

Yes. It was stupid, because she knew it wasn't real. Not really. But it was her only connection to the parents she vaguely remembered having. "I'll bring it in."

"Great. Now, how's your shorthand, kid, because I'm ready to dictate that letter."

Anna stood, shaking her head. "A letter. That's funny."

ANNA ARRIVED HOME to find Ben waiting on the steps of her building. It was hot and humid and he looked a little wilted, as if he'd been waiting a long time. She could only hope he hadn't been here all day.

Part of her filled with dread. The fact that he was here meant they were mostly likely going to have another confrontation.

The other part of her was happy to see him, of course, and she hated that part like a nagging toothache. Just. Go. Away.

Finding a parking spot, she did a quick and efficient parallel maneuver and stopped the car within six inches of the curb like a proper city driver. When she approached him, she saw he had a stack of books and two brown bags on the step next to him.

"Please tell me you haven't been waiting here since this morning or I might actually have to say I'm sorry."

"Don't be ridiculous. I left once I realized if you came out any later, you would be late for work. You're never late for work. You could have told me."

"I told you last night I would take the bus."

"You could have told me this morning."

She could have. Only she didn't want to send

him a text because then he would have her new cell phone number. A number she'd purposefully changed after she'd left him as a way to make her feel more separated from him. So much for that strategy.

"Or I guess I could have called and confirmed," he admitted more to himself than to her.

"You don't have my new number," she reminded him.

He sighed. "Anna, of course I have your new number."

Right. Because he was Ben Tyler. Spymaster. Sometimes she forgot because, aside from the crazy things that happened every once in a while—like the current president of the United States calling to get his opinion on something, Ben was mostly a normal man.

"What's that?" she asked, pointing to his stack of stuff and wanting to ignore his breach of her privacy.

"Books on pregnancy. I've gone through them and highlighted passages on morning sickness and the transitions that occur in the second trimester, which I think will make you feel better. I've also noted some questions in the margins that I'm hoping you can answer so I can better understand some things. Then I stopped at Chef Chen's in Little China. I told Mrs. Chen about your morning sickness and she made up some special soup that she assures me will fix you right up."

"That's a lot of soup," she said, desperately trying not to be affected by his attention.

"Mrs. Chen says I needed fixing up as well and threw in a quart of the house special lo mein."

Her favorite. "Okay. Come on up."

Might as well give in to the inevitable. Ben wasn't going away peacefully. Besides that, Mrs. Chen was a genius with food and could cure anything from fever to the common cold with the right blend of spices and ginger. If she said this soup would make Anna feel better, then it would.

As she walked up to the second floor with him trailing, she considered how this meeting could have been awkward. After all, last night she'd let loose with everything she'd been feeling and holding on to for all those years. Usually the day after a big confession could be weird between two people, but Anna didn't feel it.

Instead, she felt a little freer. Her secret was out there. She'd said it. Forget pride and forget rejection. Forget it all. She loved Ben Tyler. And it had felt good to say it because it was real and had been a part of her life for a long time.

She. Loved. Ben. Tyler.

He couldn't make her unsay it. He couldn't do anything but hear it.

The only thing that really pissed her off about the confession was that while he'd been staring at her as if she'd hit him with a two-by-four—looking more stunned than he had after she told him she was pregnant—she still actually thought he would say it back. It was crazy. It was insane. But she'd waited for it anyway.

She knew the man he was. She knew he was self-contained and emotionally unreachable. She was slowly coming to grips with the fact that her love could be entirely predicated on the premise that he simply wasn't capable of loving her.

But deep inside, where she was really honest with herself, she knew that picture of Ben wasn't entirely true. A man didn't read pregnancy books and make notes in the margins if he didn't have the capacity for great caring.

So what now really pissed her off was that he couldn't see it. He couldn't see what she saw when he looked at her. He couldn't know what had been shimmering in his eyes when he made love to her that night. Because there had been something there. Something more than desire. She'd seen... need. As though he had needed her so desperately in that moment. Didn't that mean there had to be something more than sex between them?

But it's not as though she could tell him. It was something he would have to acknowledge on his own.

That night she thought he had. She'd thought he was ready for what they could be. Except... he hadn't been. She knew it hurt him when she left. As much as she hurt in those three months away from him, it didn't give her any satisfaction to know he'd missed her, too.

They reached her apartment and she dropped off her purse and flipped off the sandals she was wearing. Barely into her fourth month and already her feet would swell if she was on them for any length of time. Lord only knew how her ankles would look when she was walking around with a bump the size of beach ball.

Ben set down the books on the coffee table and took the bags to the kitchen. Since he seemed comfortable in her space, she let him gather the plates and silverware. Picking up one of the books, she started to scan through the sections he'd highlighted. The man was crazy for information. He collected it the way some people collected coins. Reading, he said, was always one of the easiest ways to gather it.

She stopped when she saw a picture of a breast in the book. Next to it he'd written, *Increased Sensitivity?*

The seemingly innocuous question had her squirming and squeezing her legs together. In fact, her nipples and her breasts were more sensitive. If he were to touch them…

Whoa. Enough of that. As hard as leaving him had been, as hard as trying to imagine her future life without him had been, remembering the sex… had been just as hard.

Because she tried to imagine feeling that way

with another man someday and it simply would not come. She certainly hadn't felt that way with boyfriends she'd had before Ben.

There had been that one disaster while she'd been working for him when she tried to make him jealous by dating a hot young guy. Not only had Ben not lifted an eyebrow, but also it turned out Kevin had shown up at the office once to pick her up for their date with no cash in his wallet. He'd actually asked Ben for the money and Ben had given it to him. Needless to say, she'd been mocked ruthlessly for her taste in potential mates.

Poor Kevin. He didn't stand a chance against what she felt for Ben. Even when she knew it wasn't working with him and that she was dating him for the wrong reasons, she still tried a last desperate attempt to see if she could somehow use Kevin to get over Ben. Because wouldn't that show her boss how over him she was?

The sex had been lousy, she felt guilty as hell for using Kevin—although he really didn't seem to mind—and, in the end, she'd realized how immature she'd been about the whole thing. She'd been playing silly girl games like she was a character on a sitcom. She had no doubt that Ben would have seen right through her scheme.

If he'd bothered to care. Which he hadn't.

The next day she'd dumped Kevin, who seemed remarkably relieved at the time. It made her realize what a poor job she'd done at attempting to be someone else's girlfriend when she was so clearly Ben's…girl. Woman. Assistant. Employee. Devoted, love-sick idiot!

It was some point after that when she'd realized that maybe their relationship would remain the same. She would love him and he would need her and it would be enough.

But then he'd gotten sick and, in his weakness, he'd reached out to her.

Now he was asking questions about her breast sensitivity. After she told him she loved him.

After she told him they were over.

"Here. I brought the soup and some lo mein if you're hungry."

"My breasts are none of your business!"

"Okay."

He set the bowls on the small table she had next to the kitchen. A table she never ate at when she was home. It was mostly used for setting down her grocery bags and the mail before things were sorted and put away.

He'd even managed to find the one serving dish she owned and had filled it with the lo mein he'd recently microwaved to reheat. It was odd to watch him doing these things. These simple tasks she'd done for him for so long that he was doing for her.

She sat at the table squirming a bit because of her breast declaration. He hadn't known she'd been looking at the picture in the book when she said it. Heck, maybe he hadn't even meant anything by the question. Maybe he was curious in a nonsexual way if her breasts were more sensitive.

Yeah, right.

He handed her a spoon and a paper towel to use as a napkin—because, really, what was the purpose of buying both—then he sat across from her.

Not counting last night's disaster, this was the first time they were sharing a meal together since she'd left him. It was exactly the thing she didn't want to do because if she fell back into this pattern, she was afraid she would never break out of it.

But she was feeling tired and the soup did smell really good. She took a few cautious sips and waited for junior to approve or disapprove. After a couple of minutes, she could tell the kid seemed satisfied with the selection. She had a suspicion the kid might even let her have the lo mein.

"Are you angry I'm here?" he finally said after a few long moments of them silently eating.

"I should be. I told you that there can't be anything between us. Sitting here and having dinner after a long day is not exactly helping the situation."

"I brought books on the baby. That's perfectly within the boundaries. Besides, you didn't say there couldn't be *anything* between us. You said you weren't going to marry me or live with me."

"Yeah, so that basically covers a relationship."

"Not quite," he said slowly. "There's something you left out."

"What?"

"Sex."

Anna's stomach flipped over like fish on land and because she had just read it in the book he gave her, she knew it was too soon to blame the sensation on the baby moving.

"Anna, I'm not sure how to say this but…I guess, I would like to make your breasts my business."

Oh, my. It probably wasn't a good sign that her nipples suddenly got hard.

CHAPTER EIGHT

"DID YOU JUST SAY SEX?"

"I did. I would like to have it," he said, then added, "With you." In case that wasn't clear.

She dropped the spoon into the bowl and sat back staring at him. "Are you crazy?"

Maybe, he wasn't sure. He only knew he couldn't stop thinking about her. Couldn't stop fantasizing about her. He didn't only want to have sex with her. He wanted to have sex with her as many times as his body was able. He wanted to sink into her until it became a common event. So that some night in the future, thoughts of it wouldn't play in a continual loop in his mind, driving him to the brink of insanity.

"Anna, I can't be the first man to say he desired you sexually. I don't see anything wrong with being honest about what I want."

"No. I mean, yes. I mean, we are so not there. You walk in here with Chinese food and a book with a picture of a breast highlighted and suddenly it's okay to talk about sex? That you want it. What the hell am I supposed to do with that bombshell?"

Suddenly irritated, he threw his napkin on the table. "What? You don't care for surprising news being dropped in your lap? You told me last night that you loved me. Did you think I wouldn't consider what you said, that I wouldn't think about what it meant to me?"

"I…uh…I don't know."

"Well, I did. I thought it about it all night. What you said weren't just words, Anna. Or were they?"

"No. I was as honest with you as I could be."

"Then let me be honest with you. I don't know if I love you. Hell, I can't say for sure I know what love is. I've certainly never been so overcome with emotion or feeling for another person that it changed me fundamentally inside."

She shook her head. "I don't believe that. You've told me about your parents. How it was growing up. They sounded like warm, lovely people. You must have loved them."

"Of course, yes."

They'd been older. A couple who had found each other later in life. His father was a successful plumber and his mother was a quiet, soft-spoken woman. Having him had been an unplanned event, so Ben's childhood was more about him fitting into their worlds rather than them accommodating his.

Fortunately, Ben had seemingly been born competent and mature so hadn't required a lot of their attention and focus. His father was stern, but not harsh. He demanded discipline and he rewarded competence. Ben's mother's quiet demeanor hid a deep intellect that he admired and often sparred with.

Had he loved them? He'd been sad when they passed, of course. His father of a heart attack. His mother not two years after that of a sudden brain aneurism. Ben had been orphaned by age twenty-six.

From that moment on he had lived with the certainty that he was alone in the world. It hadn't frightened him or worried him. He'd simply embraced his solitude and lived his life for his work.

Never once had he met a woman for whom he wanted to change that life.

Until Anna had left him. Because she loved him and was tired of not being loved back. Anna wasn't prone to dramatics or tears, yet she'd cried when he asked her to come home.

Home.

The word should have registered with him. He knew what it meant to her. Knew what she sacrificed each pay period to put money aside so that she could finally have her own house someday. A house she declared would be the best home she could imagine, because it would be hers.

Those tears showed him how very serious she was about her feelings. She deserved to know how serious he was about making something work between them, as well.

He knew he wanted her in his life. She was probably his closest friend. The first one he'd really allowed himself to have when he returned to the states. Because of her he'd found himself becoming closer to the other people he worked with like Greg Chalmers, a man still struggling to overcome his own demons, who Ben found himself want to help. And Madeleine Kane, who had needed a kick on the bottom to jump start her life again. Would he have made those more personal connections without Anna having been there first? Doubtful.

"Loving your parents isn't the same thing as loving a woman," he said.

"No, it's not. But don't say you don't know how to love someone." Anna reached across the small table and laid her hand on top of his. "You're not as coldhearted as you want to believe. You would have to choose it, Ben. Decide what path you wanted to take in life."

He laughed without humor. "Choose my path? Sort of an ironic thing to say to a man who has had little choice for the past year. You want to talk about dropping bombshells, forget that I wasn't sure if I was going to live or die, I broke a long-held, self-imposed rule and had sex with with an employee. Then my long-time employee and very close friend suddenly left me at a time when I desperately needed her. In the span of weeks I realized two things—I was going to live and I was sterile. I would never have my own children, which I didn't even think I wanted, until…wait! You come back into my life to tell me you're pregnant with my child and that you have, in fact, loved me for a very long time. However, immediately on the heels of that declaration you tell me there can be nothing between us. Those are some pretty big surprises, wouldn't you say?"

She had the decency to blush. He hoped guilt motivated it. "I'm sorry. I guess, I was only thinking about…well, me. Yuck."

He turned his hand under hers so that their fingers meshed and he squeezed it in shared commiseration. "You had a pretty rough few months, too."

She nodded and he could see her eyes watering. This new pregnant Anna, he was coming to realize, was a crier.

"I was so afraid you were going to die," she sobbed. "When the first round of chemo didn't work, I didn't know what to think. I couldn't believe it could actually happen, that you might not live. I wouldn't believe it. So all I could think about was the next step, the next round of treatment.

"Then one night, out of the blue, you're sitting there with this massive erection and all of a sudden we're doing it when I've wanted to do it with you for years. Then you don't talk to me for days. Nothing about your health, certainly nothing about that night. Suddenly, you get this call and, oh, by the way, you're doing this risky procedure that might kill you even faster. And about that night…it just sort of happened and you're really sorry it did." She paused. "I had to leave. Don't you see? You left me no choice.

"Except four weeks later I'm peeing on a stick and, wow, I'm going to be a mother. I had to tell you about it. Then finally, finally after six years of holding it inside I spill my guts all over the place and tell you I love you. You say it's not over and walk out and I'm, like, what the hell does that mean? And today, after twenty-two years of not caring I finally decided to find my parents. So, yeah, I'm right there with you."

He stood and moved around the table to pull her into his arms. Hugging her like he hadn't hugged anyone in a very long time.

She sobbed on his neck and he could feel the dampness seep through the short-sleeved polo.

"You did say *massive erection*. I heard that correctly, didn't I?"

She laughed and hiccupped and then hit him on the shoulder. All the things he wanted to accomplish with that statement.

"I'm sorry I didn't consider things from your perspective," she said as she used the back of her hand to wipe away her tears. "I can't say I'm sorry I left you. Because I really felt I had to go, but I'm sorry for all the other stuff you went through alone."

"Okay. That's fair."

"Ben." She looked at him intently. "I don't think

I can do it. I mean, have sex with you. The first time it was too much. Too big. Leaving you was the hardest thing I ever did. I felt broken for weeks after and it took all my strength to get back to this place where I am. I'm not ready to go down that road…yet."

And there it was: that small window of opportunity. Ben was suddenly in love with the word *yet*.

"I get it," he said, stopping her from saying anything else, before she could think too much about it. He didn't want to screw this up. He cupped her face in his hands. Her precious face that he'd missed so much. He ran his thumb over her cheekbone, then her lower lip.

Yes, he wanted her. But not now. Not after all this stuff that had been spewed about the room. Ben could feel how the emotions cluttered up the air. On both sides. But there was one thing he had to set straight. He wasn't leaving her without her knowing what their future would look like.

"I said that I don't know if I love you. But I do want you. Desperately. Like you said…maybe love is a choice. Well, then let me try."

She shook her head, her cheek brushing against his palm. She was so damn soft. "Ben, you can't force yourself to love someone. That's not what I meant when I said you had a choice."

"I know what you meant. You meant I have to believe it can exist before I'll believe I can experience it. Fine. Then show me."

"What do you mean?"

"We can date. Like any other couple. I want to take you out and get to know you not as a friend or an employee but as something else. I want to take you to dinners and movies and buy you flowers. Hope maybe I can impress you enough so you'll let me and my massive erection back into your bed."

She rolled her eyes. "I can't believe I used the word *massive*. You're never going to let me live that down are you?"

"Unlikely."

"So we date." She paused as if considering the idea. "With maybe the potential for sex. What if it doesn't work out?"

He shrugged. "What if it doesn't? You were ready to have a relationship based only on our shared parenting of the kid. If we date and it doesn't work out, we'll still have that."

Her eyes narrowed a little. "You made me think you weren't happy with that arrangement."

"I'm not. I want the baby in my life. Full time. Not part time. But I guess that's punishment for every man who doesn't have the good sense to marry the woman first before making a baby with her. I don't get my way in this."

He watched her taking in his words, and knew that she was satisfied with them. He wasn't lying. He knew he had very little control in what the final arrangement between them was going to be.

"Okay. We can date."

"Excellent. Before I leave give me a taste. Just a taste, so I can remember…"

He didn't finish his thought. Simply lowered his head and felt for her lips. They were exactly like he remembered. At first touch they were plump and delicious, giving him a little resistance as they pushed against his own lips. That should have been enough, but when he heard the slight gasp in her throat he wanted more. His mouth opened and he pushed his tongue inside feeling the moist heat of her mouth, remembering all too well how her wonderful mouth had surrounded the head of his cock.

Holding her face in his hands, he thrust his tongue steadily against hers, hopefully reminding her of that night, too. How they had moved together so easily, so naturally.

Then he felt pressure against his chest and he knew that he was taking her too far too fast. She wasn't ready for sex. He could respect that, he would honor that. But he damn well wanted her to know that, in terms of desire for her, he had no equal.

Slowly he lifted his head and watched with satisfaction as she struggled to blink her eyes open.

"Delicious. Just like I remembered."

"You should go," she whispered. "I can't…think when you do that."

Which was the point but he didn't want to press things. He had made good progress. She'd let him back inside her apartment. She let him back inside her mouth. It was only a matter of time before he was ultimately back where he really wanted to be.

Between her legs and in her heart.

"Good night. I'll call you."

Ben left with a reminder to lock the door behind him and had this crazy urge to jog down the hallway to the elevators. For the first time in these past few crazy days with Anna he had a sense that things weren't truly over. That he could fix them.

Like any other mission he took on he simply had to focus on his goal, set a plan in motion, then make it work.

In this case he needed to make this *relationship* work. Okay, so she wanted to be loved back. It seemed like a reasonable request and he hadn't lied to her when he said he would try. Unfortunately, he knew himself too well. Love was something poetic and pretty. He wasn't a man inclined to either. But regardless of whatever he came to feel for Anna, she would never think for one second it wasn't love. He could convince her every day that she was the center of his world, and she would never have to know how he labeled his emotions.

She would be his and with her came his child.

Yes, this courtship was just another mission for him.

And when he was on a mission he did not fail.

MARK WATCHED Anna walk across the lobby of their office building, heading toward where he was sitting at the coffee shop, but not really see-ing him. Her mind was occupied and he didn't have to stretch to figure out who was filling up her thoughts.

He wished Ben could see her like this. See her and know what it was like to have a woman who was walking alone in a crowded atrium and think-ing of nothing but him. Once again Mark found himself jealous of Ben.

"Anna!"

At his shout she raised her head and searched the small café. She waved and came over, taking the open seat at the small table. Mark was meet-ing someone here shortly and he wanted to make sure he had an extra seat available.

"Sit here and save my table," he said. "I'll get you some tea."

She didn't protest having been spared waiting in line. He knew she could tire easily and after walking from the parking lot all the way through the lobby her ankles were probably already a lit-tle swollen.

Mark took the tea from the man behind the counter and handed him five bucks so the next time he saw him he would have Mark's order ready. Then he sat with Anna and watched her put three creamers into her tea. He hadn't started the search for her biological parents yet, but he wondered if one of them might have been of English descent.

"Oh, before I forget." Anna reached into her purse and pulled out a folded slip of paper.

Mark looked at the slip of paper with its embossed stamp and read the names he knew were fake.

"I know," she said. "Makes you realize how easy we make it for terrorists. Hey, here are some names and baby footprints. Instant American citizen."

"Stuff like this used to keep me up at night."

"It doesn't anymore?"

The question startled Mark because the first answer that came to mind was, no, it didn't. On the heels of that thought he realized it wasn't exactly true. He still read every piece of information he could find regarding the continuing mission in Afghanistan. He still cared what happened to the operatives and the soldiers he'd left behind.

But his first thought getting up every day was no longer about how he was going to beat the enemy. Instead, he thought about the cases he was working on, growing his business and what was his number-one priority right now.

Ben had been right. It had taken time, but he was definitely starting to make the transition from agent to civilian.

"Sometimes," he finally answered. It was accurate enough. "I need to wrap up some other things, but then I'll get started on this. Should be interesting."

"Thanks." She sighed.

"So what's up with you?"

Her brows raised in a question.

"You were walking through the lobby like a zombie. Clearly something is up."

She gave a wry expression. "I should have known better than to take up with another spy. You guys see everything. Ben wants to date me."

"I thought he wanted to marry you."

"He wants that, too, but he's willing to start with dating. I—I told him how I felt about him."

"Good girl." Mark always believed in honesty between two people. Whether it ended happily or badly, it should at least be real. Helen had understood that.

"Yeah, well, I don't know how good it is. He said he didn't know how he felt about me but that he wanted us to get to know each other as something other than employer and employee. Something beyond friendship."

"Seems reasonable." And logical. A lot like Ben. By not pressing too hard, it appeared as if he was giving Anna options. She could easily say no to an offer of marriage. Harder to reject something as simple as a date.

Anna held the cup in her hands and looked away from him. "What if…"

"What?"

"What if this is only about him getting the baby? I mean, seriously, how desperate would a man be if he knew his one and only shot at fatherhood could walk away from him at any time and take his child with her? Not that I would do that, but he would know he has no control in this. I'm sure it drives him crazy."

Mark shook his head. "He's not that ruthless. I promise. If he said he wanted to give you a chance to date, that's what he meant. Trust me. We weren't pals, but we knew each other. Well."

She smiled then, and it made him feel good. "You really think so?"

"I do. Now, I need to meet someone down here. Why don't you go up and open the office."

"You got it, boss man."

Mark watched her leave and felt a twinge of guilt for lying. But it wasn't like they had to be honest in *their* relationship, after all. Besides, he'd made her smile.

The hard truth was Ben was exactly that ruthless. If he decided he wanted the baby full time, he would take the most logical path toward achieving those ends. He wasn't a master manipulator without reason. Mark was sure Ben was confident he could make Anna believe whatever he wanted. The question was would Anna realize before it was too late that she was being played.

Mark considered talking to Ben again. Maybe more of a man-to-man than a man-to-adversary discussion. Mark had known Anna only a few weeks, but he liked her and the thought of letting her get hurt…again…didn't sit well with him. It was like watching a kitten trying to hold her own against a lion.

If he told Ben that Anna deserved better, would he listen? Mark could imagine how that conversation would go over. But the truth was if Ben didn't love her, he wouldn't be able to make her happy. No matter how good a job he did at making himself believe it was love.

No one knew that better than Mark. Certainly not after Helen. It wasn't fair to try to hold on to one thing at the expense of another. Mark cared about Anna enough to not want to see that happen to her.

Of course, there was his own life he should be concentrating on. But when had that ever stopped him? He was a meddler by nature.

"Mark?"

Mark jerked out of his thoughts, surprised he'd lost track of the people surrounding him. Maybe he was making that magical transition to civilian life faster than he realized. He stood and turned to the approaching man he'd been waiting for. Mark offered his hand but the man paused for a second then, as if reluctantly, he gave it a quick shake.

"Hi, Dom. It's been a long time."

"Thirteen years to be precise." Dom pointed to the empty chair and Mark nodded as if to suggest he'd held it for him. Mark watched as the old man planted his hands heavily on the table and shuffled his legs slowly until he could sink onto to the chair.

"How are you?" Mark asked, also sitting.

"I'm old," Dom said, stating the obvious. "It's just arthritis if that's what you're asking. I don't have Parkinson's or anything else. I move slowly most days. Some days not at all. It's not the worst thing an old man can deal with."

"No, I don't imagine it is. And Marie? How is she?"

"She's old, too. She pretends…well, it's why she wouldn't come here today. She still wants to pretend. Pretend Helen didn't die in that car wreck. Pretend her lungs aren't making it impossible to breathe, especially on such humid days. Pretend she can keep up with Sophie."

At the mention of his daughter's name, Mark's heart pinched. Sophie. For more than thirteen years she'd been only a name at the bottom of a card or email, the unknown recipient of a gift. A fuzzy face over the internet more recently. Now, she was about to become startling real and he wasn't sure if he could handle it.

"Dom, you have to know how sorry I was to hear about Helen. I moved heaven and earth to get back for the funeral in time, but the damn transport plane I caught got rerouted to the Philippines and—"

Dom held up his hand. An imperious command for Mark to stop talking. Mark figured he deserved it. After all, excuses were exactly that. He hadn't been there to help grieve with his daughter's grandparents. Worse, he hadn't been there for his daughter.

No, what was worse was that he was sitting in a café and wondering if the smartest thing he might ever do would be to start running and not look back. Yet his ass remained planted in the seat.

This is the part where you leave the life you thought you wanted all behind and start doing the right thing.

"I want to see her, Dom."

The old man nodded. "You want more than that, I think."

"Look, I know I have been the model of the absentee father, but it's not like I abandoned her. I've stayed in communication at least once a month unless I had to go underground for some reason. And being back here isn't all because of Helen. I started thinking that it was time for a change, time for me to be in the states and be a bigger part of her life. When I learned about Helen, I knew it wasn't a choice anymore. I quit my job and came to where you are. I've started my own business. I've got plenty of money to support the two of us and the truth is I'm—"

Mark didn't want to upset the man with the rest of what he'd intended to say. But it was unnecessary.

"You're younger." Dom sighed.

"Before Helen's death she was touring in every city around the country. There was also talk of another European trip. Helen could keep up with that. Can you and Marie?"

Because Sophie wasn't any average teenage girl. Sophie had the gift of music. As a child prodigy, she performed with many different orchestras showcasing her talent to audiences all over the country. Apparently his daughter was in high demand. She hadn't played any concerts since her mother's passing, but eventually that would change and she would be back on the road.

Mark tried to imagine Dom in his condition keeping up with such a robust schedule. He couldn't.

The man closed his eyes and when he opened them Mark pretended not to see they were red. "She just lost her mother six months ago. We're all she has left. She doesn't even know you other than as the man who got her mother pregnant."

Mark tightened his jaw. He wasn't about to tell Helen's father how it really went down between them. It was Helen's secret and he would honor it even in death. But he did remind his daughter's grandfather of one very important fact. "I offered to marry her. I gave her my ring. She was the one who broke the engagement."

"Yes, she did."

"I've been patient. You said to give Sophie time to adjust before rushing into her life. I've sat on my hands for six months waiting. You can't tell me that Sophie isn't ready. She knows I'm in the area. Hell, she's probably wondering why I haven't come to see her."

"We believe she should meet with you, yes. Marie and I have discussed that. But to live with you full time...I don't know if that will work."

He was holding something back. Mark could see it in his face. It was hurting Dom, which was why his eyes were still red. They were both biding time, hoping that something would change, but Mark didn't know what that something was. He only knew he wanted his daughter in his life. Neither Dom nor Marie could continue to convince themselves they could raise her on their own for much longer. Time was their enemy.

"Dom, her schedule is going to pick up again—"

"I know what her damn schedule is! Don't you think I know? Her agent is constantly pressuring us on this. We asked for this break to give her time to grieve, but now everyone has decided that six months is a perfectly satisfactory time for a fourteen-year-old girl to get over the death of her mother!"

Mark leaned back in his chair letting Dom have his say.

"We hoped maybe she would adjust to a more normal routine. School, friends. But she's...she's not like other kids her age. Certainly not like Helen at that age. All Helen used to think of was her hair and boys. All Sophie can think of is...more."

Then she's like me at that age.

"Dom, I think you agreed to meet me here because you know what I told you over the phone is right. You and Marie are her grandparents. I will make sure you remain a steady and important part of her life. But she's my daughter, my responsibility and she should be with me now."

The man didn't have to know how terrified Mark was about the idea of being a father. He was hoping it sort of came to him. Like some magic wand would be waved as soon as they were together and bam, he would be insta-father.

"And like I told you, Marie and I are still considering it."

"That's fair. We don't have to make any major changes right now," Mark agreed. "But I'm done waiting to see her. She should at least know I'm here. That I want her in my life. You can't hide her from me forever."

"Is that what you think? That we've been hiding her from you?"

"Every time I ask to see her or schedule time with all of you, you come up with one excuse after another. What was I supposed to think?"

Dom shook his head. "Son, you've got it all wrong. It's not us keeping you from her. It's *her*. We didn't know quite how to tell you, but I'll just come right out with it. Sophie wants nothing to do with you."

That was when Mark felt his heart break for the first time in his life.

CHAPTER NINE

"WAS THIS A GOOD IDEA or a bad one?"

Anna glanced at Ben who was smiling grimly. He had waited exactly two days before calling her to politely ask her out for a date Saturday afternoon. They'd had a nice, if slightly awkward, lunch at a small bistro they both enjoyed and then he'd suggested a tour of the Philadelphia Art Museum that was featuring the works of Van Gogh.

Anna had walked the creaky boards of the museum enjoying the swirls of color and light. It was odd seeing so much beauty on the canvas even though she knew that at the time he'd painted them Van Gogh had been in so much mental pain.

"Why would you ask that?"

"I don't want to bore you. I want us to have fun."

Anna couldn't say how much fun she was having. But she felt peaceful with him. At rest deep inside in a way she hadn't been in a long time. Probably since first discovering he was sick with cancer. She wondered if it felt that way for him, too, now that he was finally healing. Now that he no longer had to deal with the specter of death looming behind his shoulder. But she didn't want to ask and put his illness in the middle of their date. This was supposed to be about seeing if they could have a new future together, not dwelling on what they almost lost. Still, she couldn't help but look at the paintings and be reminded of her past in a way.

"It reminds me of a class trip," she mused, moving slowly from canvas to canvas. At a time when she'd been normal for a while. Just a girl in school who was tuning out all the things her art teacher had to say about the classics on the wall and instead thinking about whether Johnny Blanton was going to try to kiss her when he walked her home from school that day.

Now here she was again, only this time she was wondering if Ben was going to kiss her when he dropped her off. She'd already told herself she shouldn't let it happen. Kissing Ben was…powerful. Kissing Ben could make her forget all the reasons, very sound reasons, she had for not having sex with him.

"Uh-oh. You've compared our date to a school trip. The museum was a bad idea, then."

She smiled. "No, it was actually a good memory."

"You told me you hated school."

He'd been doing that all day. Showing her how much he recalled of everything she had ever told him. He mentioned her favorite color, pointed out her favorite thing to eat on the menu. It was nothing exciting—just a grilled cheese sandwich. But that particular bistro prepared it with three types of cheeses, which made it simply to die for.

Of course, she'd never doubted he was observant. The man had been trained to see and hear everything within his surroundings. However, being observant and being attentive were two different things. Like hearing what she said and understanding why she said it were two different things. In his defense, though, she'd never talked much about her past. Any details she'd shared with him had been superficial facts.

"I didn't hate school," she said slowly. It felt as if she was offering up some big secret even though this was only her personal history. It simply wasn't something she'd ever talked about with anyone before. But if they were going to make this work, if they were going to have an actual relationship, then it was probably time she gave him something of herself and the life she'd experienced growing up.

Funny, she could see now, as he quoted back all the things he thought he knew about her, how much she had kept from him. All she'd told him were the meaningless things, nothing really important or substantive about her life. She'd told herself she was in love with him, but could a person be in love with another person when there was so much of herself she hadn't revealed?

A year ago the idea that he would remember she liked grilled cheese sandwiches and the color purple would have thrilled her. A true sign they were connected.

Now, it wasn't enough.

"I didn't hate school," she repeated. "I hated being in school. I hated the age I was that made it mandatory."

"Explain."

"When you are in foster care you're not in control of anything. Where you live, what food you're given, what clothes you wear a lot of times. I hated not being eighteen. I hated middle school and high school as institutions because, as long as I was attending them, I wasn't eighteen. Those years, the only thing I could think of was getting out of the system. The foster system, the school system. All of it. I wanted it behind me."

She stopped and looked at him, wondering if she made any sense. His expression appeared stern. "Anna, you never talked about your time in the different homes you were in. I never pressed. But were you hurt? Were you—"

"No." She held her hand up. "Nothing like that. I didn't have any really bad experiences in any of the homes I stayed in. Nothing truly awful. I know there are horror stories about kids in foster homes. But there are other stories, too. A lot of the people who take in kids like me are good, kind, loving people. They're trying to help, not hurt. I'm sure there are some bad apples, but it's like that everywhere with everything. So, no, I don't mean to vilify the foster-care system. I'm only saying I was anxious to be out of it."

He nodded. They continued walking side by side down the length of the exhibition hall taking in the work without really studying it.

She had this crazy idea that he might reach out and hold her hand. He didn't.

"When you talk about it, you use the word *homes,* plural."

"I had three. The first was a really nice woman. Her husband didn't pay us much attention but she was always laughing and hugging us. She had two girls and a boy. They were older than me, closer to being teenagers. We were all fosters. At first I thought I had won some mom lottery. I didn't remember much about my own, but I knew this mom was way better. She made cookies and tucked the blankets in around my shoulders at night. I was with her for three years, but then she got sick. Cancer, although I didn't know it at the time. Eventually she was so sick she couldn't take care of us anymore. We were reassigned."

He made a sharp noise and she watched his jaw tighten. He was mad for her, but there was really no reason to be. It was simply how the system worked.

"Go on," he said.

"The second family I didn't like as much. There was an older boy, theirs, who was nasty. In hindsight probably not any nastier than any ten-year-old boy would be who had a nine-year-old girl foisted upon him out of the blue. I provoked him, too. I was mad at having to leave my last family, I guess. And I think it was then that I finally understood what my situation was and that I was different from other kids. I acted up a lot and he was an easy target for my anger. If I had left him alone… but I can't change what happened."

"What happened?"

"We would fight all the time. He would chase after me, pull my hair, sit on my chest. Stuff boys do to little sisters who annoy them and I was intentionally annoying. Only I think with real brothers and sisters there is more of an underlying affection. A sense that they are connected no matter what. Family. We never had that. We were two strangers living in this house and we didn't like each other. One day our fight got out of hand. He was squeezing me from behind, because I had taken his prized signed baseball. I reached over my shoulder and scratched his face. Then he wigged out, pushed me down and started punching me."

Anna stopped walking, remembering what it had felt like. Lying on the new carpet in the family room, the one that Mary had warned her not to spill anything on. Not able to get away as the pain grew while Howard—funny, she hadn't thought about him in years—kneeled over her with his knee pressed into her stomach as he continued to hit her with the fist he'd recently learned how to make.

"He broke my nose. Blood spewed everywhere. It was so gross. Mary and Bill came running in. Mary was shouting that the carpet was ruined and Howard was being held back by his father. I remember he started crying. Scared himself I think. He probably didn't know he had that much violence in him. Anyway they called my case worker and when she got a look at my face, she removed me from the home. But really I was to blame for part of it. I worked at making him hate me."

"I'm sorry."

Anna shook her head, purposefully avoiding looking at Ben. She didn't want to see pity in his face. "You know how many brothers and sisters fight? You know how many end up with broken noses? That's what I mean. Being in a foster home isn't like prison or hell. It's just a place."

"And the last home?"

"Two nice people. Jan and Larry. They were older and their son had just graduated from college. They were suffering from empty nest syndrome I think but didn't want someone too young. They were terrific people. I still send them cards at Christmas and they still send me a birthday card each year."

"But all that time you still hated your age. You were only what, ten, eleven?"

"Twelve by then. Yeah, but I knew any minute it could go away, right? I mean, what if Larry or Jan got sick? Or what if their son couldn't get a job and wanted to come home but didn't want me around? They were great people and did as much for me as any two people could, but there was still that fear. The knowledge that they weren't mine and that it was all temporary. I *needed* to be eighteen. Because then I would be independent. Once I was eighteen everything that was mine, was mine to keep."

"When did you come here on your class trip?"

"Freshman year of high school. It was part of our art class grade. You know, back when school still had art. I remember thinking how normal I was. I had been with Jan and Larry for almost two years. Not everyone knew my situation, just some close friends who asked because I called Jan and Larry by their first names, instead of mom and dad. I had a boyfriend for the first time. I felt normal for about ten seconds. Then I remembered. I always remembered. And I thought, only four more years to go."

"Eighteen is young to be on your own," he said gruffly.

"Larry and Jan were great that way, too. I worked all through high school at two different jobs and earned enough for a semester at community college. They let me pay board for a ridiculously low rate while I got my associate's degree. Then with a solid waitressing job and some financial aid I was able to go to Rutgers to get my bachelor's degree."

"Was that hard? Staying with them when you wanted out?"

Anna smiled softly. "You don't get it."

She could see he didn't like that response.

"It wasn't about getting out or away from them because they were bad people. It was just about knowing that if something happened, I could be the one to walk away. Nobody was ever going to *place* me again. That's all I cared about."

He looked at his feet as if he couldn't meet her eyes. She realized he did that a lot when they talked about the hard stuff. The kind of stuff they'd never talked about before with one another. "You never told me any of this."

"You never asked."

He sighed. "I wouldn't have. You were my employee and it wouldn't have been my right."

She nodded. It was hard to forget that's how he had thought of her when she had thought so differently about him.

"Ben, can I ask you a question?"

"You can."

"Why did that night happen? If you only ever thought of me as your employee, if you had all these rules about not messing around, then what made you break them? Honestly."

Again, his gaze dropped to the floor and as she waited for his response she worried that he was formulating the perfect answer. What she wanted to hear, instead of the truth. She braced herself when he finally did look her in the eye and, at least, she thought, she would be able to see if whatever he told her was partially true.

"Yoga pants."

"Huh?"

"Yoga pants. You were wearing these tight clingy pants and you bent over to get a book and…"

"And?"

"I got hard."

Anna blinked. Then she tried to see through his words to whatever game he might be playing, but she didn't think he was playing. He was answering her question as best he could.

"Okay."

"Okay?"

She could see the concern in his face that he might have done something wrong. But she couldn't be unhappy with his answer. No, it wasn't a confession that deep down he'd been pining for her for the years they had been working together. They both knew that wasn't true.

This was something else entirely. He'd wanted her. He'd lusted after her. And that desire had been strong enough to make the great and almighty Ben Tyler break his hard-core rules.

All things considered, it was a pretty complimentary answer. Who knew she looked that good in yoga pants.

"I'm tired," she announced. It happened this way sometimes. Suddenly. Just like the nausea. All of a sudden she felt as though she could lie down where she was and take a nap. Given that they were in the middle of a museum, she figured she needed to rally a little bit longer.

"Me, too."

That was nice, she thought. That he'd admitted his fatigue rather than tried to hide it so she didn't feel like the weak one.

"Let's blow this Popsicle stand, then."

"This is a great museum, not a Popsicle stand… but I heartily concur."

BEN DROVE THEM to Anna's place and didn't ask before getting out of the car and escorting her all the way to her door. He waited while she opened it and, once it opened, he began to turn away.

"Do you want to come in?"

The offer surprised him. He knew she was exhausted. He could see the faint tightening around her eyes. And as much as the idea of spending more time with her—possibly even ending up with the two of them making out on the couch—appealed to him, he hadn't lied when he said he was exhausted, too.

The truth was he hoped he had enough energy left to drive home. If not, he would have to find a place to park and rest for a while. He'd learned through his recovery process that if he went with his natural tendency to push his body too far, then he paid for it later.

This wasn't like a cracked rib or a sprained knee where he could deal with the pain and muscle through. Hell, he'd once been shot in the shoulder and had continued to move over difficult terrain for three days before finding someone to take out the bullet. A cakewalk when it compared to battling this new postcancer body of his.

He knew if he tried to fight the fatigue, then he would relapse for a time and find himself achy and miserable for days after.

"As much as I'm intrigued by the offer—and, really, I can't believe I'm about to say this—I simply don't have it in me."

Her eyebrows rose. "Seriously? You think that was an offer? You're dead on your feet. Me, too. If I was ready to have sex with you, which I'm currently not, I don't think either one of us would be awake for the climax. I was offering you a place to crash temporarily."

How humbling. "It's only four in the afternoon. We're pathetic."

"We're a pair of wimps. Deal with it."

He would. Because the prospect of getting to spend more time with her after he woke up was enticing. They could eat dinner together. He liked eating dinner with her. It felt right to him, and since she'd been gone, nothing he'd eaten had tasted as good as when he was with her. The Reuben sandwich he'd had while he watched her eat her grilled cheese sandwich...delicious.

Decision made, he moved past her into her tidy apartment. The purple couch was going to be a problem.

He pointed to it. "It's too small for me."

"You can take the bed. I'll take the couch. It's where I usually nap anyway."

Her bed. Her sheets, her pillows, her scent. The thought made him groan inwardly. He would smell her again. He hadn't really gotten to smell her since that night. Maybe a little when he'd hugged her after she broke down sobbing, but that hadn't been enough. Not nearly enough. And when he'd been kissing her, all he'd paid attention to was the feel of her. This would be different.

Lying in her bed would be like she was surrounding him and he wondered if he would be able to sleep at all or if he would suffer endless memories of their bodies intermingled.

"Let's be clear. This is not a nap."

Her lips curled as she clearly struggled to keep from laughing at him. "Sorry, I forgot. Big bad Ben Tyler doesn't nap. The bedroom is over there. There is a blanket on the bed you can use. With the AC on high you'll need it."

Ben walked to the room and stepped inside what was decidedly her territory. He considered it a positive sign that she trusted him with this space. The queen-size bed was neatly made, and on the end of it was an old-fashioned-looking throw blanket that appeared to have been hand knitted. Something a grandmother might make her, if she had a grandmother.

"Make sure you take off your shoes," she called to him.

Ben eyed the bed again. Her bed and he knew suddenly that he didn't want to sleep in it alone. "Come in here. Please."

His words weren't loud but his message carried. She leaned against the door, her shoes already removed. The sight of her painted toes made her seem vulnerable to him and he had this vague image of what she would look like with her belly swollen and full.

Barefoot and pregnant and beautiful, he mused. He chose not to share that thought with her.

"Did you need something?"

You. "The bed is plenty big enough. We should both sleep here. It will be more comfortable for both of us."

She gave him that look he was coming to know too well. The hell-no face.

"Anna, as you already pointed out, we're both exhausted. Nothing sexual is going to happen and this makes more sense. Besides, if this does work between us, we will be sharing a bed in the future. We should get used to sleeping together."

She said nothing, but he could see she was at least considering his suggestion. Hoping to convince her without words, he kicked off his loafers and placed them at the foot of the bed. He'd worn khakis and a polo shirt for their date. Not the most inspiring outfit, but he'd thought jeans would be too informal. He'd wanted her to know that he considered their date a very serious occasion. Lying down, he unfolded the blanket and then made room for her beside him.

"I sleep on the right."

Instantly he moved over to the left side. She wore only a loose cotton dress that fell to her knees. Moving to her side of the bed cautiously, as if he might try to pounce, she awkwardly lowered herself as he tossed the blanket around her shoulders.

There was approximately two feet of space and a mile of unresolved stuff between them. But Ben still thought it was progress.

After a few minutes of stillness, Ben finally conceded maybe this hadn't been such a great idea. They both needed to sleep, but their tense bodies wouldn't let them.

"This is weird," she mumbled.

"I sense that. I'm not sure why."

"It's really…intimate. I mean, we're sleeping in the same bed."

"Anna, I've been inside your body. We've made a child together. I'm not sure that sleeping together while fully clothed should be considered more intimate."

"Probably not. But it is."

He sighed then moved closer to her. Wrapping his hand around her waist he pulled her back against his chest and tucked her into the curve of his body. She resisted at first, but when he settled on the pillow next to her, he could feel her starting to relax.

"Why didn't you say anything after that night? Why did you wait days before even bringing up the subject at all? You could have confronted me and told me how you felt then."

He wasn't sure where the question came from, but she was right. Lying together in a quiet bedroom in the middle of the afternoon listening to the sound of the air-conditioning unit hum was intimate. Like anything they said to each other would be okay. Would be real.

"I don't know. Part of it was stubbornness. I wanted you to bring it up first. When you didn't, I assumed you didn't want to rehash it. Then I thought…it's so stupid."

"Tell me."

"I thought maybe we didn't have to talk about it. Maybe we could just slip into this relationship without you having to admit how you felt and it would be easier for you. Less messy."

"Or having to admit how you felt, either."

She twisted her neck so she could see him. "I guess so. I guess it makes me a little bit of a coward. I should have come clean with you from the start. But then I felt you pushing me away…"

"I wasn't. I mean…I didn't want you to feel like

that. I just didn't want to fight you about the stem cell procedure."

She was quiet then, but he sensed she wasn't done asking questions.

"So, if I had told you that I had feelings for you before you got sick, what would you have done?"

He would have fired her. He would have fired her rather than admit that somewhere deep inside he craved those feelings from her. "I don't know," he lied.

"I thought so. I think we both knew it was easier for us to say nothing. And that was true before and after that night."

Ben pulled her a little tighter. "Maybe, but saying nothing cost me. I lost you for weeks because of it. So I'll say this. I had a really nice day today."

He could feel her body react to his words. "Me, too."

"This feels nice with you in my arms."

There was a moment of hesitation then finally she sighed. "I guess."

"We're going to make this work, Anna. You'll see."

He fell asleep quickly, content in the knowledge that he had made progress that day. And it didn't worry him at all that Anna never replied.

ANNA LISTENED TO the sound of his even breathing and wondered if she slipped the pillow out from under her head carefully and started beating him repeatedly with it if she could make those soft, even sounds go away.

It wasn't fair. He was relaxed and on the verge of snoring and she was staring at the wall, still exhausted but completely unable to sleep.

Had she ever only slept with someone? She didn't think so. There was sex. There was dozing after sex. There was leaving quietly after sex. There was pulling away from Ben and making sure he was covered with a blanket and then going to her own room after sex.

There had never been any sleeping. Lying in someone's arms. Trusting herself completely in his care. Being vulnerable enough to let go with another person in this very simple way.

Wow, it was harder than she'd thought.

He'd been her boss. They had worked together. She'd spent six years thinking she was in love with him. But lying in this bed with him, listening to his even breathing, feeling his chest move up and down seemed way too...real.

What if she snored? How completely mortifying it would be if he knew that. How...personal. There was no hope for it. If she tried to sneak out, she would wake him up. He was too sensitive to movement and sound not to know she was escaping...*leaving*.

As tired as he was, he needed the sleep. It was important for his total recovery. So she would simply lie next to him and wait until he stirred. Then

after he left, she could collapse into bed…alone…
and feel free to sleep for as long as she wanted.

But, man, was she tired now. Her eyes were so
heavy. She imagined there was nothing wrong with
closing them. Certainly, she could doze for a bit.
Dozing wasn't exactly like sleeping because some
part of her mind would still be alert to her surroundings. Dozing would allow her to rest without
completely abandoning control to hard-core sleep.

Eyes closed, warm in his partial embrace, she
fought against losing consciousness. She wouldn't
sleep. She couldn't sleep.

She fought it for as long as she could but eventually junior took over and demanded control of
her body for a time.

And so she slept. With Ben.

Totally weird.

CHAPTER TEN

MARK LOOKED AT the birth certificate and frowned. So far nothing. He'd done only the most preliminary checking on the names. He'd run down all the obvious leads he was sure Anna had already tried. He always felt when you were after information a checklist approach was very helpful. Sometimes the process of taking something off the list as not viable was almost as important as finding information that was.

Typically, when you could cancel out all the obvious options, what you were left with was the answer. Only he was nowhere close to that with Anna's parents.

What had that felt like? he wondered. The moment when she realized that not only had her parents abandoned her, but they had gone one step beyond that and had given her no road map back to them.

At least Sophie knew who her parents were. It probably hadn't occurred to his daughter that she should be grateful she knew her mother loved her and didn't want to leave her. Even though her father had had nothing to do with her other than cards and gifts for the past almost fourteen years, she was way better off than Anna had ever been.

Maybe he could get Anna to talk to her. Explain that Mark wasn't the lowest form of humanity known to man.

She doesn't want to have anything to do with you.

How could that possibly be? She didn't even know him enough to not like him. At least he deserved a chance, didn't he?

Mark groaned in the empty office, putting his face in his hands and wondering where the hell it all went wrong. A soft cough had him looking up.

Leave it to Ben to find him at his worst.

"Can I come in?"

He was standing politely just outside Mark's office door. Mark imagined he looked clueless, because it was exactly how he felt. It wasn't a sensation he was necessarily familiar with.

"Sure."

Ben walked in and took a seat. "I'm here to take Anna to her doctor's appointment."

"She's not back from her errands yet."

"So I see."

Right. The man was, like, Sherlock Holmes observant. He would have deduced that Anna wasn't here based on her vacant desk. Mark felt foolish stating the obvious, but he hadn't wanted to take the chance of Ben possibly questioning him about what was the source of the no doubt nearly anguished expression on his face.

He knew what he looked like because he actually felt anguish. His daughter didn't want to know him.

"What do you have her doing these days? Still just keeping her to the computer work, I hope."

Right. Anna. That's all Ben would ever want to talk about with him.

"Not quite, I've got this unsolved serial killer case. Seems the guy only goes after pregnant woman. I make Anna wear one of those Baby-in-Here T-shirts—you know, the ones with the arrow down her belly—and I send her about the city hoping to lure the murderer out of hiding."

Ben didn't as much as blink. "I'm sure there are others who find you entertaining, Sharpe."

"But you're not one of them. I know. She's dropping off some packages for me." Gifts he'd picked out for Sophie in advance of their meeting. Like any good strategist, as soon as he'd learned of his daughter's feelings for him, he'd set upon a course to win her over.

He planned to start with pink Uggs. If need be, he'd end with a car she wasn't old enough to drive yet. A desperate man had to take desperate measures.

"Thank you." Ben eyed the certificate in Mark's hand. No doubt trying to read it. His eyes narrowed as he obviously made out her name. "Is that Anna's birth certificate?"

Mark opened the drawer of his desk and put the paper inside.

"It's Anna's business. That's all you need to know."

"She told me she made the decision to find her birth parents." Ben frowned. "I didn't realize you were involved."

"It's what I do."

"It's what *I* do. You can stop the investigation. I'll take it from here."

Mark laughed. At least this was a distraction. "You have got to be the most arrogant SOB on the planet. Your days of giving me orders are over, Tyler. Anna asked me to do this for her, and I'm doing it. Frankly, you stepping in here and trying to play the part of her hero is a little...dramatic for you."

"I'm not trying to be anything. I'm going to marry her—she's going to be my wife. If anyone should be involved in finding out about her past, it should be me."

"Hell, I'm surprised you haven't already. Not like you to leave questions unanswered about the people in your life," Mark said. "But did you say *marry* her? Didn't you guys have your first date this weekend? That's a little bit of a stretch."

"Not when she's carrying my child it isn't. It gives me...a head start, I believe you would call it."

Mark assessed his former boss. The ruthlessness he'd seen during his days with him on the Farm was still there. Civilian life may have tempered it, but it hadn't squashed it. He had no doubt now Tyler had simply listed Anna as a prime target. An asset to be cultivated with any means necessary.

Only love and relationships weren't like war. Well, not exactly like war anyway.

"If you push her too hard, too fast, you're going to lose her," Mark warned.

"I don't need love advice from you."

No, and Mark wasn't really sure why he was trying. He knew Ben would reject anything he had to say about Anna, but he couldn't seem to keep his mouth shut.

"Maybe not. Hell, I wasn't really any better at relationships than you. Other than the seduction part."

"Yes, that habit you formed of identifying any woman I was attracted to and seducing her before I had a chance. Quite a skill that."

Mark couldn't apologize for it. He'd taken too much satisfaction in it, even if it did make him a jerk. "Look, my point is I know you. I've seen you hunt down targets for months, hell, even years, with a merciless single-mindedness that always seemed to work. That was fine for terrorists. It won't work for Anna. I've known her now for—"

"Three months to my six years," Ben interjected. "We've had this conversation, remember? Please, though, do educate me on the subject of Anna."

Mark sneered. "You know, at first I was worried about her. Worried she was at risk from being played by someone who is a master manipulator."

"And you're not?"

"No, but I'm not trying to fool anyone into thinking I love her just so I can get my hands on my kid."

Ben made a sudden motion forward as if he wanted to attack, but then he must have remembered Anna would return shortly. No doubt she wouldn't like the idea of her former boss strangling her current boss. Ben settled into the chair.

"You don't know what the hell you're talking about," he snarled.

"It doesn't matter. Now that I know her better, I think she'll see right through you. She's smart, but beyond that, she knows you, too. She'll see through your high-handed seduction methods if they are simply a means to an end and not born from real sincerity."

Ben snorted.

"Fine. You go ahead and think you've got it all figured out. But I'm here to tell you if you screw this up, if you piss her off beyond forgiveness, then you'll be a stranger to the child you say you want to know."

"What would you know about it?"

"I have a child. A child I'm a stranger to."

Mark watched Ben's forehead crease as he tried to access the information he had on Mark. Maybe at one time he knew Mark had a child but that information had been deemed unnecessary and long buried back in his brain.

"I forgot. I'm sorry."

"Well, it was pretty easy to forget considering I didn't talk about her much."

Or at all. There were no pictures in his wallet, not that an operative at that level would have carried any personal information anyway. Still, he didn't have a picture of her anywhere period. The last time he'd even seen her was a year ago on her birthday. They'd had a Skype chat for a few minutes. She'd seemed bored with him. And the picture hadn't been all that clear.

His daughter.

"What happened?"

Mark startled a little. A personal question from Ben? A question that had nothing do with gaining useful information for a specific purpose, but rather was a subject he was curious about? That was a first. Mark supposed the least he could do for this old colleague was to paint a picture of what not to do with Anna.

"Her mother was my college girlfriend. We dated most of my senior year. She was a junior. She expected to get married after I graduated. I expected to work abroad for the CIA. I guess she thought she was losing me. She told me... It's so stupid when you think about it, what a man will be willing to believe to get his uncovered dick inside a woman. She told me she started taking the pill. She lied about it and got pregnant instead."

Helen. He never once thought of her as devious or manipulating. He'd never really given her that much credit. He could only imagine she'd been scared out of her mind for lying. If he'd been listening to her, really listening to her, he was certain he would have known what she was trying to do. Hold him. Keep him. But back then half of all his thoughts were firmly locked in the future. Not enough of him had been in the present to know he was being set up by a really bad liar. A setup that had major consequences.

"What did you do?"

"I proposed," Mark snapped. "What the hell do you think I did? Helen was a nice girl. She came from a good family. She wasn't…sneaky. She was just desperate. I mean, it's hard to get all righteous on a woman who got pregnant because she loves you that much."

"But you didn't marry her."

Mark shook his head. "No. A couple of months into the engagement, she could see that while I was making all the right motions—I applied for the FBI instead of the CIA, filled out a few applications for law school—I wasn't happy. She told me she screwed up and that she knew she didn't want to live with a man who would always want to be somewhere else. She promised she would raise our daughter with love and never let her know how she was conceived. Then she returned my ring accompanied by an application for the agency. I never looked back."

"Until now."

"Yep." Until now. Now, he was here and Helen was dead and his daughter didn't want to see him.

"Do you regret it?" The question wasn't judgmental. Ben was merely curious.

"No." He had to hack the word out of his throat, but it was the truth. "No, despite how it ended, I never would have given up those years. Makes me a son of a bitch, doesn't it."

Ben shrugged.

"Anyway, that's what I'm doing here. In Philadelphia."

"Really? Not here to steal all my employees, then?"

"Oh, that, too. I understand you have a couple of investigators who work for your troubleshooting group. My plan was to steal them, as well. After I secured Anna. But that's for sport. You understand."

There was a semblance of a smile. "So you are here to reconcile with the mother and get to know your child?"

The sadness and regret that had weighed Mark down for the past few months bubbled up like fresh sparkling water then quickly fizzled out. Those feelings he'd once had for Helen were a long time ago. He wasn't sure how strong they had been, but they hadn't been nearly strong enough to hold him to her. No, he never would have come back for her.

"The mother, Helen, is dead. I'm here because my daughter needs her father now. Even though she doesn't actually realize that yet."

"I'm sorry."

"Me, too. Which is why you can believe me. Don't screw this up with Anna. If you really want her and the child, you're going to have to be honest with her. At the end of the day if you can't love her, then she deserves someone better. Someone who can give her what she needs. You're going to have to live with it."

Ben stood as the door to the outside office opened.

"That's where you're wrong. You had a choice and you took it. I've already made my choice and I'm not going anywhere."

Anna entered the outer office and stopped. She took in the scene of the two men together in the same room and her face took on a suspicious expression. Slowly she approached and opened the door.

"Everything cool in here?"

"Yes, we were speaking as I was waiting for you," Ben said. "We have your appointment and I didn't want to be late."

Anna turned to Mark. He thought of a hundred things he could say that would make Ben's life difficult in that moment. Things like, *Watch out,*

Anna, it's a trap. But he couldn't do it. He felt a sudden affinity for Ben. For all his posturing about what he was or wasn't going to do, they both knew that in the end it would be Anna's decision.

Which meant Ben was in a place he'd never been before…out of control. For that the man deserved Mark's sympathy.

THEY SAT IN the waiting room of the doctor's office with several other pregnant ladies. Anna studied the belly sizes of the only just pregnant, mostly pregnant and *really* pregnant women. Glancing at her own stomach she thought it was definitely bigger than it had been three months before, but, man, it couldn't get as big as some of these women, could it?

She watched as one woman basically rocked from side to side to gain enough momentum to get out of the chair she was sitting in after her name was called. A few of the other women with equal-size protrusions actually laughed along with her as she finally made it to her feet.

What the *hell* was funny about that?

Anna was counting on a basketball-size thing while these women were sporting Volkswagen Beetles. Cautiously, she glanced at Ben who sat next to her, seemingly unaffected by the women around him.

"You're what? Six-two?"

"Six-one and a half," he answered without hesitation as if he knew exactly what was going through her mind. "Don't worry. The kid will fit. Barely."

"Anna Summers."

Anna lifted her head at her name. The nurse was smiling, holding a clipboard in her hand and waving her over.

Anna and Ben stood together. Something she wasn't exactly expecting.

"Uh…"

"Can I come in with you?"

Awkward again. Anna thought back to the weekend when they had both attempted to act like the normal couple they weren't and wondered if this would be like that. She thought about what she would be required to do for this visit. She already handed in her early-morning pee in a cup to the nurse so she was spared that indignity.

She had to get weighed—she could make him turn around for that. They would only pull up her shirt to poke around a bit. Then they would use the stethoscope to listen for the heartbeat.

Yes, he would want to hear that. A man who had come so close to losing his heartbeat would love the sound of a newly created one.

"Okay. But don't go asking a ton of questions, all right? You're not grilling the doctor like an enemy agent. This is my body, my pregnancy."

Ben frowned and she knew he was currently dismissing the list of questions he'd already formulated in his head.

They were escorted into an office where Anna was asked to sit on the examining table and Ben sat in an uncomfortable chair in the corner. The last time they had been in a doctor's office together it had been a very different situation.

The last time he'd been in a doctor's office by himself he'd been making a life-altering decision without her. She couldn't forget that.

Anna swallowed and started to wonder if what they were attempting to do was even possible. In the harsh light of reality, with the euphoria of her feelings stripped away she tried to imagine the two of them together.

Lying together in bed had been odd. Not horrible and eventually she had fallen asleep despite her desire not to, but it hadn't felt natural.

Because it had been so new for them.

Maybe she was to blame for that. Not only hadn't she shared her past with him, she'd also never done anything to change their future. She never suggested they go on a date. Never made any sexual moves toward him. Never once led him to believe she wasn't completely content simply being his executive assistant.

He was right to ask her why she had held on to her feelings for so long. She couldn't have said she fell in love with him immediately after starting work, but certainly after two years she'd pretty much locked up her heart against anyone else. Four years was a long time to hold on to something that big.

In those four years she'd worked with him, talked with him, joked with him and battled with him. All the while telling herself that what they had was good enough. It was better than most marriages, she thought. They had each other's backs. They didn't play games. They enjoyed each other's company. They didn't hurt each other intentionally.

What a crock of shit.

She hadn't given him anything of herself. Her fears and her hopes. Only her brain and her time and her caring. That wasn't love. That was the illusion of it.

He'd been her work husband. She'd been his work wife. They had settled into professional married bliss. What he probably thought constituted a fine working relationship. Yet, she thought it was something more. Something that entitled her to be part of his decision-making process when it came to his health. How naive of her.

"Are you okay?" he asked.

"Yes, fine."

"You're quiet."

"So are you. I thought maybe being in a doctor's office…" She was deflecting. Ben wouldn't let something like his near-death scare result in a permanent phobia of doctors or their offices. He was too practical for things like that.

"Trust me. This in no way reminds me of my

doctor visits." He pointed to the pictures on the wall, which featured a steady progression of a growing fetus inside a woman's uterus.

Finally the nurse came in to weigh her and Ben dutifully turned around. Then she took Anna's blood pressure and glanced at the chart as she was writing it down.

"Blood pressure is a little elevated. Can you think of any reason for it?"

I'm embarking on a relationship with a man who I thought I loved for maybe six, but definitely at least four years, only to realize now I'm not sure what love is. Also, I'm going to have his baby.

"No, not really."

"Well, it's not too high. Nothing to worry about, but we'll want to keep an eye on it."

"Okay."

"You can undo your pants and lift up your shirt. The doctor will be in shortly."

The nurse left and the silence in the room grew worse. She forgot about the unbuttoning the pants part. The truth was there was nothing she would like better than to unbutton her pants. The push of the material on her stomach was making her want to pee and the grim reality was the pants were too tight before she'd needed to pee.

"Do you need me to turn around again?"

How awkward would that be?

"Hi, Doc, here is the father of my child. But I really don't like him to see me without my pants on

so I'm going make him face the corner. You cool with that?"

"No, that's fine. Can't be squeamish, right?" She undid the buttons of the casual black pants she'd worn and as soon as the zipper slid down she let out a sigh of relief.

"Getting too tight?"

"Mmm. Just a bit."

He stood then and moved toward her, looking down at the belly still covered by what she called her granny whites because they were becoming the only underwear that fit. She looked down to see what he saw and the round bump that was now her stomach was glaringly obvious.

"It's huge," she moaned.

"It's not. It's a little mound."

"I'm a porker already and it's only month four."

"It's barely there. It's not like your stomach was exactly flat before."

That took a moment to process. "Are you saying I was fat before I was pregnant?"

He huffed and mumbled something about women under his breath. "You were not fat. At all. But if memory serves, and trust me it serves me too damn well these days, you had a little...a gentle roundness to your belly."

"You are so dead."

"I mean, come on, Anna, you have to admit it's not like you could bounce a quarter off the damn thing."

"You need to stop. Right now."

He opened his mouth then shut it again.

"That's right," she nodded. "We'll just pretend this didn't happen."

"I liked your stomach," he said quietly. "I like it better now. Can I touch it?"

Could he touch it? No! Again, weird. Ben Tyler touching her stomach…that was filled with his baby that he put there because they had sex. Sometimes it was hard to remember that night because she thought about how she had been with him and what she'd done with him that she'd never done with anyone before. Almost like it hadn't really been her.

Then other times it was impossible to forget. How easy it all felt. Like they had been doing it for years.

"Please."

Anna held her breath and gave a tight nod. She leaned back a little on the table to give him access and watched his large hand descend on her lower belly. Skin touched skin. She could feel the warmth immediately and it seemed to heat up her whole body like he was some faith healer laying hands on her and she was being cured.

Then he started to make slow circles with that hand, pushing a little against her flesh, stroking a lot until his fingers dipped under the waistband of her embarrassing underwear. She looked at him, ready to question what he was doing but his face was intent on the place his hand covered.

Color rose in his cheeks and she could see his nostrils flare. Not that he was the only one impacted by his touch. Her heart started to pound heavier and her legs shifted in reaction to his touch. She could feel herself grow damp and she thought about what it would be like for him to slide those fingers a little lower, just a little lower...

"And how are we today?" the doctor asked as she entered the room.

"I'm the father!" Ben announced while he jerked his hand out of her panties.

The small and serious looking OB/GYN smiled. "Let's hope so."

CHAPTER ELEVEN

"DO YOU WANT TO HEAR the heartbeat?" the doctor asked Ben.

"Yes, please."

Ben watched Anna lean back again and tried not to think about what he really wanted to do between her legs. It was almost unseemly given their current surroundings. He'd been worried since their date over the weekend that he was somehow losing his connection to her. After they had woken from their *rest* he'd sensed a change in her. A certain distance. Like every time she looked at him now she was reassessing her feelings for him. Examining them in some new light.

Maybe entirely rethinking her claim that she loved him.

She was probably right to question her emotions. He couldn't recall one moment during their long working relationship when he'd done anything to merit her love. He was a fair boss. Yes, they were friendly with one another. Probably spent more time together than other employers did with their employees outside of work. He could honestly say the bounds of their relationship had transcended beyond that of merely professional. Certainly even more so when he'd gotten sick. He'd depended on her then. Leaned on her in a way he never had with another person before.

But love? Had he been love-worthy? He never remembered her birthday, she always remembered his. His Christmas gifts to her were typically impersonal gift cards, while hers were always thoughtful. She'd found an out-of-print copy of a book that detailed spying strategies during the American Revolutionary War including those of Nathan Hale. The guy who regretted only having one life. Ben had loved that book.

She gave him six weeks of Italian cooking lessons once, because he'd made an offhand comment about wanting to learn how to make pasta. He had, in fact, learned how to make excellent pasta and he could remember having her over to dinner to enjoy his cooking, never once thinking that she thought those invitations might have meant something more.

Every year she found the thing he wanted most without knowing it.

Every year he gave her money to places like Ann Taylor Loft and Barnes & Noble.

It was a crazy idea that she loved him. But when she'd confessed why she'd taken his dismissal of what had happened between them so hard, he grabbed on to it with both hands. If she loved him, she wouldn't leave him again. If she loved him, she would let him be with this miracle child.

If she loved him, she would marry him.

Yet when that didn't happen instantly he had to resort to proving his worthiness and so far he found himself coming up short. Chinese food and some books on pregnancy seemed like a pale version of romantic gifts.

There was the other thing he'd bought for her when he feared he might die. He'd wanted to make sure she had security if he wasn't around to provide it for her. But when she left him and he didn't die, it seemed like a thing she might not want to have from him. Maybe too clumsy of a gesture. Maybe too much. He couldn't say because he didn't know women that well. Didn't know Anna well enough.

But now he was here. The doctor was putting something on her stomach and then turning up the dial on a monitor. The whir and bump of something moving at a high speed caught his attention.

"That's it?" he asked, feeling a creeping sense of awe fill his body. It was like seeing the Egyptian Pyramids for the first time, only so much more intense.

Bump, bump.

"That's it. In four weeks you can make an appointment for your sonogram and at that point you'll be able to know if it's a boy or a girl."

"Shhh." He'd done it unconsciously. He didn't want any noise interfering with what he was hearing. Was it normal that it beat that fast? Did it sound like a healthy heart? Did boys' hearts beat faster than girls' hearts and if so, how did this one sound? Because he wanted…he didn't know what he wanted. He wanted this life.

"He's still coming to grips with the whole thing," Anna said.

The doctor took away the device and Ben almost snarled.

"Sorry, but she's all checked out," the doctor told him. "Make sure you pick up a sample cup before you leave and I'll see you in four weeks."

"Thanks, Dr. Connelly."

"No problem. And congratulations."

Ben nodded and waited for the door to close. When he looked at Anna, he thought he had no words.

She reached out and cupped his face and he pressed her hand against his skin. "I know. Crazy, right? It's alive!"

He laughed as he imagined was her intent. But the intensity of the moment wouldn't leave him. He'd been staring death in the face four months ago and now he'd helped to create life. It seemed so miraculous.

And yet completely mundane. Something couples did all the time.

"Please marry me," he whispered. The idea of not having her and the beating heart inside of her body as his was incomprehensible to him.

When he looked to her for an answer, she smiled at him gently. "No. But I will go on another date with you."

"I'll take it. Let me take you to lunch." He helped her off the table and watched her hide that precious belly under pants that he could now see were definitely too snug. Women, he decided, could be ridiculous about things like going up a pant size. He made a mental note to pick up some things for her. Something stretchy that she might like.

"Can't. Have to get back to work."

"Then dinner tonight. My place this time."

She had to think about it and he wondered at the hesitation. She'd promised to give him a chance. That meant *dates*. Plural.

"What?"

"I don't know. Maybe we should keep it to a restaurant."

"Last time I took you to a restaurant for dinner you upchucked in a public bathroom. I would think you would prefer the privacy."

"It feels like we're moving a little fast."

This frustrated the hell out of him. Of course he was moving fast. He had only five months left to convince her to tie herself to him for the rest of her life. Reining in his impatience he used sound logical reasoning.

"For almost four months you practically lived with me. Now coming over for dinner is moving too fast?"

She shrugged. "That was work. This is a date."

"I'm not going to pounce on you if that's what you're thinking."

Not that he didn't want to. Hell, he'd been a few steps away from sinking his fingers into her and making her come while she lay on an examining table in a doctor's office, of all places. Pouncing was the least of all he wanted to do to her.

The very idea of having her in his house—potentially wearing a comfortable pair of yoga pants—was enough to make him salivate. But he was determined to move at her speed. Which meant what he wanted didn't matter.

"Fine. Then a restaurant."

"Wow, you caved pretty fast. That's not like you."

"I call it compromising."

"That's not like you, either."

"I'm growing," he growled.

She laughed and it sounded sweet to hear. How long had it been since she'd laughed with him? Even though she was mostly laughing *at* him. He was her straight man and in the beginning of their relationship he'd found it incredibly annoying that he was so amusing to her. After a while, he would purposefully say things he knew would inspire her humor. Just so he could hear her laugh.

"Okay. I'll come to dinner at your house. But we agree no funny stuff. I'm not ready for that yet. Not like you had a chance after you called me fat anyway."

"I didn't call you—" Enough. He'd won. She was coming to his house for dinner. It was all that mattered.

ANNA LOOKED AT the computer screen on her desk then at her cell phone she placed next to it. Then at the screen—which hadn't changed—then at her phone again.

It would be the easiest thing in the world. She could call him and tell him she wasn't feeling good or was too tired and simply cancel their night together. It happened. Dates got canceled. It wasn't like she was shutting him off completely. He would, no doubt, ask for a rain check and she would gladly give it.

They could reschedule for the weekend when she had more free time.

They could reschedule for next month when she wasn't so freaking freaked out.

Anna dropped her head back and moaned. That's what was happening. She was scared and she couldn't really define why. Watching his face when he realized he was listening to the beating heart of his child was like nothing she'd ever seen before. Not out of Ben Tyler.

Ben Tyler was stoic. He was whiplike smart. He was responsible and in charge of every element of his life.

A man in firm control.

That he should find awe in anything didn't feel right. Not for him. Yet it had been plain to see he'd been shaken to his core by the sound of a heartbeat.

Then he'd proposed again and she knew with that proposal only the child occupied his thoughts. She couldn't blame him. When she listened to the sound of that beating noise for the first time it got to her, too. She instantly wanted to take it out of her belly so she could hold it and sing to it and say, hey, you're my baby.

It was crazy because she never thought of being a mother. Maybe it was a result of being raised in different foster homes. It wasn't like she felt any link to her past that needed to be continued into the future. She was Anna. She was on her own. She'd never felt any urgent need to procreate.

Added to that were all the other natural concerns. Many people parented their children the way they had been parented. Anna's mother and father abandoned her. While she didn't see that being something she could possibly do to her child, she knew in the deepest corners of her heart that, in many ways, she'd abandoned Ben when he needed her most.

She could tell herself all day that she'd left him because she'd given him her heart and he'd dismissed it out of turn. But deep down in her soul where she didn't like to go very often because it was a scary place, she knew that part of the reason she left was fear.

Fear of losing him. Fear of being left behind. Again.

Running from that fear made her a coward.

Sort of like canceling on him at the last minute would make her a coward.

So fine. She would go but she wouldn't pretend that anything he said or did wasn't all about the baby. It had nothing to do with her. It would be crazy to think otherwise. Not after all the years when she hadn't meant anything to him other than being a competent employee.

A competent employee who looked decent in a pair of yoga pants apparently.

LATER THAT NIGHT Anna rang the doorbell and braced herself. She was edgy. Once she'd made the decision not to cancel, she'd started feeling as if any minute she might snap at someone. Like suddenly all of her patience was gone, and she was this raw live nerve. She'd gone home after work and changed out of her uncomfortable pants, deliberately putting on a pair of stretchy pants that, while they were not *the yoga pants,* were pretty darn close.

Looking down at herself she could see the bump of her belly under the tank top she wore. That the thing making the noise in the doctor's office was, in fact, growing inside of her body.

It was so utterly strange when she thought about it.

The door opened to Ben who wore a loose, short-sleeved shirt and jeans. He looked good. Better today than when she'd first seen him after his stretch of quarantine. And he would only continue to grow stronger and fill out even more. Back to the old Ben with the broad chest and the steely blue eyes that she could get lost in for hours when he spoke.

It dawned on her that this could be problematic. She'd been able to get away from Ben at half strength. Ben at full strength? It was hard to know.

"Come in. I've got the grill on out back. The humidity has died down so it's not so bad out there."

She followed him through the house for a stop in the kitchen where he offered her a variety of non-alcoholic, non-caffeinated drinks. In the end she went with club soda and lime. Following him outside, she picked a lounge chair on his deck and settled herself in to be wowed and amazed by the act of Ben cooking. For her.

No, for the baby. This was all about the baby. She needed to repeat it over and over again like a constant loop running in her brain so she wouldn't think that he was doing any of this for her.

"How did the rest of your day go?"

"Fine," she muttered.

"Any new interesting cases?"

"Nope."

She watched him take out the tongs to turn the grilling meat, probably thinking up several more innocuous questions that might trigger a pleasant conversation.

"Mark told me he's helping you find your birth parents."

"Yes, so?"

He tensed then slowly shut the lid on the grill. "I would have helped you if you had asked."

"I didn't."

"Why now?"

"You know." She pointed to her belly. "The whole genetics thing. I mean, if I have relatives out there somewhere, I should probably know about it. If there are any medical conditions we need to know about, it's important to have that information."

"I've thought about that. I've been doing some reading and we can save the placenta after the birth. Freeze it and, in case there is ever a need, the baby will always have its own stem cells to use."

That had her eyes widening. He was already worried about their kid getting cancer. It was thoughtful, but the thought of freezing her parts after they came out of her body... "Gross."

"No, smart. As a precaution."

"Fine. But I still think I should find my parents if I can. Or maybe even their parents. Obviously my mother had addiction problems. But we should see what else is out there."

"Do you remember her?"

Anna shook her head. It was more accurate to say she didn't want to remember her. If there were memories—and there were a few—she forced them out of her head until they were gone. Like the sound of her mother's voice calling her name. Or a lullaby she knew had been sung to her. None of it needed to be remembered, because in the remembering there was only pain.

"Then how do you know? I mean, about the addiction."

"The smell." Sickly sweet and awful. It had filled the room where they lived and Anna had instinctively known it was a bad smell. Maybe melting crack or heroine. She remembered how it made her feel scared because after the smell came, her mother would be different. She couldn't touch her or talk to her. Then all those very vague memories filled with a sense of wrongness.

"Can I ask another question?"

She shrugged.

"Why Mark?"

"Why not Mark? He's an investigator."

"I mean, why not me?"

"I don't know. I guess with everything going on between us, asking you for a favor right now seemed a little over the top."

He frowned. "We're supposed to be starting a relationship."

"Trying to start. Not in one."

"And you felt more comfortable going to Mark for help."

"Yes."

Everything was more comfortable with Mark. Because he didn't make her feel this way. He didn't make her feel any way. He was her boss. She wasn't in love with him. They could talk about anything. Everything was easy between them. Not like this.

As if making a deliberate attempt to back off, Ben returned to the grill and lifted the lid, studying the contents within very thoughtfully.

"I've got steaks on. I hope that's okay."

She wasn't sure where this need to fight with him came from. But the dark edginess she'd been feeling since she decided not to cancel the date had taken up residence in the pit of her stomach and it wouldn't let her go. It was taking over and she didn't think she wanted to beat it back. Let him see this side of her. Let him know that it existed.

"Um, do you have anything else? I'm not really into steak anymore."

He stopped and she could see his mind spinning. How long had he prepped the steaks and marinated them in some special recipe he'd found? Because he knew she liked steak. She'd always loved steak. Of course he would think enough of her to serve what he knew she loved.

"I have some chicken breasts. In the freezer."

"Okay."

He looked at her then but didn't say anything. "You want a refill on your drink while I'm inside?"

"No, I'm good."

He headed inside. A few moments later and she could hear the beeping of the microwave as he unthawed the chicken she didn't really care about. When he came outside with a plate of pale meat and barbeque sauce she grimaced.

"What?"

"It looks weird."

"It's raw chicken. This is what raw chicken looks like."

"Okay, but I want it plain. No sauce."

"You love barbeque sauce. You put barbeque sauce on French fries instead of ketchup."

"I don't like it now," she argued. "I want the chicken plain. Is that okay? I mean, I am a guest, right? You want to please me, don't you? That's the point of this whole shebang."

"You're more than a guest."

"Right, sorry. I'm also the mother of your one and only child."

"Anna…"

She spoke over him. "How long do you think it's going to take us to eat? Because *The Bachelor* is on television tonight and I don't want to miss it."

"The Bachelor?"

"Yeah. I know you don't watch unreal reality TV. But I do and I don't want to miss an episode."

"Isn't that what a DVR is for?"

"Yes, but then I can't tweet at hash-tag Bachelor with everyone else watching at the same time. Talk about what the girls are wearing, predict who is going to get the boot, that kind of thing."

That was doing it. Now he was getting annoyed.

"We're supposed to be on a date. I hoped we could spend the time talking, not watching television."

She shrugged. "Sorry. This is me on a date."

"This is you in a snit."

Perfect, she thought. Anna moved her feet over the edge of the lounge and stood. "Look, if you don't want me here, I can go."

But moving a little too fast she tripped over her flip-flops and the glass in her hand fell to the deck shattering around her feet.

"Don't move," he barked at her.

Anna stood motionless while Ben bent to pick up the largest of the jagged glass around her feet.

"Sorry about the mess," she mumbled.

He said nothing. Simply picked up the pieces and took them inside to throw away. When he came back he had a damp towel in his hands. "Sit down."

Anna sat on the lounge chair while Ben crouched in front of her. He carefully removed her flip-flop and then used the towel on her ankle and foot picking up any stray bits of glass that might have hit her. He did the same routine with her other foot, picking it up, running his hands around the bottom of her calf and ankle checking for the tiniest pricks of blood.

Then he used the towel on the flip-flops making sure not a single shard remained. When he was done, he slid the shoe on each foot and looked at her.

"You want to tell me what this is about?"

No, she really didn't. "I think I should go. I'm obviously in a mood. Let's blame it on hormones and call it a day."

Ben straightened and cupped her face in his hand. "It's not hormones. You're acting like someone who has been backed into a corner against her will. You're frightened. I know fear when I see it. But why? I told you I wasn't going to jump you as soon as you walked through the door. Even though you and I both know you wore those pants to be provocative."

Anna stood and Ben was forced to step back from her.

"I wore them to be comfortable."

"You wore them to tempt me. Or maybe test me. I'm not sure. Did you really think something as simple as clothing would make me break my word to you?"

No, it wasn't that. It wasn't any of the things he thought. She simply didn't want to be here with him. It was too hard. It was too much to think about and worry and wonder about. It was too hard to keep her wits about her when he was rubbing her feet and checking for small pieces of glass in the event she might have been pricked. Too hard to remind herself that he did that because of the baby and not because he cared about her.

He cupped her face again, moving closer until she could see the individual hairs in his eyebrows, and the new gray streaks that were appearing at his temples as his hair grew in. "Anna, talk to me."

"I want to go," she said quietly. She felt weak. She felt so impossibly fragile. She felt as though if he continued to touch her the way he was doing, then she would shatter, just like the glass had.

"You mean run. Again. Only this time I won't let you."

"Because of the baby." She swallowed. "I knew it. I'm trapped with you because of it."

She saw a faint reaction in his eyes. Pain. Pain she'd inflicted.

"Why are you doing this? I thought…I thought you said…"

"What? That I loved you?"

"Yes."

"I thought I did."

"Thought. You. Did."

Anna caught his wrists and pulled them away from her face. She couldn't look at him when she said it. She wasn't nearly that courageous. She looked down and all she could see were their feet so close together. "I don't know. Maybe it was an infatuation or a crush. These past few days I realized there is a ton of stuff we don't even know about each other."

Ben didn't say anything, although she could still feel his scrutiny, still feel him studying her. Like she was some fascinating new specimen of humanity.

"I was, what, twenty-two when I started to work for you? Hell, what girl that age wouldn't be in awe of the mighty Ben Tyler?"

Again, nothing.

"You didn't even see me until that one night. Never looked at me. Really looked. How could I love you when you didn't even know who I was as a person?"

Ben shook his head. "I saw you. But Anna you were my—"

"Assistant. I know." She felt hollow. Like she'd purposefully thrown away her most treasured possession and now she could see she was nothing without it.

He would give up on her now. He would run through her words again and realize they made sense. How could she have loved him when she wouldn't let him know her? And he had already said he didn't love her. Didn't know if he could love her.

He was smarter than she was. He knew what they were, while she didn't. All she was to him was a moment of lust for a man who had been facing death. Really, what man wouldn't take that opportunity to have the last screw of his life?

She was pathetic to think this might have worked between them. Pathetic to think that something would change between them when, for six years minus one night, nothing ever had.

Now that she was being difficult and temperamental, he would stop trying to woo her. Stop wanting to date her. Stop thinking that they had a future. She would pop the kid out and they would set up an every-other-weekend visitation thing like all other couples who had a one-night stand that resulted in a child.

She lifted her chin, daring him to do it. To tell her this obviously wasn't going to work out between them. But when the silence continued and she could tell he wasn't going to be the one to say it, she opened her mouth to end this permanently.

But he stopped her with a finger on her lips, keeping the words bottled up inside her mouth.

"I have something for you. Something I think you should see. Do you trust me?"

Trust him. The mighty Ben Tyler. If nothing else, of course, she trusted him.

"Okay, what is it?"

"It's not here. I have to take you there. Will you come with me?"

She could say no. She could say she was tired. She could say any other bitchy thought that came to her mind and let go of this night and let go of this man forever.

Instead she nodded.

CHAPTER TWELVE

THEY GOT IN THE CAR without speaking a word. Every once in a while Ben looked over at her, but her gaze was firmly fixed out the passenger window. It was getting close to eight o'clock and the sun was starting to go down, but they would still have enough light and plenty of time for her to see it.

It. What was it? It wasn't a gift, or even something he'd planned to bequeath. Because it wasn't something he had before he thought about giving it to Anna. He'd seen it after being diagnosed and bought it for her. At the time it seemed perfectly logical that she should have it.

In hindsight, given everything that had happened tonight, he wasn't so sure it was the best idea to show it to her. Yet he felt as though he was losing ground, as though there was quicksand beneath his feet and he needed her to know that she'd been more important to him during those years together than she realized.

He had no idea how she was going to react to it though. Given her mood tonight she might think this was about the scariest gesture a man had ever made on behalf of a woman. But he owed it to her to show her.

He hadn't seen her?

It's what she said to him and it seemed almost comical. Especially after years of forcing himself *not* to see her. Years of telling himself her hair was too red, her freckles were too prominent, her smile was too big. Years of thinking how completely inappropriate in every way she was for him romantically. Years of putting her in the messy pile of life. A place he stayed very far away from.

And she thought he'd been completely indifferent to her except for a pair of snug yoga pants one night.

He could tell her the truth, he supposed. The truth he'd hidden from himself for so long. The truth he'd only recently let surface and openly acknowledged.

The truth that he'd wanted her all the time they had been working together. So much so that it required effort to convince himself how much he didn't want her. So much so that it got harder and harder to fall back on his rule never to get involved with an employee.

He'd wanted her before that night and he wanted her now. But she seemed like she was desperately trying to pull away from him, while he was desperately trying to hold on to her. She'd shown up to his place with an agenda and it had nothing to do with giving them a chance at a relationship.

"So how long is it going to take to get there?"

"Not long." They weren't far from his home. Their destination was a couple of blocks away. He hit his turn signal and drove up the small hill of a street that ended in a cul-de-sac.

Five houses lined the circle with large yards stretching out front and equally large yards in the rear if he recalled correctly. They were newly built, but each one was a custom-designed home so that they weren't cookie cutter in appearance yet still blended together in a way that suggested this was a single neighborhood.

He'd met two of the other home owners when he'd visited with the real estate agent. There was a middle-aged couple with grown children, one who still lived at home, and a young couple who had two children under the age of five. He, of course, had had no way of knowing then that having young children around would be a good thing.

"What is this?"

Ben didn't answer her. He parked in one of the driveways and got out, circling the car to open the door for her. The sun was setting but, as he'd predicted, there was enough light to show what he wanted her to see.

Anna stared at the darkened house not understanding.

"You bought a new house?"

His tongue felt thick in his mouth. What had been such a rational decision at the time now seemed very irrational. Probably, no, certainly, he'd completely overstepped his position in her life. Which might not have been a problem if he had actually died. It wasn't like she could have called him out for it once he was buried. However, exposing himself like this, while still quite alive, was much more difficult.

"I bought *you* a house."

Anna blinked. "You bought me a house?"

He held up the key he'd stuffed in his pocket before leaving his place. "Want to see it?"

"You bought me...a *house?*"

It was hard to interpret her tone. Disbelief was probably the most distinguishable emotion.

"I know. I'm not going to say it's not a little crazy—"

"*A little crazy?* It's insane! It's a freaking house." She waved her arms at him. "Ben, I told you I wasn't ready for marriage and, all of the sudden, you rush out and buy us a house? Was I supposed to be happy that you're trying to buy me off with real estate? Is this some kind of massive bribe? I get the house, you get the baby... Wait a minute. This doesn't make any sense. You already have a house. If I said I wasn't going to live with you there, what made you think I would change my mind about living with you here?"

"I don't think that. This house isn't for us. It's

for you. And I didn't rush out and buy anything. I bought it months ago."

Her jaw dropped and he could see her processing the information. He figured it would be better to have the discussion inside. He didn't know if her neighbors were nosy, but there was no point in taking the chance. He was fairly certain this would turn into a raised-voices kind of a battle. He didn't want her to set a bad first impression.

He walked up the driveway to the front door and unlocked it. The electricity and plumbing he'd kept on not wanting the house to be completely devoid of energy. He'd programmed the thermostat to keep the house at eighty degrees and automatic light switches that went on at timed intervals. While it was still stifling in the summer heat, it was at least bearable.

Wordlessly, she joined him in the foyer following him as he pointed out the empty rooms. "The living room, a smaller den. The dining room. The kitchen and great room straight back."

She stopped and walked into the middle of the empty living room. Hardwood floors and newly painted white walls.

He could see her taking in the crown molding, the light fixtures and the number of outlets along the walls.

"I'd been by here a few times as they were being built to check them out. I had been thinking about getting something different for myself. Then the

diagnosis came and obviously I had other priori-
ties."

"When. Exactly."

It was a demand not a question. "After the results of the first round of chemo. I wanted to make
sure you were set up…in case anything happened
to me. I wanted you to have a place to go. Something that was yours and not mine. I didn't imagine you would care for me leaving you my house,
but I thought something new, that was yours alone
would allow you to take it. I bought it outright. The
deed is in your name."

"It's a house."

"It's your home if you want it to be. I thought
about telling you when you let me know the lease
was running out on your apartment, but I was
afraid of how you would react then. Not going to
lie, I'm still afraid of how you're reacting now."

She turned to him, lifting her arms up only to
let them fall listlessly at her side. "You did this. For
me. Because you thought you might die."

"You said I didn't think about you or notice you
except for that night. You said I didn't know you.
But you're wrong. I know what having a home
meant to you. You talked about it frequently. You
said mine was an architectural mess and that a
real home should be comforting and embracing.
When you talked about having a house your face
would change. Like it was this mythical thing you
couldn't ever imagine actually owning. I never un-

derstood why that was. I would tell you all the time I could help you with a loan for a down payment and help you with arranging a first-time buyer mortgage you could easily afford. But you never seemed to want to do that."

She still hadn't said anything. He could see the dust he was pushing around with his shoe. The place needed to be cleaned.

She stepped toward him. "I didn't buy a house because it had to be perfect. I was waiting for everything to be perfect. Although I'm not sure what that *perfect* is anymore. Or maybe what I was really waiting for wasn't just walls and a ceiling… but a home. A real one, with more than me in it. I think what you saw in my face when I talked about having a house was more about having a family. Someone to come home to. Someone who was mine."

"You have a family now, Anna. Forget what you do or don't see with me in the future. That little bit in your belly with the beating heart will always be your family. From now on."

Her shoulders dropped then and great sobbing cries echoed throughout the empty rooms.

Oh, shit, he thought. More crying.

He reached out as if to pat her on the back but she leaped into his arms and held on to him as if she would never let him go. This, he thought, this is what he wanted when he'd brought her here. There was probably something ethically wrong with buying a home just to get a woman to hug and sob all over him, but he didn't care.

"I saw you, Anna. Every damn day. I swear it. But I didn't know what the hell to do about it. If I'm being honest, I still don't."

She looked at him and smiled, her face was a hot mess and tears still streamed down her cheeks.

"I was such a bitch earlier."

"I noticed. *The Bachelor?* Seriously?"

She half sobbed, half laughed. "I'm scared. I'm really freaking scared."

"I know." He wiped her face with his thumb. "I don't know of what, though."

She shook her head and when he looked into her eyes he saw the fear, but also maybe something else. Maybe something like hope. Hope he could work with.

"I'm going to kiss you now."

"I thought you said no pouncing."

"Kissing isn't pouncing. A kiss is just a kiss."

She frowned. "Isn't that from an old song?"

"Anna?"

"Yes, Ben?"

"Shut up."

It was, he decided, their first kiss. *That night* didn't count because it was all too blurry and rushed and had happened before either of them knew it was happening. Then that time in her kitchen he hadn't given her any choice. It was something he needed without thinking about what she needed.

This, he thought, was two people dating who got to kiss for the first time. Something they both wanted. He could taste the salt on her lips and feel the soft plumpness of them. Everything about Anna was soft. He ran his hands into her hair to hold her head at the exact right angle so when he pushed his tongue into her mouth it was deep and they were connected.

It felt more right to him than anything he ever remembered. Better than that night, better than the last time in her kitchen. And he wondered if every time hereafter it would get better still. It seemed impossible.

Her tongue played with his, her hands on his back, her breath mingled with his breath. He could feel his body stretching forward toward her, wanting her, needing to feel all of her against him. What should have been just a kiss was about to become actual pouncing if he didn't back off.

As he pulled his head away and could still feel the little pants of her breath on his mouth he struggled for control. In his life he couldn't remember a struggle as intense. But she said she wasn't ready for more and he wasn't going to do anything to jeopardize the fragile headway he'd made tonight.

"I should take you back."

She nodded and he could see the flush of red in her cheeks, the glassy, unfocused look in her eyes.

She wanted him, too. She wanted him the way he wanted her and for a second he wasn't sure why he thought it was so important that he stop.

But the reality of the empty house intruded and the last place he intended to have a pregnant woman was on a hardwood floor.

Unless, of course, she was on top the way she had been that night, riding him, taking him deep—

"Ben?"

He jerked out of his thoughts and finally brought himself ruthlessly under control. Anna was still walking around the room, the sound of her flip-flops echoing off the empty walls.

"This is really my house?"

"Yes. When we get to my place I'll give you the paperwork. You can move in whenever you want. With the mortgage paid, and your salary—assuming Sharpe isn't a cheap bastard—you will more than be able to cover the utilities and taxes."

"Move in to *my* house. Where I'm going to raise *my* baby."

Our baby. He didn't voice the correction because he didn't want to upset her. Tonight was about her, not about the baby. While he was glad she loved his gift, and satisfied she knew that he had done this before there was even an idea of a baby, it didn't change his strategy for their future together.

Yes, he'd given her this house. And he couldn't wait to see her turn it into a home. Then he planned to attack it like a medieval knight, bringing down the barricades and storming the walls until he, too, was safely inside it alongside of her and their child.

"Since learning about the pregnancy I checked into the local school system," he said. "It's got an excellent reputation and there are also a number of well-reputed day cares not fifteen minutes in either direction."

She held up her hand to stop him. "Yes, yes. I'm sure you've got a list of the best grocery stores with the highest quality produce and the best dry cleaner and hairdresser and all the rest, too. I just… I just want to take it in for a few minutes."

"Do you want me to leave?"

"No. I want you to stay."

Anna left the room and made her way back to the foyer and the wide staircase that led to the second floor. Four bedrooms, he told her continuing his commentary on the house. There was a smaller one next to the master bedroom that could easily be used as a nursery.

She sat on the stairs and he sat next to her feeling slightly awkward. In a way it was like when they had tried to sleep together. Both of them unsure and stiff together, compared to how easy it had been when they were working alongside each other.

Ben still wasn't sure he understood when the situation between them had changed. He didn't think it had only been them having sex, or even Anna leaving him. Something else had shifted and made them out of sync. Nearly discordant, and he felt helpless to put it back the way it was. To make them the way they had been before.

But for now, they were together and she had cried because he gave her a house. They had kissed again and it was nice. And she didn't want him to leave.

It was enough. For now.

"WHAT DO YOU MEAN I can't paint?"

Mark walked into his office the next day to find his exasperated assistant talking into her cell phone like she was dealing with a slow child. Or more likely a very stubborn man.

"I'm on Google right now and it says nothing—" She stopped and Mark couldn't help but look over her shoulder at her computer monitor. The first page contained all kinds of warnings about exposure to paint fumes while pregnant.

"Okay, fine. I can't paint. Yes, yes, I'll let you hire painters. But I'm picking the colors."

Mark chuckled and made his way to his office. She'd left the mail there and the folders of a few cases that he'd recently agreed to take on. One was the death of a teenage girl many believed was a suicide. An anonymous tip, however, indicated differently.

"Hey."

Mark lifted his head. "So how did date number two go?"

"He bought me a house."

These two were definitely not on the traditional courting path. A proposal first, then dating, now home buying. Huh. "A little over the top for my taste—I'm more of a flowers guy. But what are you going to do with a guy like Ben."

Anna smiled and sat in his guest chair, her hands instantly moving toward her belly, which was still barely there but growing every day.

"Can I talk to you?"

"Isn't that what we're doing?"

"I mean as a friend. I don't have many and Maddy is in Detroit right now being fabulously in love with her fiancé. I don't think I can talk to someone so happy with love right now."

"Then you've come to the right place. I'm nowhere near happy with love right now."

"What's your beef?"

"Well, there was this charming redhead I met who I would have liked to get to know better. Sadly, she was already committed...and pregnant."

She batted a hand at him, dismissing his heartbreak, but he had to admit it wasn't all harmless flirtation. Leave it to Ben to snatch her up first. Leave it to Mark to be always a step behind.

A house, he thought. Ben obviously wasn't taking any chances. Could there be a more perfect gift for a woman who had grown up in the foster-care system? Mark only hoped the gesture had been made out of sincerity and not strategy.

"I'm serious, I don't know what to do."

"About the house? Worried it's a bribe?"

Anna shook her head. "That's the problem. It's not a bribe. He bought it for me months ago. When he was sick."

Not strategy then. Just sentimental feelings. Ben Tyler with sentimental feelings. The very idea seemed completely unsupportable, but the truth was glaringly obvious. "He really thought he was going to die, didn't he?"

Anna nodded. "You've never seen a man look so betrayed. When we got the news after the first round of chemo that the cancer was still there, it was like he'd personally failed at a mission. He was devastated. Not because he was still sick, but because he hadn't successfully destroyed it. I should have known then that he would have done anything to beat it. That he would be willing to take any risk…just to win."

That sounded a lot like Ben. "So let's recap. You have a man who you say you love. This same man who bought you a house when he thought he was dying so you had somewhere to go after his death. This man who is also the father of your unborn child—"

Anna winced. "Yeah, I get it. I'm being stubborn and ridiculous. I should just marry him and make a home with him and raise the kid. Easy answer."

"Anna, I wasn't trying to talk you into anything. You said you're being stubborn and ridiculous. Isn't the question why? He's been back in your life for a couple of weeks now. First, you were afraid he didn't love you. Then you were afraid he only wanted you for the baby."

"That still could be true."

"No, it can't. And you know it. Because he didn't buy that house when you were pregnant. Isn't that what's scaring you most of all?"

She looked at him then and he could see an anguish that belied her normally easy nature. This woman had been hurt in ways Mark didn't remotely understand.

"What if, in the end…he doesn't love me?"

"I don't see how that's possible."

She gulped and he could see she didn't entirely believe him. Whether it was her fear of not being loved, or her fear of being abandoned after she committed herself, it had a remarkably strong hold on her. Why shouldn't it?

Her parents had left her. A foster mother she cared about got sick and so she was taken away from her. Ben got sick and he was almost lost to her. Mark wondered if Ben knew how scared she was. If he understood the real reason she'd left him when he got sick wasn't because he didn't include her in his decision, but because she needed to leave him before he left her?

Anna was a woman who was lacing up her sneakers and getting ready to flee. Mark could see it. He wondered if Ben did.

"I don't know what's gotten into me. I've taken

up enough of your time. This is my job and I'm sitting here talking about my love life."

"You can always talk to me. We're friends, Anna."

She smiled halfheartedly and returned to her computer and whatever tasks she had lined up for the day.

Mark thought about calling Ben to tell him he needed to be even more cautious with her. Then Mark considered Ben's reaction the last time he'd tried to talk to him about Anna. No, Mark was done interfering. Ben was on his own when it came to love.

But as much as Mark liked to consider Ben a rival, he was, in his own way, kind of rooting for the guy. Obviously Ben had powerful feelings for her. But if he pushed her too hard and went too fast—the home buying a case in point—he wouldn't give her enough time to accept that what he was offering was real and permanent.

Anna wasn't much better than a rabbit right now. And while Ben was holding up a really big carrot, and she was desperately hungry for it, one false step and she might decide she was better off without it. Safer, anyway.

Yes, she was pretty messed up. Because her earliest memory started with an epic betrayal.

Was this how Sophie felt? Had she felt that one of her parents had abandoned her at an early age because he wanted to be a spy instead of a dad?

And now the one parent she counted on the most had done the most unforgivable thing and died, leaving her practically an orphan.

Of course, Sophie had her grandparents so she wasn't living at the whim of the foster-care system. But what if something happened to them?

Wasn't that exactly what Dom was afraid of and why he'd taken Mark's phone call in the first place? He and Marie were too old to escort Sophie all over the country. Between his arthritis and Marie's emphysema things were getting harder for the two of them, not easier.

Mark needed to fix this. Now. Or at some point in the future Sophie would be the one lacing up her running sneakers getting ready to bolt any time a man tried to get close. What if she never gave herself a chance at real happiness? Mark would always know that it was partly his fault.

Maybe he couldn't save Anna, maybe he couldn't help Ben. But Mark sure as hell could fix things between him and his daughter.

He picked up the phone and dialed the number he had committed to memory. Dom's voice was instantly recognizable.

"I'm done playing around, Dom. I don't care what she wants. I'm coming for Sophie."

CHAPTER THIRTEEN

MARK PULLED ALL his courage together as he approached the house. Dom and Marie had been living in the same home in the upper-middle-class suburb of Philadelphia known as Bryn Mawr for as long as Mark had known Helen. He'd had no trouble remembering how to get here. As he parked the car in the driveway he noted that his hands were as sweaty as they'd been the first time he'd met Helen's parents.

Sweatier even than the time they had come to tell her parents she was pregnant and they were getting married. Funny, because he didn't remember her being nervous then. It was almost like they were an afterthought to Helen.

His parents hadn't been thrilled with the announcement, knowing what it would do to his plans to apply for the CIA. His father was a former military man who thought serving the country was a man's duty, not a choice. While he'd originally imagined Mark following in his footsteps as a career soldier, he'd at least accepted the CIA as the next best thing. Certainly better than, say, the Coast Guard.

Of course, his parents had been even less thrilled when he told them the wedding was off. His mother seemed to know that, while biologically she was a grandmother, she wouldn't be one in reality. That had certainly borne out. Sophie had disappeared into Helen's family and his parents had gotten to see her only once as a baby.

He would change that. His father had passed away two years ago, but his mother deserved the chance to know her grandchild. Thankfully his older sister had given her two others to keep her occupied or she might have been more insistent about seeing Sophie and that might have created conflict between the two families.

But now, come to think of it, he wished she had been more insistent. Maybe if his mother had forged some bonds on the Sharpe side of the family, this meeting wouldn't be quite so nerve-racking. It was too late now. What was done was done.

He got out of the car and started up the trail of steps that led to the front door with the flowers clutched in his hands like a sword he might need to defend himself. He rang the bell and waited.

A few moments later a solemn-faced Dom opened the door and let him inside.

"You're early," Dom noted.

"I'm anxious."

"They're waiting for you in the living room."

Mark followed the older man, purposefully slowing his gait to match Dom's arthritic steps. He thought of the many steps outside without any kind of railing and wondered how Dom still managed them. There was also the size of the house. It felt like it went on forever, sprawling over several thousand square feet. It must take the man an hour to get from the foyer door to the kitchen.

After what seemed like an eternity later, they finally rounded a hallway that had an archway opening to a much larger room than Mark remembered.

Or maybe it was that he felt smaller.

It wasn't until he saw her, wearing a green dress with her hair in a heavy braid down her back that he let out his breath. She was beautiful in person. So much like her mother. He'd forgotten how pretty Helen had been.

She looked at him, her face expressionless. Marie made a coughing noise behind her hand that sounded feigned and Sophie immediately rose and walked over to him. She held out her hand and met his gaze head-on.

"Father."

Father? He took her hand and watched her dip into a small curtsy.

"Did you just curtsy?"

Marie shuffled over to them quickly. "Sophie often has to greet dignitaries and sometimes foreign heads of state when she's traveling. A curtsy is always appropriate."

Except he wasn't a dignitary or a head of state. He was her father and she'd shaken his hand as though he were a stranger.

Then again, he *was* a stranger. But he was here to change that.

"Marie, I brought you some flowers."

"They are lovely. I'll put them in water while you two chat."

Left in the center of the room, Mark didn't have a clue what to say. There she stood, perfectly still and elegant, while inside he was shaking like a leaf. Wasn't she supposed to be the teenager, and he was supposed to be the grown-up?

The grown-up thing to do, he supposed, was make the first attempt.

"I'm sorry about your mom. I tried to be there for the funeral but…" He didn't think she would understand about cargo planes being routed to the Philippines. "Anyway, I'm sorry."

She blinked then, but said nothing. Looking around the room his gaze landed on the large black grand piano. It made sense that it was the focus of the room. He wondered how many times her family had gathered here to listen to her perform.

He latched on to it. "I was hoping I could hear you play something."

"I've prepared a piece for you this evening."

She looked like a girl, he thought. The green dress she wore was formal satin with a large bow belted in the back. He thought it looked like something a doll might wear. Not a teenage girl. And she sure as hell didn't sound like a girl—teenage or otherwise. She sounded like a middle-aged adult.

He certainly wasn't going to mention either, though. She'd obviously taken care to dress appropriately and prepare a piece of music to play for him. And she hadn't run screaming from the room as soon as he walked in. That had to be a good sign.

"So what's the situation with school? Are you thinking high school next year? You would be, what…a sophomore?"

"Given my travel schedule it's easier for me to be tutored at home and on the road."

"Sure. But don't you want to go to high school at some point. For the experience?"

Now she looked at him as if he were dull-witted. And pitted against her formidable IQ, he might very well be. "I believe the experiences I have performing with some of the best musicians in the world while traversing the globe far outweighs any I might have at a pep rally. Did you think I might want to be a…cheerleader?"

Uh-oh, deep waters, sinking fast.

"Of course not. Not that there is anything wrong with cheerleaders. Your mother was a cheerleader, after all."

"Sophie, darling, why don't you play," Marie suggested as she and Dom reentered the room. "It will be a wonderful way to start the evening."

Mark could have hugged Marie—who was not a huggable woman—for intervening. He felt like a man sliding down a steep slope with nothing to hold on to. He could see the abyss in front of him, but he couldn't stop.

Dom and Marie moved to two high-back chairs that he was sure were their assigned seats for every performance. That left the elegantly patterned love seat facing the piano to him. He sat and watched as Sophie situated herself on the bench as if she'd practiced just that—sitting on the bench—more than a thousand times.

She went through a few warm-up runs then stilled her fingers and her hands until the anticipation was almost too much for him to bear.

Then she began and it was like heaven cracked open the gates and beauty spilled forward in a slow, steady stream. He knew the piece—one by Beethoven. The sad one. But he'd never heard it played like this. Never so chillingly poignant, so achingly beautiful. He wanted to weep for no other reason than it was that good.

This was his daughter. This creature who could make this incredible sound with her fingers on a large piece of what he'd more or less considered noisy furniture. This was art and she was a master artist.

It was a moment after she finished before he even realized she had stopped. So enraptured he'd been by the story she had spun with the music and the sadness it left in his heart.

"Sophie that was…that was the most amazing thing I've ever heard."

She looked at him then. "That was for my mother."

"I don't know what…I don't what to say."

She smiled then. Considering how evil that smile was he really should have seen it coming.

"I do. Screw you."

With that she stood and marched out of the living room with her head held impossibly high. Not so many minutes later the faint sound of a door slamming from above could be heard.

Okay, he thought. So she was a teenager after all.

"YOU'LL HAVE MY REPORT tomorrow, but overall I think Davis was pleased with the negotiations."

Ben looked across the desk at his colleague Greg Chalmers and thought that it felt good to be back in this seat. Listening to Greg break down his last assignment as a consultant for Davis Industries felt like old times. Like things in his life were finally returning to normal.

"Was anyone lying?" Ben asked. Greg's particular talent was being able to identify the physical tells when people were lying. He'd been a hell of a psychologist in his day until he screwed up his practice and career with a gambling addiction.

Now his talents were used for more commercial purposes.

"Hell, they were all lying. But only one of them paid us to tell them who and when. Mercer is completely overstating the value of his company. I recommended to Davis he either walk away from the deal or drop his asking price significantly."

"That's his call. Ours is simply to provide the information they need."

A knock on the door had him frowning. Joyce Mellon was the assistant handpicked by Anna to replace her. She wasn't quite the partner Anna had been. Mostly Joyce kept occupied with the more menial tasks of what he required from an assistant. But she was prompt, hardworking and efficient.

She'd been an executive assistant for years and had only reentered the workforce after losing a large chunk of her retirement savings in the recent financial collapse on Wall Street. For her this job was only temporary until she could rebuild some of what she had lost, but Ben was grateful to have her for as long as she wanted to stay. Good help was hard to find, after all. The Annas of the world didn't happen very often. In fact, the Annas of the world only happened once in a lifetime.

So it wasn't like the very efficient Joyce to break protocol and interrupt him while he was in a meeting. If she was doing so, it was because she had a reason.

"Come in."

Joyce opened the door wearing a concerned expression. "I know you said not to disturb you but you also said—"

"Relax, Joyce, he'll realize why you interrupted him once he sees it's me." Anna breezed past the woman and instantly Ben stood. Like his body simply rose from the sheer excitement of her presence. She'd come to see him. Purposefully. Without him having to ask her.

She wore a sleeveless pink dress that flared out around her. The color should have clashed with her red hair yet it didn't. It made her look youthful and fun.

More youthful and fun than he had ever been in his life.

Greg also got to his feet. Lanky and tall, it was more like he unfolded himself rather than stood.

"She's back!" Greg said gleefully.

"She's not back."

"I'm not back," Anna corrected Greg, moving forward and stretching to kiss the tall man's cheek.

Ben noticed she didn't kiss his cheek. Sure, the desk was in the way...but still.

"You're not back, but you're here."

"To see Ben."

"To get your job back? Which he will not be so stupid as to deny you."

"No," Ben snapped. "She's not here about work. Greg, I'm not sure if you're aware of this, but Anna and I are...well...we're engaged in a...um... What are we doing? What am I supposed to tell him we're doing?"

"We're dating." Anna smiled at Ben's discomfort he was sure. But he still nodded to her in recognition of the lifeline she had thrown him.

He'd never talked about his personal life with his employees before. Certainly he never told anyone of his feelings regarding Anna, although he had a suspicion Madeleine had guessed there was something between them. To tell people who had never known them outside the context of work that they were now dating felt awkward.

Like people would suddenly see something in him they had never realized was there before. However, he had to admit it also felt good. Like he wanted Greg to know someone like Anna would choose to be with a man like him.

"You two? Seriously? In like a hundred years I wouldn't have thought—" Greg shook his head. "Never mind."

"Well, maybe we wouldn't be dating, but the truth is he knocked me up." Anna tilted her head in Ben's direction and Greg's eyes widened tenfold.

"Anna!" Ben shouted.

"What? In a couple of weeks it's going to be very obvious. Were you planning to hide me away like some dirty little secret? Stuff me in some nunnery until the kid hatched?"

Of course he wasn't. And it wasn't like he wanted to keep anything about him and Anna secret. But if he thought he was giving something of himself away by admitting his attraction to Anna, then he was certainly offering all sorts of information by letting his colleagues know he'd slept with her.

"Uh… Congratulations," Greg said. "To both of you. So you're just…dating?"

"I offered marriage immediately, of course, but Anna wanted to take things slow," Ben stated. Then he looked to Anna who seemed to be enjoying herself. "Do you see what you have done? People will think I'm a cad."

"I don't think *cads* actually exist anymore, but whatever." She laughed and he knew for a fact the imp had enjoyed his awkwardness. Nothing pleased her like unsettling him. It was her favorite game.

"May I ask why you felt the need to come here and offer up our personal lives to your former co-worker?"

"I knew you were in here with Greg and I wanted to say hello to him. Also, people should get used to me being around here in a non-professional capacity. I figure if Greg believes we're dating, then everyone else will, as well. It's not as though we could pull a fast one on him."

"Well, I'll be honest, you two don't strike me as each other's type. But if the look on Ben's face when you kissed my cheek is any indication, I would say you are on the up-and-up." Greg winked at Anna. "I'm out of here. Talk to you tomorrow, Ben."

"Goodbye," Ben said.

The door closed behind Greg and Anna smiled again. "Did you seriously give him a look just because I kissed his cheek?"

"I think it had to do more with the fact that you didn't kiss mine."

Anna set the straw bag she carried on the chair. Then with a casualness that Ben couldn't tell if she truly felt, she moved around the desk and leaned forward to kiss his cheek. He got a hint of her shampoo, her scent.

Anna.

Since the kiss they had shared the other night, he'd been preoccupied with getting her in his arms again. More accurately, he'd been preoccupied with getting her in his bed again. The memories of their night together were no longer enough. He was starting to forget what her nipples felt like, forget how tight she'd been around his cock.

He needed reinforcement to keep those memories alive. And he needed new memories. He needed to be on top of her this time, where he could show her how strong he'd become the past few months. How capable he was of protecting her and the baby.

He imagined this was how cavemen must have done it. Impregnate the woman then convince her you are the caveman strong enough to hold on to her and the baby. Not really a bad plan.

She rocked back on her feet. "Happy?"

"No." He turned and wrapped an arm around her waist, pulling her body against his. He could feel her surprise and her gasp of shock when he lowered his head and took her mouth in a searing kiss. It wasn't sweet or light or intended to be a gesture of greeting. It was simply what he wanted from her.

What he realized he'd always wanted from her. With an effort that showcased the strength he knew he'd regained, he picked her up by the waist and turned her until she was sitting on his desk.

Her pink dress rode up revealing most of her legs from the thigh down. He stepped between them and put his hands on either side of her hips, trapping her there.

"Did you ever think about this?"

"What?" she asked a little breathlessly.

"All those times we were here in my office. Working late. Did you ever think about me putting you on this desk and doing this?" He took her mouth again and she opened to him more readily. As if she was coming to accept the idea that they were two people who kissed whenever they liked.

Her hand circled his neck and he could feel the delicate stroke of her fingers against the short fuzz of hair that had grown back. It made him shiver.

"Yes, I used to think about it."

"And what did I do to you? What did I make you do to me?"

She blushed and it thrilled him. He liked knowing she thought about him this way when he'd done the same. It used to take sick effort to suppress those thoughts when she was around. He had to work to smother any sexual thought that might enter his mind. But some days…some days either when he was tired or feeling particularly stifled and he would let them come.

Anna sitting on the desk just like this, her arms around his neck holding on to him. Her legs spread around his hips. Her panties torn from her body while he worked his erection deep inside of her all the while knowing anyone could come in and see them entangled. See that Ben Tyler was screwing Anna Summers and she was liking it.

Only this wasn't a fantasy. This was real and she was pregnant with his child. She needed to be cherished, not screwed on a desk.

"I'm sorry," he said moving away.

But she was still sitting on the desk panting a little. "I'm not. That was hot."

Hot was where he wanted to take it. But not here. Not with Joyce sitting on the other side of the door.

"We shouldn't do this…here."

"I know," she said. "This is crazy."

She hopped off the desk and smoothed down her dress and Ben had to work to stem the disappointment. Before he could offer another apology, she cupped his face in her hand. Her small palm brushing against his skin seemed to soothe him, as though he was some lustful beast needing to be calmed.

"I used to make you do wicked things to me in my fantasies. And I did them back to you."

He smiled and ducked his head. "I don't suppose I could convince you to come home with me and demonstrate."

Her lips were turned up and he knew she was thinking about it. She had been the one to suggest that they take the sexual side of their relationship slowly. With good reason. She was right that, in many ways, they were only starting to truly know each other. But that didn't make him want her any less.

It seemed he was waiting for trust. She was like a girl who had gotten pushed into the deep end of a pool once and, having had that experience, she was now more cautious. Dipping her toe in first, then perhaps wading in a bit farther. It was agonizing to wait for her to get over the caution, but until she swam into his arms he had to be patient.

"I'm…considering it."

"Consideration is an excellent thing."

She laughed. "You've been good about not pouncing."

"Not going to lie. What just happened there was a little bit of pounce."

"It was. But you pulled back before taking it too

far. You're thinking about me, not only about sex and that means a lot to me."

"Would you have let me?"

She didn't answer, but the faint blush on her cheeks was still there and he cursed his noble self.

"Okay, we need to stop talking about this," he said, sitting slowly in his chair even as he adjusted his pants over his not-fading-fast-enough erection.

"Am I frustrating you?"

"Immensely."

She moved around to the opposite side of the desk and sat across from him—a safe distance away—a thoughtful expression on her face. "I don't mean to be a tease, you know."

"I know."

"I want to make sure this is…right between us before we start doing it. I mean, the last time it happened without either of us thinking about it, or talking about it. It changed everything and I'm afraid—"

"Anna, you don't need to explain. I get it. I don't like it because I do want you. Badly. But I do get that you want it to be more than sex the next time it happens."

"Right."

"But so we're clear…it *will* happen."

She didn't say anything but she wore an expectant expression, like a cat that had been offered a pint of ice cream. Another excellent sign.

"Now, did you come for a visit or was there something else?"

She opened the large straw bag she'd set aside. "Two things. Here are the color samples for each of the rooms. I've labeled the room on each sample so the painters know what goes where."

Ben had already hired the contractors to paint the house to her liking, ensuring she was nowhere near an open can of paint. Once the house was finished and completely dry, she planned to start moving in her things, having already given notice to her landlord.

For him the move couldn't happen soon enough. He loved the idea that she would be living in the house he provided, loved, too, that she accepted his gift. When he'd bought the house he remembered thinking that by the time she learned of it, he would be dead. She would have no choice but to accept it as his last gesture of what he wanted. He didn't think she would deny him that.

When he told her about it the other day, he knew there was a possibility she would reject it outright. That the house would make her too beholden to him and she had too much pride to take something of such value.

But no. She'd looked at those papers that declared her the sole owner of the home and she'd put a hand to her belly and nodded as if it all made perfect sense to her. As if he'd been right to give it to her.

It certainly made perfect sense to him. She was only a couple of blocks down the road from him. No matter what happened between them, she would always be close. If they had to share custody of the child, her proximity would make that easier, too. Hell, when the kid was old enough he could walk between their houses.

Of course, that wasn't Ben's ultimate plan. The plan was to get her to let him inside. And once he'd gained access, he would do everything in his power to never leave again.

"This is the color for the nursery. Since I'm not sure yet if we're going to find out the sex and because I'm not really an all-blue, all-pink person, I went with soft canary cream. What do you think?"

Ben looked at the sample intently. He saw yellow. It was nice. But he knew that she would expect him to care about this. This was the first step they were taking together to prepare for their child to be a part of their lives. What color would the room be where he or she spent those first few years. Where the child would remember nothing about the decor.

"I think it's very nice," he said thoughtfully. "Calming. Yet cheerful. Soothing but…"

This time she laughed outright and took the sample back from him. "You're such a faker."

"It's yellow, Anna."

She looked at the sample. "Soft yellow and I think it's perfect. There, that's done. The other thing I was thinking about is some furniture shopping. If you want to come along, that is. But you totally don't have to."

"Of course I will."

"It will be boring. You'll probably hate me when you see how indecisive I can be about these types of things. I'm very careful with my selections. I'll be even more so shopping for this place. I want everything to be perfect."

"It won't be boring. I'll be with you. I can help your decision making."

"Okay." Then she reached into her bag again, this time for a manila folder. "I brought this, too."

He took the folder and opened it. It contained a copy of her birth certificate. "What's this for?"

She looked down at her hands, which were twisting in her lap. "I thought about what you said. About going to Mark for help instead of you. The truth is, before everything happened I never once thought about finding them. I don't know what happened to my father. I have no memory of him at all. But her, well, I know she deliberately left me, so it was, like, who cares what the hell happened to them. But now it seems important. Since you are an important part of my life now and you have experience tracking down information I thought that it was right that I give it to you, too. I'll let Mark know. Of course, he'll probably want to make it part of this crazy competition between the two of you, but, really, if anyone is going to find them, it should be you."

Ben closed the folder and said nothing. He looked at her face, its open expression, and swallowed. This thing that she'd given him. This was trust.

Suddenly it scared the living hell out of him because he didn't know what would happen to them if he ever broke it. He set down the folder carefully and thought about the lengths he would go to for this woman. There was nothing he wouldn't do for her. To make her happy, to keep her safe and to stay a part of her life.

Since you are an important part of my life now...

He'd been her boss. That had to have been important. He'd been the man she thought she loved. Surely that had to qualify as being significant in her world.

Only now she was saying that things were different. That he was different to her and even more important.

No, there was nothing he wouldn't do for her. And there was nothing he wouldn't do to keep her protected. Even if it meant lying to her.

"I'll take care of this," he said. "Trust me."

CHAPTER FOURTEEN

ANNA STARED AT HERSELF in the cheval mirror she kept in her bedroom. Naked, she turned to her side and stood as straight as she could and sucked in her belly as hard as she could.

It was no use. The bump was there and it wasn't going away. Beyond that, her breasts were getting bigger. They were bursting out of her normal bras to the point where she'd actually bought her first maternity bra. The cup had a snap, too, so it could be used as a breast-feeding bra.

She tried to imagine the idea that, in the near future, she would be thrilled to pieces to have some little creature basically eating her. It didn't exactly come, but she figured once the kid was out everything would change.

For now she had to deal with the damage the kiddo was doing from the inside. Next on her shopping list were the pants. Definitely the ones with the stretchy waist and the space for a bump.

Yes, it was time for the clothing to start covering her more completely. But for now, looking at herself completely naked, she had to admit she didn't hate what the bump was doing. It was as though her body suddenly had this new purpose it never had before. She looked ripe and lush and filled with expectation of this big event that was coming.

Not the worst look in the world. Ben didn't seem to mind it…at least not while she wore clothes.

Anna tried to imagine what Ben would think when he finally saw her naked. Because that was coming eventually.

The electricity between them was only growing and the sexual tension from him—and her—seemed to be keeping both of them in a perpetual state of heat. Heck, she'd almost encouraged him to take her on the desk in his office, with his assistant no more than ten feet away from his office door. Thank goodness he'd had the presence of mind to stop, because she hadn't. With all of his chasing of her and all of her running from that chasing it had been easy to overlook a basic fact.

She wanted him. She'd always wanted him and now it seemed exacerbated because her body was acting against her better judgment. Hormones plus desire equaled horny.

So, yes, soon he would see her body in all its glory. She definitely wasn't skinny. Not that she'd been overly skinny before as he'd already mentioned, pointing out the gentle slope of her non-flat belly. But now she really wasn't skinny. Instead she was fecund. With boobs and hips and a bump.

Since she'd committed to dating him she'd told

herself the reason she'd put off having sex with him made all the sense in the world. She was uncertain of her feelings, uncertain of his. She was afraid of why he wanted her and then afraid of what it meant if he did want her as much as he said he did. Could she handle that level of passion from Ben and still protect her heart?

But beyond all that, she had to deal with the reality of him seeing this body. Granted, she wasn't full-blown, mamma jamba pregnant yet. She couldn't imagine yet what that would look like, but she *was* different.

It would be an adjustment.

The last time the sex had been surreal. As if she'd been watching from outside her body while some other woman who looked like her had sex with him. Frankly, she'd been impressed. After that many years of going without, she fell right into a rhythm with him.

She'd remembered that it actually hurt. That first full thrust of him inside her had burned a little. But she'd been so over-the-moon happy that he was finally inside her that the pain seemed trivial.

The next time it happened would be normal couple sex—what almost every couple who dated and liked each other enough to take their relationship to that next step did. She and Ben had gotten the kissing part down pat. He kissed her every time he saw her now. He kissed her when he picked her up for lunch and kissed her when he dropped her off after a date. He kissed her in the car before he started the engine.

Sometimes he would kiss her after he paid the check for their dinner.

It was strange, too, because she didn't see Ben as a kissing kind of guy. Sure, when he was going to make love to a woman he would engage in earth-shattering, mind-blowing kisses. That seemed totally his style. He wanted to overwhelm the enemy, er, the woman with sex appeal and pleasure.

But kisses for the sake of affection, or a quick peck just because he could, seemed slightly out of character for him. Especially in public.

Maybe it's because it's all you'll let him have.

Anna dismissed the voice in her head. She didn't need an inner monologue to know she'd kept Ben at arm's length solely out of fear on her part. But the fear and the panic of what they as a couple might look like was starting to recede. She and Ben had only four more months to work out the details of what that image would be before they became parents. Then it would change again. So they needed to get this right.

One thing was for sure, in four more months there wouldn't be enough room inside of her body for the baby and Ben's penis, so if they were going to do this, now was the time.

Putting on the bra that fit, Anna picked a loose green cotton maxi dress. It cut in right under her breasts and actually highlighted the bump. She looked like a mildly chubby woman with a belly or a newly pregnant woman just starting to show.

Either way it wasn't horrible.

The doorbell rang and, looking at the clock, she knew without a doubt it was Ben. He was exactly on time. There were days she wondered if he arrived early and simply stood outside doors waiting for the second hand on his watch to clear the twelve before hitting the doorbell.

Today they were going non-baby furniture shopping. Like any couple did who was furnishing a house they might one day live in together. Taking a deep breath, she made her way into the living room and opened the door.

He was wearing a pair of jeans and black T-shirt that clung to his chest, which was filled out now thanks to him eating more and working out regularly. In another month or two he would probably have put on all the weight he'd shed and no one would know that the world had almost lost this man.

She would know, though. She would never forget, either.

In a way, it was odd seeing him in jeans. It was yet one more thing to get used to in this new Anna/Ben 2.0 version. They kissed, they took naps together and he wore something other than business attire—or his robe and pajamas—when they were together. They definitely were no longer that working couple they used to be. They had turned into something else, and she found she really liked it.

"Will you humor me at least and ask who's at the door, even when you know it's me?"

"Who is it?"

"Excellent. You're in funny mode today. I love it when Anna aspires to wittiness."

She flashed him a smile and waited for his corresponding growl, which he granted her. It occurred to her that no matter how different things were, there was still some element of the old Anna/Ben 1.0 left in them and that was nice, too.

This was how it used to be between them. It felt as though they were finally getting their precancer groove on and it made her happy. Yes, they still needed to find a way for the old and the new to fit together in harmony. But she was starting to believe it could happen. Really believe.

"Are you ready?"

Anna nodded. "Yes, I think I am."

"Then let's go."

Eventually they ended up at the IKEA store near the King of Prussia mall in the outskirts of Philadelphia. They wandered the displays and, sadly, it didn't take long for them to become locked in a ferocious battle of wills.

"This bed is prettier," she said.

"This bed is bigger," he said, pointing to the king-size bed he preferred.

"I've never needed anything bigger than a queen."

"Well, I need a king. If the plan is for us to be sharing this bed one day—and, as far as I'm concerned, that is still the plan—we will need the big one. I like to have room…to work."

Anna turned to him, exasperated. They had been picking out furniture for her new house for hours now and it occurred to her that Ben's primary motivation was making sure the piece was of good quality and large enough to accommodate them having sex. The chair had to recline fully, the couch had to be big enough to support them both if they were lying side by side, which her purple couch would not.

"Is sex really all you can think about?"

He considered her question. "Yes."

"You want me that bad?"

"Yes."

Anna laughed. "I don't get it. How do you go for years without thinking about doing it with me, then suddenly one night lose control over a pair of yoga pants and now all you can think about is getting me back into bed."

"Into the larger bed, yes. I should never have told you about the yoga pants."

"Ben, I'm being serious."

"Anna, I don't know what to tell you. I didn't think about having sex with you for six years, because I wouldn't *let* myself think about it. Sometimes a thought or two…I couldn't help that. But mostly I would suppress it. Then in a moment that night… I don't like to refer to it as losing control—"

"You wouldn't, Mr. Control Freak."

"I prefer to think of it as letting the moment take over."

"That's such crap."

"The point is now the deed is done. You are no longer my employee. You are, instead, the woman carrying my child and the woman I'm attempting to court. The fact is I think about taking you to bed quite often. So when you take me furniture shopping and you ask me which piece I prefer, I imagine making love to you on said item and that helps in my decision-making process."

Anna tried to wrap her brain around the concept of him wanting her like this. The way he said what he was thinking blew her mind.

"It is the craziest thing. If you were any other guy on the planet, I would know to take this as flirting, perhaps with intent to seduce. But you are actually dead serious."

He closed the distance between them so that less than an inch remained. Less than a breath really. "I'm deadly serious about wanting to take you to bed. I have been since I had my first erection after my treatment. I would not be lying if I told you it occupies many of my day-to-day thoughts. Does that answer your question?"

Anna caught her hand around her throat as she tried to calm her breathing. This man was seriously getting to her. First on the desk in his office. Now today with this completely honest admission of what he wanted from her.

"Let's get the bigger bed."

His smile was more wolfish than anything she had ever seen before.

"Hey, Anna, Tyler."

They turned at the greeting. Mark approached them with a seemingly reluctant teenager in toe. The girl wore a pair of shorts and a T-shirt that read Music Is My Life, What's Yours? Her expression let anyone looking at her know how unhappy she was with her current circumstance, whether it was shopping or the company she was with was hard to say.

"Sharpe," Ben said, glancing at the recalcitrant teenager. "Can we hope you didn't kidnap her?"

"Don't let the I-would-rather-be-anywhere-else-than-here look fool you. We're having a great day."

"Whatever," the girl muttered.

"Anna, Ben, this is my daughter, Sophie Warren. Sophie, this is Ms. Summers—I told you about her. And this is Mr. Tyler. We used to work together in the CIA."

"Oh, did you abandon your children, too?"

Mark's smile was big and tense. "Fun. We're having fun. Sophie is helping me pick out the furniture for her room, which I'm setting up in my condo."

"Which I'm never going to visit, so I don't really know why we're bothering."

"Look, can we hold the snarky commentary for five minutes? I wanted my friends to meet you."

Anna smiled through the awkwardness, remembering exactly what it felt like to be fourteen and on display for people. While Jan and Larry had been terrific with her, they did like to show her off her to any first-time visitors as an example of their good deed.

"Oh, and look, we've taken in a foster child. See what we're trying to give back to the world."

That was when Anna developed the bad habit of rolling her eyes that irritated Ben so much.

"Hey, can I give you some advice?"

The girl wanted to say something, but caught herself. She clearly had no problem expressing an attitude with her recently reunited father, but she'd been raised well enough to know it wasn't acceptable to behave rudely in front of other adults.

"He's going to buy the furniture anyway. Don't pick out the stuff you hate just for spite. You'll kick yourself later."

The girl seemed to flush a little with guilt.

"I knew you didn't like that green chair," Mark said. "I mean it's really foul green. Now we're going to return it. Which means we accomplished absolutely nothing today."

"Don't let us hold you up," Ben said.

"Yeah, hey, Tyler. I need to talk to you." Mark's face was suddenly serious.

"Regarding?"

Mark shook his head. "Not here. Can I stop by your office tomorrow?"

"Yes. I'll be in after ten."

"Great, see you then. Enjoy the rest of your day."

The two walked off with Mark still muttering about the green chair and Anna smiled. "What do you think he wants to talk to you about?"

Ben didn't answer. Instead he shrugged and only said he'd learn that tomorrow. They found a sales-clerk to take the order for all the items they selected. Anna paid for them all with what she'd called her house savings. Now that she actually had the house, it was time to put that money to good use.

The bump took over and demanded food. Ben was happy to treat her to lunch, which included a tuna-fish sandwich with an extra pickle and a brownie with whip cream that she insisted on eat-ing first. He merely expressed his gratitude that she wasn't eating them together.

By the time they arrived at her apartment and he walked her to her door, she was in a crazy state. Nervous, but excited. Queasy, but exhilarated. She was ready. This time when he made his move she would let him take over.

They were going to do this. They were going to have sex. It would be nice, it would be thoughtful, not just some random happening. Then they would get to find out what kind of couple they would be going forward. At least in bed.

"Anna, today has been lovely. Thank you."

"You're welcome. Actually I was going to—"

"I'm exhausted. I'm sure you are, too. So, I'll leave you to rest alone. I'm convinced that sleeping was so difficult for you last time because the bed was too small. We won't have that problem with the new one."

He bent down and kissed her firmly, but briefly, on the lips then headed away from her before she finally got the chance to say what she wanted.

"But I think I want to have sex with you."

The empty hallway, however, didn't respond.

BEN WALKED into his home office and saw the couch waiting for him. He imagined how good it would feel to get off his feet and close his eyes and lose himself to sleep. It had been a good day today. He'd definitely felt as though progress had been made, especially when she'd agreed to the larger bed.

And, for a moment, when she'd looked at him then at the bed, he imagined that she was seeing them in it together in the near future. Maybe not precisely the way he did, with him above her and inside her, pinned to the mattress so that she would never think about leaving him again.

No, he doubted she would know how desperately he wanted to possess her. Instead, he thought she imagined them as an ordinary couple, as two people who belonged in the same bed, which was a good thing.

When he'd left her with nothing more than a kiss, had that been disappointment in her eyes? Had she expected him to make a move on her? After all, he'd flat out told her he wanted her and he'd seen the reaction in her eyes when he had.

Maybe she thought he intended to go inside her apartment with her. Hell, maybe she'd intended to do the asking herself but he'd cut her off.

The idea brought a smile to his lips. If he'd left her a little...deflated...then that might be a good change for them. He'd made his feelings regarding sex known. Maybe it was time for Anna to start admitting that she wanted him, too.

The way she'd looked at him...then at that large bed...

Of course, Sharpe had interrupted them and removed all thoughts of bed-sharing. Ben walked over to his desk, deliberately holding off succumbing to the couch and its temptation for now. He saw the folder on his desk, the one he knew contained Anna's birth certificate.

He had to believe that whatever business Sharpe wanted to discuss with him revolved around Anna and her missing parents. Maybe Mark had found something and wanted to let Ben know about it first, as a courtesy.

Ben doubted it, though. He had firm suspicion

that Mark's first loyalties were to Anna. Whose wouldn't be? The woman practically inspired it with her spirit. In seconds she'd managed to make a connection with Mark's daughter that he doubted Sharpe had been able to do in weeks of communication.

Ben looked again at the birth certificate and thought about the woman who had come from a childhood like Anna's. He thought about the heartbreaking stories she'd told him of her time in foster care. Stories she didn't see as heartbreaking, instead simply accepted them as something that had happened to her. Even now a surge of rage bubbled in him when he thought of some punk-assed kid who was bigger than she was, holding her down and hitting her face so hard he broke her nose.

Ben took a breath and controlled the urge to seek out that kid and return the favor. He knew she wouldn't appreciate it.

Now she wanted to go further into her past. She wanted Ben to take her deeper into where her life had truly started and where it all went wrong. It was probably time to admit, at least to himself, that it wasn't a place he wanted her to go.

Especially now. With so much of her life in turmoil between him and the baby. The house had been the first step to giving her the security and comfort he wanted her to have in life. Unraveling the truth about her past now might shake that foundation of security at a time when she needed it most.

He was supposed to protect the mother of his child. Not upset her. It was self-serving logic. He knew it, but he didn't care. He would talk to Sharpe tomorrow about stopping the search for Anna's parents.

Ben opened a drawer and put the certificate away where he couldn't see it.

Then he made his way to the couch and released a deep sigh as he laid down. His body would finally get the rest it needed. Fatigue was still his mortal enemy, sometimes sneaking up on him and hitting him like a fist in the gut. The doctors told him it would most likely be a year before he was truly back to normal. He could see how right they were.

Hell, the sad truth was if Anna had wanted him to make a move today, he doubted he could have made the event very memorable. No, this was better. Let her wait for it, the way she made him wait for it.

Letting his arms and legs relax and his eyes close, Ben's last thought was that it was good to be alive.

And better than being alive was wondering what might happen the next time he saw Anna together with the king-size bed.

CHAPTER FIFTEEN

"NICE OFFICE," MARK COMMENTED as he sat in Ben's guest chair. "But why here and not in the heart of the city where all the action is?"

"I don't need the flash of Center City. This is a nice, growing community and it serves its purpose."

Right, Mark thought. Ben was always about efficiency. He'd never had much use for the extras. That included small talk.

"So I'll get right down to it. Anna told me that she gave you her birth certificate."

"She did. I'm glad you brought that up. I know I asked this of you before, but now I'm being serious when I say I would like you to stop your investigation. She's trusted me with the task. I'll take it from here. There is no point for you to waste your time."

Mark should have been surprised, but he wasn't. He'd already told Ben he had no plans to back off, but that had been before Anna brought Ben into the investigation. She, too, probably would prefer that Mark drop the matter and let Ben handle it.

There was no doubt the man was completely capable of finding out whatever Mark would find out.

Sitting in this office, he felt a little silly now. He'd actually come here to offer a wager. It's why he hadn't wanted to discuss it in front of Anna when he saw her at the furniture store. Seemed a little insensitive to use the woman's past as a challenge between him and Ben.

Only it had been months since he'd felt anything remotely challenging work-wise. Even the cases he took on seemed like no-brainers to him. He'd been polite when the officers had thanked him for his uncanny work in identifying clues and bringing new eyes to the case, but the truth was he thought whoever had worked those cases to begin with must have been fairly incompetent—or at best, overworked and under-observant.

No, the only real challenge Mark had faced since returning to the states was trying to win the affection of a teenager who hated his guts. So that wasn't proving to be very satisfying. Since nothing got his juices going like matching wits with Ben, Mark thought he might use Anna's situation for his own purposes. His conscience was appeased as long as Anna got the information she wanted. He figured no harm, no foul and a win-win for both of them.

Only Ben wanted him off the case. And, Mark realized, he felt like a jerk. "I haven't changed my mind on this."

"Look, Sharpe, it's pointless to have us both looking into the matter. I'm the more obvious choice to do so—"

"You are?"

"I'm her… We're going to be… What I mean is—"

"As far as I can see you're still only her baby daddy and nothing else," Mark said. "She gave the case to me first."

"You have a business to run. You should be taking cases that pay."

"I can do both. Besides, you know how I feel about Anna." Mark watched a muscle in Ben's jaw tick and he took an inappropriate amount of pleasure from it. After all, needling Ben was almost as fun as competing against him.

"No. Tell me. Exactly how do you *feel* about my Anna?"

Mark flashed the older man a smile. "She's my friend. My only friend in the states really. And because, for some reason, she seems to like you, I won't upset her by letting her know you referred to her as *my Anna*. I mean, really. Dude, it's the twenty-first century."

"If you won't back off, then why did you come here today?"

"I thought we could… Well, it seems kind of stupid now." Mark shrugged. "I thought maybe we could bet."

"Bet? On what?"

"First man to find Anna's parents."

Ben actually laughed but it wasn't a very funny sound. "You are unbelievable, Sharpe. You're that desperate to prove you're the better spy that you think we could race against each other to uncover Anna's past?"

Was that what Mark was doing? Was he trying to prove something to himself? To Sophie?

"Look, it was a bad idea. I just thought— I need something. Something I can...win."

"Still not getting along with your daughter?"

"You met her. You heard her."

"She's a teenager." Ben offered the words as if they were explanation enough.

"She is and she isn't."

Mark thought about the performance he'd attended a few nights ago. The mayor of Philadelphia had hosted a fund-raiser and had asked Sophie to perform along with a few singers and dancers. Mark had insisted on accompanying her as a way to better understand the life she was living.

He had sat with Marie backstage and watched as, once again, Sophie did something to the piano he'd never seen another performer do. She didn't play the instrument. She brought it to life. She didn't make music. She told amazing, complex and wonderful stories.

When it was over, she'd graciously greeted the mayor and many of his guests. Answering the questions about her gift, her age and how she kept up with her schooling and her plans for the future. She behaved like…a professional.

A grown-up woman in a girl's body. When he'd driven them home, he'd tried to pay her compliments to that effect. It seemed ridiculous to say, since he'd had nothing to do with raising her, but he'd been proud of her. Not only her talent, but her poise, as well.

She hadn't responded to any of his comments and Mark was starting to feel as if he would never get through to her.

"I heard her play once," Ben said now. "She has a spectacular gift. You didn't say anything about that when you mentioned you came back for her."

"I'm still coming to grips with simply being a father, let alone the whole prodigy thing."

"You understand you need to give it time. A father-daughter relationship can't happen instantly. At least, I would imagine that it can't. I might have better advice for you if the baby is a girl."

Mark nodded. It didn't matter that Ben didn't have a child yet, his advice made sense. Of course Mark needed to give it time. That's what he was doing. Inch by inch. He accepted every invitation the Warrens offered for dinner or lunch. He took every opportunity to be with Sophie alone when her grandparents didn't give her a choice to refuse his company.

He tried to be funny, he tried to be open-minded.

He tried to be a cool dad. What teenager didn't want the cool dad?

His apparently.

"Of course, if you push her too fast, it will only make her dig her heels in harder."

Mark listened to the words he'd said to Ben only a few weeks ago and knew Ben repeated them intentionally. "You think you're being funny, don't you?"

"I'm not attempting to be humorous…although I won't lie and say it didn't feel damn good to give you some of your own medicine. Because while you weren't wrong, now you know how I felt." Ben seemed to lose the icelike facade he'd always maintained around Mark. It was as if he acknowledged their common bond. And they were finally talking to each other, man-to-man. "Patience used to be our strong point, you know."

"Tell me about it. I could sit for hours in an unventilated room with temperatures outside spiking over a hundred degrees and simply watch a window across an alleyway on the off chance someone would show up for a meeting. Now I feel like I can't stand being in my own skin for five minutes at a time. When I'm with Sophie I have this ridiculous urge to pick her up and start running without having any idea where we're going. God, I can't believe I said that out loud."

And that he'd told Ben, of all people, how crazy he was feeling was the total kicker. Mark could only imagine how uncomfortable his former superior was right now with what had been a healthy dump of too much information.

Except when Mark looked at him, Ben didn't look uncomfortable. Instead he looked…sympathetic.

"Yes. That's exactly what I want to do most days with Anna. It's…unnerving. Unfortunately, we find ourselves with two people who wouldn't particularly appreciate that experience."

Mark could see that, maybe for the first time, Ben understood what drove Mark to compete with him. They were more alike than they were different.

"It was ridiculous to use Anna's past as some kind of wager between us."

"It was."

"Are you going to tell her?"

"No. You weren't trying to be insensitive. You're simply having trouble adjusting to civilian life. And the reason why you're making this adjustment doesn't seem to be giving you a break."

"A break? Try not a crack. She hasn't given a smile or word freely. I don't know what the hell to do because I don't think she understands that this is about more than only letting me into her life. This is about us making a life together."

"What are you saying? You want that room you're making for her in your home to be permanent?"

Mark could hear the surprise in Ben's voice. Because it was one thing to have a relationship with his daughter. It was a completely different thing to want to finish raising her. Did he want that? Had Dom and Marie been fifteen years younger and in better health, would he have been okay with letting Sophie stay with them while he continued to watch her life from the sidelines? He'd like to think he wouldn't have. He'd like to think that no matter what, now that Helen was gone, it was time for Sophie to be with him.

"She might not have a choice. You haven't met her grandparents. They're in their seventies and not in very good health. I might be the best option for Sophie at this point."

"Then you'll figure it out. If you want it to work as badly as I can see you do, then you'll make it happen. You're not a quitter and I've yet to see you not get what you want."

"Thanks." That meant a lot coming from Ben.

"Will you back off Anna's case and let me handle tracking down her parents?"

Mark could have accepted what Ben had said earlier. It didn't make sense for both of them to look for the same thing. He had no doubt both of them would find whatever information was out there to learn. They were too good at what they'd done in their former lives to not be able to handle a basic request for information, even with an obstacle like false names.

But something in Ben's expression made Mark pause. Despite playing it cool, Ben wanted him to back off. Badly. This was more than suggesting Mark would be wasting his time by doubling Ben's efforts.

"Will you tell me the real reason why you want me to back off?"

Ben tilted his head. "No."

Wrong answer. It meant Ben had an agenda and, for Anna's sake, Mark couldn't live with whatever consequences came from that agenda. At least he could provide Anna with some neutrality. For everything she'd done for him, he felt as though he owed her the simple courtesy of finding her parents.

"Sorry. I made a promise to her. She asked me to find them. I'm going to find them."

"You won't. Not before I do."

"I've had the birth certificate for weeks longer than you've had it. What makes you think you'll beat me to the information?"

"A hunch." Ben shrugged.

"Okay, well, we said no bet. But I don't see anything wrong with using your little statement there as…motivation."

"You're pathetic, Sharpe."

"Don't I know it?"

Mark left the office feeling lighter than when he'd gone in. For a few moments there, it had felt as though Ben were a friend. There simply to listen and let Mark get some of the shit he was feeling about his relationship with this daughter off his chest.

Two old adversaries who could see how their lives had changed and take comfort from each other in knowing that neither would forget the past. Maybe Anna wasn't his only friend in the states after all.

"CAREFUL, CAREFUL."

"Lady, we got it."

Anna stared down the mover and he stared back hard. Considering he was holding up one half of her dining-room cabinet, she let him win. "Sorry. I'm a little anal about this stuff."

"Really," he muttered. "Couldn't tell."

Deciding it best to avoid the surly moving man who was sweating through his blue uniform shirt, Anna left the dining room and made her way to the living room where Ben was carefully measuring the wall.

"Geezus, Tyler, pick a spot in the middle and hang it up."

Ben turned to give Mark a scorching glare. "To be properly centered I need the length of the wall."

Mark walked over and put his finger on a spot. "Trust me. That's the middle of the wall. I'm a crack shot and have an excellent sense of topography. I know where the middle is."

Ben continued his measurements. "If you would

like to be useful, I'm sure there are other pictures that need to be hung."

"There are. Upstairs in her room. But, nut job that you are, you won't let me in her bedroom."

"There is no reason for an employer to be in his employee's bedroom. Yes, while I concede that I am, in fact, calling the kettle black, it doesn't change that I'm right. You stay downstairs and out of my way."

Mark turned toward her. "Anna, will you talk to him?"

Anna smiled and watched as Ben finally tapped in the nail to hang her favorite painting. It was a print, not an original, but it was signed and numbered and she considered it her first big art purchase. A man and a woman in formal dress dancing on the beach. Very romantic.

Funny, for all the times she'd ever looked at it, she never once thought of her and Ben in the scene. She didn't see him taking off his shoes and socks and rolling up his trousers to spin her around on the beach. He was far too practical.

But it never bothered her, his lack of whimsy. She loved his stability instead. Maybe that was why she liked the picture so much. Knowing it was a fantasy and nothing more. She would much rather have the man with the leveler and tape measure in his hand than some flaky guy on a beach without his shoes any day.

"It's perfect," she said as she approached them.

For the first time as she stood next to him and admired his precision, she wrapped her arm around his waist. She could feel him startle and his muscles tighten, but she didn't let go.

Last week following the furniture shopping, she thought she was ready for sex. But after that moment at her door had passed, she hadn't followed up on initiating the sex. Anna had assumed Ben would press again and when he did, she was prepared to give in. Perhaps it was silly, but she thought it was important that he initiate it when they did finally have sex again. That way there would be no confusing what was happening between them.

They would both know that he was openly acknowledging he wanted her. Even though he'd said as much to her over these past weeks, his deeds were what counted.

Only, after days went by and there was no move on his part did she start to understand something she'd never realized before. Ben needed something from her, too. He needed to know, maybe as much as she did, that she wanted him, also.

It wasn't like her to make the first physical gesture. To take his hand first, or kiss him without any prompting. But she was coming to understand that if they ever were going to make it to that next step, she needed to show him how she felt.

He glanced at her and the look on his face was hard to read. Eventually, he relaxed, too, and circled his arm around her, pulling her closer. She leaned her head against his shoulder and she tried to imagine them as a painting. A man with a leveler and a pregnant woman staring at a fantasy that would never be them.

She liked it.

"Hey, lady, we're done."

The loud shout from the foyer broke them apart. Anna did a final walk-through with the movers then signed all the necessary paperwork. She had the check ready and a tip in a separate envelope for each of the men, thanking them for all the heavy lifting. Between what had already been delivered by the furniture stores and her personal effects, the house finally felt complete.

She was home. Her home, with her colors and her taste and her stuff and no one could ever make her leave it.

Ben had done this. He'd given this to her. Not a possession, or a property but, instead, a lifetime of security.

She could feel the tears coming and tried some shallow breaths to stop them.

"Oh, no. Here she goes," Ben muttered to Mark. "Turns out she's a pregnant crier."

In retaliation Anna offered him a discreet view of a particular finger centered on her hand.

Mark chuckled. "There are worse things. See you two later. I'm having dinner with Sophie and her grandparents."

"Good luck."

"I'll need it. Last time I had dinner with them I got her to speak five words. But only two of those were together. This time I'm going for a record-breaking ten. Maybe even a full sentence."

Anna wiped her eyes as Mark left and suddenly the house, which had been a beehive of activity all day, was still.

"I can't believe it's done," she said, joining Ben once more in the living room. "I can't believe I'm here."

"You've spent the past few weeks doing nothing but getting ready for this day. I imagine you're allowed a sniffle or two."

"You're so generous. Want a final tour?"

"Of course."

She held out her hand and he took it, giving hers a gentle squeeze. She walked him through each room and talked about the colors she'd chosen and what she was trying to accomplish with the furniture. All her dishes and knickknacks were still in boxes, but she had everything labeled and waiting in the appropriate room to be unpacked. It shouldn't take her more than a day to have all that work done.

She led him upstairs and took him to the nursery first. She hadn't yet decided on a crib, but she had found a soft rocking chair that looked like it had been swallowed in pretty soft green pillows.

Sitting in the chair she rubbed her belly as she

pushed her foot against the floor. "I mean I know all those old-fashioned rocking chairs look great, but let's face it, they're not very comfortable. If I'm dealing with the fact that this kid will wake me up in the middle of the night, I should at least be comfortable while I'm feeding it, right?"

Ben nodded. "Sounds like a reasonable theory."

"I'm having a mural artist come paint a scene. All the catalogs I've looked at show the nursery with fluffy clouds on the ceiling. I'm not sure why the kid wants to think its outside, but whatever. Since I can't draw a stick figure, I'm leaving it up to the professional. I think we'll do a blue sky with clouds and then maybe some cartoon animals."

"I've always been partial to Bambi."

"Then when that's done, I'll get serious about the furniture. I joined this online new-mommy group and I can't tell you how much stuff this kid is going to need. Forget the crib, there are, like, a hundred other pieces of equipment it will require, not the least of which is something called a Diaper Genie. You don't even want to know what that's all about."

She knew she was rambling, but he didn't seem to mind. He simply leaned against the door with his arms crossed over his chest taking in everything she said.

"We'll need two car seats. Everyone says that's the most practical. To leave one in each of our cars so we're not always swapping one out. Then there are the carriers—the backpack kind and the newborn baby kind. I don't necessarily see you wearing one of those sling things, but you could probably make it work. Then there's all the bags I'll need to hold all the stuff to cart this kid from point A to point B."

"Anna, you're going to be a good mom."

She looked at him. She could see in his expression that he heard the fear in her voice. "How do you know?"

"You're one of the most caring people I know. Sometimes you put on a front and act tough, but I know deep down there is soft goo under the act. It's why you used to scare me so much, I think."

"I scared you?"

"Yep. You were this chaotic mess of light and softness. Sometimes I used to worry if I touched you, I might break you. But then I found out you're strong, too. Lord knows you could always put me in my place. So strong, in spite of all the soft goo I know fills up your heart. You'll love this baby and that will make you like a lot of other moms. But you'll protect this baby with ferocity and that is what will make you a great mom."

She smiled and tried to let what he said fill her up so she could really believe it. Because she desperately wanted to. "Every once in a while you say really nice things."

"You're welcome."

"I think, though, that I'm probably going to be scared until the kid gets here and I can prove to myself I'm nothing like my mother. I mean, what if she was like me in the beginning? Buying stuff and painting rooms, looking forward to meeting me and curious about how I'd be. But then when I was born it all changed."

Ben looked at his shoes a moment then met her gaze. "You've talked about some memories. Ones that weren't bad. Like the damp cloth on the back of your neck. So she must have cared for you."

"Yeah, but watching over me when I was sick sort of gets canceled out by the fact she left me. Why did she do that?"

Anna rubbed her hands on the mound that was her stomach. It baffled her—she didn't even know this kid's name yet and already the idea of being separated from it was like tearing off a limb.

"Anna—"

"No, I don't want to talk about that. Or her. This is my first night in my new home. My forever home. I want it to be a happy one. I want to remember it, always, as the best night ever."

"I think I can handle happy. For you, I'm guessing that means pizza with mushrooms and anchovies—which continues to boggle my imagination—and a quart of some type of ice cream you will name at the very last minute."

Anna's stomach rumbled at the mention of pizza. It had been maybe only an hour since she snuck in a peanut butter and banana sandwich, but suddenly she found herself craving something she couldn't name.

"Then we can segue from pizza into a movie. Something sappy that will have you in tears, which you will insist are happy tears, whatever the hell those are."

No, she didn't want a movie or pizza or ice cream. Suddenly Anna realized the thing she was ravenous for was *him*. It was as though a rolling wave of desire slammed on top of her, filtering down from her head to her knees to her toes.

She wanted him.

This wasn't about trying to make them work as a couple. This wasn't a relationship experiment. This wasn't some random moment of weakness that they would try to brush under the rug after it happened. It was her, Anna Summers, wanting a man in her bed, wanting to get sweaty and hot with him. Wanting him to touch her. Claim her.

She scared him. He'd told her so. It was the most romantic thing he could have said because simply knowing that she had the power to make big, bad Ben Tyler afraid made her own fear less powerful. Less controlling.

"I don't want the pizza or the ice cream or the movie. Well, maybe the ice cream, but later."

"No?"

She shook her head. "I want something else entirely. I want you."

Ben smiled and offered her a hand to help her

out of the rocking pillow. She accepted it and let him pull her close until her arms were circling his waist and her round belly was pushing against his.

"Yeah, I sort of figured that out."

"You did, huh?"

"You're looking at me like I'm the ice cream."

"That's funny because I do have the word *lick* on my mind."

She felt a vibration flow through his body. "Anna, don't tease me. I'm on a very short trigger."

"No teasing. I want this. I'm ready for it. Really ready this time."

He frowned. "You sound like you're bracing yourself for a dentist visit."

She rubbed his chest in a soothing gesture. "No, I'm excited. Nervous, but excited."

"You know, we have done this before."

"That night was a Dali painting. This will be real. I want it to be different."

"I thought we did pretty okay last time."

She shook her head, knowing she has having trouble explaining herself. "Last time everything seemed to happen—like it was happening to us. We weren't thinking. Not really. We were going through the motions without really being aware of one another."

He lifted her chin so she could see the truth in his eyes. "You're wrong. There wasn't one second I didn't know who was in my arms, Anna. You were always there. I just didn't handle the after part correctly."

"To be exact, you fell asleep after," she teased, trying to lighten the intensity she felt from him.

"And I imagine I will do so again. But if it makes you feel better, I'll call out your name several times during the act so you'll know I know who I'm screwing. Now let's go."

"Yes, sir!"

CHAPTER SIXTEEN

ANNA SAT ON the bed and watched as Ben shucked his T-shirt and toed off his sneakers. He'd worn shorts in deference to the early September heat and she admired his calves and the muscled bulk of his thighs. Then he lost the shorts and the underwear and she was admiring something else entirely.

For a moment she took in the sight of him. Tall and lean with corded muscles. His hair had grown in all over his body and she could see that he'd spent time outside without his shirt on this summer because his skin had a nice healthy glow to it. She knew he enjoyed swimming and had probably spent time at his club rebuilding both his endurance and strength.

Before the cancer, he had been a man who always looked ten years younger than he was. Now, as he recovered, she could see he was returning to form.

She remembered a time during the first days of his treatment when the impact of the chemo started to make itself known. She'd been kneeling beside him in the bathroom while he'd retched for what felt like hours but was really only minutes. When his stomach finally stopped heaving, he looked at her and she saw the fury in his expression. That his body had betrayed him, that it had brought him to his knees in front of her, his assistant. She remembered thinking that if his cancer was a man, Ben would have killed him.

Now, he stood in front of her naked, proud and strong. Like a warrior, he'd fought with everything he had. Ben was a man who vanquished his enemy, he never surrendered.

She should have had more faith in him. When he told her his plan to have the embryonic stem cell transplant, she should have believed more in the power of the man to overcome death. Instead, she'd run scared.

She wondered if he would ever truly forgive her for that. She could see now why he'd been so hurt. It wasn't only that she'd left him, it was also that she hadn't believed in him.

She should have. She should have believed more in Ben than in the cancer.

"You're beautiful," she whispered. Her very own original work of art.

"Men aren't beautiful." He ran his fingers softly over her cheek. "Your turn."

Anna squirmed a bit under his gaze. Now was the time of reckoning. She stood and kicked off her flip-flops. She took off the oversize T-shirt she'd bought as a transitional maternity top.

Her boobs seemed to pop out and instantly his hands cupped them. "Wow. They're huge."

Anna grumbled. "They're bigger, they're not *huge.*"

"Anna, we're talking grapefruits on their way to becoming small cantaloupes."

She crossed her arms over her chest and instantly he recanted.

"You're right. They're barely there. I can hardly see them. It's probably the bra."

"You're not making this any easier," she said tightly. "This is the first time someone is seeing me naked and pregnant. Where before I was only... you know, naked."

"I loved you naked. And I'm *really* liking the start of you pregnant and naked." He pulled her hands away then slid his hands around her back to unhook the bra. It released its precious weight and slid off her body. The skirt she wore was a stretchy black cotton thing that clung to the belly she no longer could hide from him.

"I can't wait to get my hands on this," he said, pressing his palm to the bulge of her pregnancy. "I didn't think it would be such a turn-on, but—" He slid his hands inside the skirt and her panties and started to push them down her legs in one inexorable motion until they drooped around her ankles and she kicked them loose.

He fell to his knees and rested his face on her belly. She could feel the scratch of his late-afternoon beard, but it didn't bother her. In fact, it made her think of other places on her body where she would like to feel his cheek.

Sitting back on his haunches, he ran his hands over her bump, as if memorizing each curve, each ripple. He was totally entranced by her body.

There had been no reason for her to be nervous.

"Who would have thunk, Ben has a fetish for pregnant women."

"I have a fetish for *you*. Seeing you like this, knowing it's my child inside you... I never thought... I never thought I would have this moment in my life. Thank you."

The sincerity in his eyes made her slightly uncomfortable. She knew she'd been ready to take their relationship to this place for a little while, but, for the first time, Anna considered how this would change things between them.

Adding sex to the mix would only make the intimacy grow and deepen. She would have to give more and more of herself to him and she would expect more and more of him in return. Only she didn't know if he had more to give her. It was a big risk for her. Because she didn't know what would happen after this night. But she sensed—no, worried, deep within—that she would need him even more.

He stood and nudged her gently onto the bed. She thought about where he might like to be touched and what she should do next, but he didn't give her much chance to act. With his legs between hers he spread her thighs wide then he bent over her to kiss her mouth, plunging his tongue deep inside her as if he were announcing this kiss as something different. This wasn't a kiss to claim, or a kiss because it was all she would allow. This kiss was the beginning of sex.

He moved from her mouth to her neck and began to find spots to nip and lick. Her earlobe, where her neck met her shoulder. Then her nipples. He didn't give her any lead-up, preliminary kisses or any soft touches. Instead, he sucked a firm nipple between his teeth and pulled deep until she could feel an answering rush of wetness between her legs.

She thought again about what she read, how hormones and pregnancy could cause horniness, among other things. Irony at its finest, as far as Anna was concerned, that when a woman was her most round, she wanted sex more than ever.

But she was starting to believe the effects as touch after touch of Ben's mouth on her body instigated a tidal wave of sensation throughout her. She wondered if he tugged a little harder on her nipples, then she might come from that alone, which had never happened to her.

It seemed they had only started and already she was running her legs along the outside of his thighs and tilting her hips to touch the hardness that was just out of reach of her body with the way his hands were braced on the bed beside her head.

"Ben," she moaned.

"All right," he grunted. "We'll play next time."

He shifted and she could feel the blunt head of his penis at the spot where she wanted him. In a slow, steady thrust he was deep inside her. She could hear herself whimpering, seeking another long stroke from the master, but she didn't care.

Then he started to move and she closed her eyes and let the feelings all roll over her. She could feel the easy rhythm of his body as he plunged then pulled away. This *was* different from last time, she thought. She was more aware of him. More in her mind than in her body. She was thinking and feeling.

This Ben. He's inside me. Oh, it feels good. We're having sex and now it's going to change us. We're going to be a couple. We're going to do this all the time.

A relationship. A real relationship.

Family...

As the words filtered through her body she found herself coming close to that peak that would take her to bliss. His hand cupped her ass and tilted her closer to him, allowing him even deeper. The pace of his thrusts increased but he was still careful not to push too hard or put any pressure on her belly. Her breasts were bouncing and, even in that, she felt a tug and pull of gooey heat rocketing through her body.

The pleasure built and the urgency of what they

were both reaching for grew. She started to shake inside. The fear of what would happen when she opened herself completely and let him inside her life as well as her body began to take over.

Suddenly she had this crazy idea that when she climaxed, when he pushed her to that point, she would finally crack fully open and he would pour himself into all of those little open crevices and she would be filled with him body and soul.

She would never be able to separate herself from him again.

What if he leaves? What if he leaves after that happens?

The dark thoughts intruded through the haze of pleasure and she found herself retreating, tightening up. She needed to hold back. It was the only way she could keep herself protected.

Let him finish. Just pretend. He doesn't have to know you got scared. He won't know the difference if you cry out his name.

"Anna!"

His shout had her blinking her eyes open. His face was a tight, brutal mask of sexual ferocity. But it scared her less than her own thoughts did.

"Don't you pull back on me now. Come with me."

She closed her eyes, shut him out and reached for the arm that he was using to brace himself above. "Yes, yes. Now."

But it was as though he could see her through her act instantly.

"Open your eyes and look at me."

She didn't want to. She didn't want to see him, not when she was running away, even while she was in his arms. Even while he was in her body.

"Look at me, Anna."

Unable to deny him the truth, she complied. He slowed his rhythm and leaned in to kiss her. She parted her lips willing to give him anything he wanted as long as she could hold on to some part of herself for a little more time.

He kissed her forehead instead.

"It's okay, I've got you. I won't let anything happen. You can let yourself go."

The hand that had been holding her hip shifted, inserting itself between their bodies. She could feel the brush of his thumb right on the physical spot that seemed directly connected to that inner space she was so desperate to hold on to. Then his hips rolled until she felt as though she was being screwed into the bed. The feel of him expanding inside of her while his thumb tweaked the swollen nub between her legs was too much. It pushed her over the edge and into the abyss.

Suddenly she was bursting all over and the sound of glass breaking around her wasn't hard to imagine. He thrust again then groaned like a dying man who happened to be in a great deal of pleasure. Together they rode out the ecstasy until the sensation subsided from their bodies, leaving them limp and satisfied.

Carefully Ben pulled away from her. He lay beside her on the bed and arranged them so that he could hold her from behind.

She felt his hand drift over her damp skin and watched as his palm settled over the womb he was so enamored with. For a time their breathing labored before settling. She could feel all of him behind her. His furred chest. His body heat. His solid presence.

She could feel his semi-hard erection pressed against the back of her thighs. Wet because of their passion.

Grateful that he couldn't see her face she let the tears leak from her eyes while her body and mind tried to assimilate what had taken place.

In her life she'd never felt so exposed.

No, maybe once. When she'd been standing in that noisy room with people all around her, bumping into her, until the woman in the blue uniform knelt in front of her. Anna had felt this way then. As if she had no control over what would happen next.

"Are you okay?"

She swallowed. "Yes."

"You're sure?" he asked, moving closer and pressing his chest more firmly against her back. She tilted her head in invitation and immediately felt his lips where she wanted them, a gentle suction on that spot where her neck met her shoulder that made her body want him all over again.

Too late. I'm done. It's happened and I can't protect myself anymore. Now, I don't want to think at all.

His hands roamed over her body, down her arm, her back, brushing over her bottom, then smoothing along her thigh. She could feel his erection grow between her legs. And when he lifted her leg and placed it over his heavy thigh she knew that the first time hadn't nearly been enough to satisfy him.

"Can I have you again?"

He was almost apologetic in his request. As if he couldn't believe his desire had built again so quickly. But this, she thought, was exactly what she wanted. She needed to be completely mindless right now. She didn't want to think about what she'd surrendered to him. She didn't want to worry about what that would mean for them tomorrow.

"Yes. Hard."

He chuckled then and his wandering hand settled on her breasts, cupping them. He pulled and tugged on her nipples so gently it seemed he understood how sensitive she was and only wanted to give her the faintest echo of pleasure without pushing her too far.

Too bad that wasn't what she wanted. She didn't want him to be sweet and caring and sensitive. She didn't want him to put his hand on her belly where their child grew. She didn't want to believe that everything he offered—this house, her baby and a life with him together—could be so wonderful.

"Now," she said, tilting her bottom back and rubbing it against him until she could hear his faint moan. The sound of a man on the brink of losing control.

"Anna, baby, we've got all the time in the world."

She could hear this satisfaction in his voice. Knew that earlier when he'd said they could play later that he imagined them romping in bed all night. Maybe even making love again in the morning.

Like any new couple might.

But in that playing she would have time to think. And when she started thinking, she knew, the fear would return. She was so sick of being afraid all the damn time.

"No, please. I need you now. Inside me. Please, Ben. Please."

She could feel the words jolt him and, before she had to ask again, he slid into her. Once again, their bodies connected with such wonderful ease. It felt blissful. It felt mind-numbing. Exactly what she wanted.

That's it. Take me. Take me hard and don't let me think and don't let me run. Just let me feel.

She rocked her hips into his and she could hear his muted growl in her ear. She knew what he wanted. A slow, leisurely act that would build up the pleasure in stages and drive them both into a long, torturous, wonderful climax. Like dessert hours after the main course. Deliciously sweet and satisfying, but not truly the thing that filled you up.

There was too much time in slow and leisurely.

"Harder."

"Anna, we have to be careful."

Careful because she was pregnant? Or careful because this was fast becoming too much for her to handle? Ben was curled around her. Ben was sliding inside her from behind. Ben. Not anyone else. Only the man she'd wanted for six years and now, suddenly, he was almost hers.

Almost.

She pressed down on him using a rotating motion with her hips that brought him high and deep within her. He clasped his hand on her hip, gripping her with enough force to still her, but not enough to bruise her.

"Geezus, Anna...what..."

She heard the question in his voice. This was supposed to be his show. After all, he'd told her how long he'd been waiting for her. He'd thought of little else but her since his recovery. He'd told her all those things. He'd given her that power. She knew he wanted to please her. She knew he wanted to bring her to those gentle but wonderful orgasms time and time again as some proof of how good her life would be like if she let him stay around.

None of these things mattered to her right now.

"What? I'm not allowed to move?"

She knew he would recoil at her words. The idea that he restrained her, controlled her, wouldn't sit well with him. She knew he wanted to be in charge, but she also knew he wanted her to be free to enjoy it.

Maybe that was the trick. Maybe if she pushed him, taunted him and teased him, then he would give her the pounding she craved. If she could make him lose control, he wouldn't be able to stop and she could get to that place she needed to be.

A place of mind-numbing pleasure. The key words: *Mind. Numb.*

Only this was Ben. Ben didn't lose control. Unless, sometimes, it was with her.

"Of course...I want to make you happy—"

She angled her leg higher and pressed down harder. Reaching behind, she grabbed his ass and squeezed with enough force to show him the urgency she felt.

"Do you want me to beg? Is that what you want?"

Because she would, she thought. She would get down on her knees in front of him and beg him never to leave her. Never to abandon her.

No! Don't think it. Don't let the words form!

"Ah," she cried, sounding like a woman on the edge. Maybe that would be the trigger he needed. To hear how truly frantic she was.

"Okay, okay. This." He held her tight and pushed deep. She could practically feel him all the way through her body. "This is what you want?"

"Yes, yes. More."

He complied, but even in his compliance he didn't really give in to her desire. He didn't slam into her. He didn't push her so hard her head smacked against the headboard knocking all sense and reason and fear from her brain.

Instead, he pulled nearly all the way out of her body, holding himself at her entry with the head of his penis stretching her and making her gasp with anticipation until he pushed deeply into her. Then did it again and again. One full thrust after another.

No, he wasn't banging her, or slamming her, or balling her brains out. But he was taking away her ability to think. All she knew was his hand on her breast, his hair-roughened thigh scraping against the inside of hers. His groans in her ears each time he slid home.

She felt the drag of his penis inside her. Relentless and unforgiving until her body contracted around him in this massive, gaping chasm of pleasure. Nothing had ever felt like this before. Nothing had ever been so consuming.

He shouted and she could feel the pulse of him inside her and the flood of his own pleasure filling her.

That was it. That was what she wanted. The way she felt now, she might never think again.

BEN LOOKED AT the sleeping woman sprawled across his chest, breathing gently. He thought he had her trust now, but maybe only because she wasn't conscious. His body was replete and he should be asleep since fatigue weighed heavily on him. He couldn't remember the last time he'd made love with someone so frequently in such a short span of time. But after he'd come the first time, his first thought had been that he didn't have her all the way with him and he needed that. He needed her totally and unconditionally with him.

He thought the sex started okay. But at some point, he could tell, she'd tried to pull away and he had no idea why that would be. She was the one who had instigated their lovemaking. She said she was ready for it. He'd sensed that about her all day long. The way she reached out to touch him first. The way she turned to him, time and again, seeking him.

Yet while they were naked and giving each other pleasure, it was as though her brain took over for her body and, while she didn't tell him to stop, he sensed she had mentally separated herself from the act. She didn't look at him and, for a moment, he could actually see her faking her responses.

Ben couldn't have that. If he was honest with himself, he wasn't completely sure why that was. It wasn't only a masculine pride thing, it went way beyond that. He needed her to belong to him. Even in his own heart that sounded somewhat barbaric, but it was the truth.

When he'd started this process to woo her and

convince her to marry him, his goals had been
simple. He wanted Anna and the child in his life.
It was a logical thing to want. She was carrying
his only child. She and he were obviously compat-
ible. A marriage with a child between them would
only make them more so. Emotions hadn't come
into play.

Now, however, the more he tried to tug her close,
the more he could feel her trying to pull away. Not
because she didn't want him—what they did together in bed showed him the level of her desire for
him. Even if she'd wanted to fake an orgasm, she
couldn't because he set off all her sexual triggers.

But she was obviously afraid of something, or
fighting something and withholding because of
that. He needed to overcome that. He needed to
show her what their life could be like and that there
was nothing to fear from him.

It wasn't only about what he saw as their future
together. It was about *her* and wanting all of her.

He was sure the something holding her back
was her past. That experience of being abandoned
probably drove her fear. It made her cagey and elu-
sive even when she craved having someone close.

Ben considered what he'd learned about her parents and wondered if he shouldn't tell her the truth
now. Although he thought about why he'd held on
to the information this long and decided now was
absolutely the wrong time. He needed more time
with her like this, more time to overcome her fears

without adding to them. With every weapon at his disposal he needed to bond her to him completely. So the idea of her life without him in it wouldn't make sense.

Once she was truly his, then he would tell her everything.

CHAPTER SEVENTEEN

AS THEY WAITED for the lab technician to show up Ben grew increasingly frustrated. It had been a few weeks since they had begun what he liked to refer to as the sexual part of their relationship—a fact that made him gleefully happy. But that development certainly hadn't made Anna any more malleable in her opinions.

Clearly, she was not a woman to be controlled by intense sexual gratification. Damn it.

She squirmed on the examining table, clearly trying to find some relief for the pressure on her bladder while he attempted to overcome her stubbornness about a topic they'd surprisingly butted heads on.

"We're two intelligent people," he began, attempting another logical approach to persuade her to his way of thinking.

"We are."

"Then let me please present you my rational and sound argument one more time."

"Go for it."

"If we find out the gender now, we will be more

prepared as parents. First, we can eliminate an entire spectrum of names to consider, which should reduce the chance of a conflict between us as your pregnancy advances. Also, we can buy the appropriate type and style of baby clothes we should have in preparation for this blessed event. Finally, while I believe we shouldn't necessarily conform to any gender stereotypes, we can begin to cater the child's toys."

"Those are all really good reasons."

"So when the technician comes in can we tell her we want to know the sex?"

"Nope."

Ben imagined if the sonogram technician found him with his hands around the pregnant woman's neck, it might not look good for him. No matter how justified he might be in his actions.

He gritted his teeth together. "I don't suppose you can provide me with a logical reason for your decision."

"Nope."

"You see how unfair this is?"

"Uh, buddy, take a look." Anna pointed to her exposed and quite round belly. "I'm sitting here about to burst with pee while I continue to get bigger by the minute. My reason… I think there really aren't many surprises left in life except maybe this one. So I say, let's be surprised."

"It's going to drive me insane knowing this information is out there but I do not have access to it."

She smiled. "Uh, yeah. That's part of the fun, too."

The technician chose that moment to enter the room and Ben considered it a small miracle that she found him doing nothing more menacing than scowling at the mother of his child. Seriously, Anna would drive him insane.

He watched as Anna's belly was covered with clear goo and the technician took a wand to her belly.

"Gotta pee, gotta pee, gotta pee."

"Hold it a little longer," Ben ordered as he stepped closer to take her hand.

After glaring at him, Anna politely told the woman that she did not want to know the gender. The technician went about her work, pointing out various features of their child on the screen along the way.

Ben was shown a nose and a chin and hand and a foot. He didn't recognize any of the above amongst the grainy images. And even though he couldn't recognize any of the prominent features, he still tried to search for some clue as to the sex of his child. Surely a man would recognize a penis on a screen when he saw it. But even his formidable powers of observation were no match for this technology. He was out of luck.

Finally, the ultrasound was finished and, while

Anna wiped off the goo from her belly, Ben helped her off the table and found her the nearest bathroom.

Afterward they were led to another exam room to meet Anna's OB/GYN. This state-of-the-art practice was located adjacent to the hospital where the doctor would deliver the child. All the facilities necessary for monitoring a pregnancy through to birth were contained within the one campus. Ben felt reassured by the proximity of the doctor to the hospital.

Anna, wearing a pair of stretchy yoga pants that had reached their absolute limit of stretchiness and an actual maternity top, was vastly more comfortable having made use of the bathroom.

"I'm telling you it's almost criminal to make a pregnant woman drink that much then tell her to hold it."

Ben was nodding while in the back of his mind he reviewed his list of questions for the doctor. The last time he'd been here he'd still been getting used to the idea that he was actually going to be a father and Anna had prevented him from asking much. This time he was better prepared and he had no intentions of letting Anna stop him.

A different doctor from the last time entered the room.

"You're not her doctor."

The woman put her hands in her pockets. "I'm Doctor Bradley and I work in the practice, too. We like our patients to rotate through all of us because we won't know who will be on call when the time comes to deliver. Nice to meet you."

Anna shook hands with the woman as did Ben, but he remained skeptical. "How many doctors are in the practice?"

"There are four of us. All women."

Dr. Bradley was older, maybe in her fifties, with steel-grey hair and a pleasant demeanor.

"What if we prefer one over another? Can we have our choice of doctor to deliver the child?"

"Ben," Anna chided. "We're not going to have a problem with the doctors."

"If you truly have a problem with one of us, then yes, you should let us know," Dr. Bradley answered calmly. "We can try to make arrangements as Anna's time grows closer. Now, let's take a look at you, Anna."

"I'm huge!" Anna announced as she pulled up her shirt.

"Not too huge," the doctor told her as she gently palpitated her stomach. "You're at nineteen weeks and it looks as though the baby is growing on schedule. Your ultrasound looks good. I see you didn't want to know the gender of the baby."

"No."

"Do you know?" Ben asked. "When you looked at the pictures could you tell?"

The older woman seemed to assess him before she answered. "No, I couldn't tell at all. The baby wasn't in a position where the technician would have been able to tell you regardless. So, in this case, it's actually a good thing you didn't want to find out."

Ben was satisfied until he saw the doctor wink at Anna.

"Now, Anna, do you have any questions?"

"I have questions," Ben said.

Anna shrugged at the doctor. "You might as well sit down, Dr. Bradley, he's going to have you here awhile."

Ben frowned but proceeded with his list. "I'm concerned about sex and the best positions for it as she grows larger."

"Ben!"

"Well, I am," he said, refusing to be embarrassed. The woman was a doctor. There was no reason not to be frank. He had every intention of continuing to have sex with Anna up until the point she no longer found it pleasurable. But he had concerns about any impact intercourse might have on his unborn child.

"Well, I would say that's up to Anna. She can best let you know what feels comfortable and what doesn't."

"I can't...hurt the baby?"

The woman had the decency to not smile. "No. As long as her pregnancy remains normal with no bleeding or amniotic fluid leakage, sex is perfectly fine."

"What about her diet? She's eating an abnormal amount of ice cream. Should I restrict that?"

"Ben! I do not. Dr. Bradley, do not answer him." Anna struggled to sit up until Ben reached out to assist her. "I am perfectly capable watching over my own health and *you* will not be restricting anything. Enough of these questions unless you have something serious to ask."

Ben frowned. "Fine. Doctor, you may not be aware but I was recently treated for leukemia. It's our wish to preserve the placenta after the birth. Who do I need to contact about making sure that happens?"

The doctor nodded and made a note in Anna's folder. "We'll have that on her record. I'll give you a few contact names of the companies who handle that kind of storage. Anything else?"

"I have a question. You know, me—the actual mother. When will I feel the baby move?"

"I would say anytime. You might not recognize it at first. But usually by twenty weeks you'll feel something."

Ben watched Anna cover her belly with her hand. He tried to imagine what it might be like to feel life from the inside of his body reach out to touch him and failed. Women, he thought, were certainly the better choice to carry the newborns. Anna seemed to adjust to her changing body with aplomb.

Ben didn't imagine he would be so serene about

it. He certainly hadn't liked it when he was losing his hair and weight by what felt like the hour.

They finished with the doctor and Anna made her appointment for next month. The next time they came for the appointment she would be at twenty-three weeks and already more than halfway to her delivery. It was crazy to think how fast time was moving.

"Can I ask you a question?" Ben asked as they were leaving the clinic.

Anna glanced at him. "It had better not be about a sexual position. I can't believe you talked about that with my doctor."

"Technically she's the baby's doctor, which makes her our doctor. I wanted to make sure I didn't hurt you or it. We've been…engaging in sex quite often."

The reality was they had been going at it like monkeys. Really horny ones. If he took her out for dinner or if they stayed in to cook, they would end the evening in her room, in her bed.

Her bed.

And once ensconced in her domain, Anna happily let him be in charge. It was exactly where he wanted to be and how he wanted things to be. At first, he wondered if the frequency and intensity of the sex was somehow linked to his recovery. That he was happy to be alive and be with Anna. He'd believed that her responses were about her matching need for him.

Lately, though, when he watched her face and listened to the sounds she made in the back of her throat, he could sense that sex was part of an escape for her. A way to not think about how things were changing between them. He supposed that shouldn't bother him. After all, sex was about physical pleasure, not necessarily an intellectual activity. The fact that she threw herself into every experience and let him overtake her with pleasure meant she trusted him. When it was over she now slept in his arms, the two of them sexually completely content.

Still, he felt as though something was missing.

Most likely he was overanalyzing this and his conclusions were ridiculous. He was more than thrilled to satisfy her every desire, especially if the act of sharing pleasure was bringing them closer. He was convinced each time they were together the ties between them got stronger and more difficult to break.

On the nights he didn't see her—because every once in a while she would say she needed some space, a gesture, he thought, made mostly to be perverse—he was edgy and nervous. As though with each minute that passed while he was away from her, he was losing some of the ground he had gained.

Ben didn't do nervous and edgy well.

She was at nineteen weeks already and, while they had fallen into a normal pattern of domesticity, suddenly he felt like it wasn't enough. He wanted more of a commitment.

"Call me crazy," Anna said, pulling his attention to this moment. "But I thought you were happy engaging in sex…quite often. Right now, however, you don't have a happy look on your face." She bit her lower lip in a way that drove him wild.

"Of course I'm happy with our sex life. Hell, we're standing in a parking lot in front of a hospital in the middle of the day—the least romantic place I could possibly imagine—and still I'm thinking of taking you. Against the car with your impossibly tight pants around your ankles."

"Ben!" Her eyes widened in shock, but he could also see a gleam of answering desire.

"I can wait until we're home. But that's what we need to talk about, Anna. Home and where it is."

"I don't know what you mean."

He took a deep breath. It was a risk, and maybe he was pushing too hard and too fast, working against the advice Mark had given him. But it seemed to Ben that everything between him and Anna hinged on these months before the baby was born. They had to have their relationship defined and solid. Because after the baby was here and she had her family, she might not need him anymore.

"I want to know if you're ever going to ask me to move in with you."

Her jaw dropped and Ben decided that wasn't the answer he was looking for.

THE DOORBELL RANG and Mark jumped up from his chair. He turned off the TV and jogged to the door. Deep breath first, then he opened it to three slightly unenthusiastic guests.

"Hi. Welcome. I'm glad you could finally make it."

Marie gave Sophie a gentle nudge and the girl crossed the threshold as if she were doing so at gunpoint. Marie followed her, but turned quickly to watch Dom's progress. He was using his walker today, which meant the arthritis in his legs was making walking a chore.

"Age is a bitch," he said as he slowly made his way to the couch where he fell into the cushions with a groan. Marie propped a supporting pillow behind his back and hovered over him until he waved away her fussing. By the time she sat down, Mark could hear her slight wheezing. The two were definitely a pair.

But they were here. Finally. After many invitations—initially to Sophie alone, but extended to Dom and Marie when it was clear Sophie would not come to him alone—they'd consented to a group visit. It was a major advance as far as Mark was concerned. While Sophie had agreed to a few lunches and shopping trips, coming to his home seemed to cross a line in the sand she'd drawn.

A line Mark knew he had to erase. And the first step in doing that was to stop giving away home court by always going to her grandparents' place.

If you couldn't beat the enemy on his terms, then you beat him on yours. A creed that had served him well during his years with the agency.

Not that Sophie was the enemy, Mark reminded himself. Just the prize.

"Sorry you're having a rough day," he said to Dom.

He pointed to the windows that overlooked the Philadelphia skyline. Dark clouds had rolled into the area and rain was threatening. "Humidity and rain make it worse."

Mark considered suggesting that staying in Philadelphia through August and September wasn't the best way to avoid humidity, but he kept his mouth shut. There would be no rocking the boat for this visit. The rocking could—and would—come later.

"Sophie, I thought you might want to see the room I had decorated for you."

After their little adventure at IKEA, Mark hadn't trusted Sophie to make the best calls regarding her room. Regardless of Anna's advice to the contrary, he suspected Sophie would continue to let spite dictate her choices. Instead, he hired an interior designer and told the man exactly what he wanted—the most perfect room imaginable for a fourteen-year-old piano prodigy. Budget nearly unlimited.

The man understood and Mark was pretty happy with the end result. Not that his opinion mattered if Sophie wasn't happy.

Evidently she wasn't making a move, so Marie stood first. "All right, let's have a look. This… apartment…is where you'll be living for the foreseeable future?"

Mark could appreciate her concern. An apartment wasn't a house and Sophie had always lived with a yard. "I think it's for the best. I've never owned a home or taken care of lawn or anything like that so I'm not sure what I would even do with a weed whacker. Between starting the business and well…Sophie, I've got to be careful where I spend my time. It's not like I need to worry about the correct school district for Sophie. And these units are all condos so I own this outright."

Sophie, who had been looking out at the forty-story view of the downtown Center City, acknowledged that she was actually listening to the conversation.

"What do you mean you don't have to worry about a school system?" she asked. "You don't have to worry about anything with regard to me."

"Come see the room, Sophie." Mark hoped that once she saw the room, saw that he was serious about meeting her needs, she'd better accept him in her life.

"Why do I need to look at a room I don't plan on ever staying in?"

Frustration mounting, Mark decided this was one of those moments that necessitated changing tactics. For months he'd been playing the nice guy. Months of pandering to her every desire in the hope that she might give him the time of day. Months of calmly accepting every snotty response to every question he asked. Months of tolerating her incessant eye rolling as if he were the least intelligent man on the planet and only she knew it.

He was done with being the patient, nice guy. She was his daughter. He was her father. It was time she understood the facts.

"Marie. Tell her."

Marie instantly jerked and looked to Dom for support. "This wasn't the plan. We said a few more weeks. She's not ready."

"She's not ever going to be ready," Mark said. "This isn't working and she needs to know what's happening in her future."

Dom nodded his head slowly. "He's right. We can't keep putting it off. You might as well tell her."

Marie opened her mouth but the only sound that came out was a sob. She made her way to Dom. "I can't do it," she said. "I just can't."

"Fine. I will." Mark walked over to Sophie, who straightened, suddenly much more attuned to what was happening around her. "Come see your room, Sophie. Now."

He added enough heat to the last word to actually send her in motion. They walked past the spacious kitchen to the hallway that had a linen closet, a bathroom and two bedroom doors.

"The bigger bedroom is mine, obviously, and I

have my own bathroom." Mark opened the door to his room and cringed when he realized that the bed was still unmade and he'd left his clothes on the floor. Shutting the door quickly, he opened the door to her room. "This is yours. You have a connecting door to the bathroom next to it."

Sophie didn't comment. The theme of the room was purple, but it wasn't overdone. The bed had a musical motif comforter on it and enough pillows to make a harem happy.

Mark had purchased the electric keyboard Marie had said Sophie had her eye on and it was set up with a music stand along one wall. On the other side of the room there was a desk that held the latest iMac computer. Bookshelves framed the desk, but Mark had left those mostly empty. He figured she would want to fill them herself. Same with the closet that he'd had fitted with an organizer to be able to make the most out of the space.

"Okay. I saw it." She crossed her arms over her chest. "Happy?"

"No. No, I'm not happy. I'm not happy your mother died in that car accident. I'm not happy about the kind of father I was while you were growing up. But I can't change those things, Sophie, and you need to realize that we have to get over this in order to move on."

She whirled on him with real anger in her eyes instead of the usual contempt. "I don't need to move on from anything. My mother died and it sucks. But I'm dealing with it the only way I know how. You need to know though that losing her is the only thing that is changing in my life. Do you understand? I will live with Gram and Granddad. I will continue to perform and I will continue to be tutored in my home. I don't need you. I don't want you. So you can crawl back under whatever rock you crawled out from. Just because I lost her doesn't mean I suddenly want you."

The words hurt. But even more wrenching was the utter grief he heard in her voice. In all his efforts to get her to make a space for him in her life, he'd nearly forgotten that she was still a little girl who had lost her mother at the wrong age.

"You won't be living with your grandparents anymore. You're going to live here. With me."

"*What?* No way! Gram!"

Mark moved out of the way as Sophie bolted past him. He gave Marie and Dom time to explain the situation. After a few minutes, when he entered the living room tears were streaming down his daughter's face.

"I don't understand," she wailed.

"Honey, you have to. We have to sell the house. We've already bought our unit in the seniors' community. Your grandfather's health is declining, he needs more care. My lungs aren't improving. I'm going to need to be on oxygen soon. That big house and the stairs…it's too hard for either of us to move around."

"We can get help. You can move into one of the bedrooms downstairs."

"Sophie, I'm sorry," Dom said, trying to reach out for her hand, but she avoided his touch. "I'm sorry I couldn't be better for you. We wish we were twenty years younger. We wish…we wish our Helen hadn't died." He sighed. "Sophie, this move to the seniors' community had been planned long before her death. After we lost her we canceled the sale. Of course we did. We thought we could take care of you together. We thought with you being so mature we could handle raising you. But these past few weeks have made us realize that Mark is a better option."

"He's *not* an option. He's nothing to me. He's just some name on a birthday card or a Christmas present."

Mark stepped forward. "Sophie, your grandparents and I have discussed this a lot. You know them. Do you seriously think they would let you live with me if they didn't think I could offer you a better option? Dom and Marie need the care. You're a smart girl so you know this. They can't keep traveling with you and you're too young to travel by yourself. And they can't continue with the way things have been just to make you happy. It's not fair to them."

"Not fair?" She was screeching now in a total teenage meltdown. "Not fair? What about what happened to me? My mother died. That's not fair.

Now my grandparents—the only family I have left—are going to leave me, too. To you?" She turned on Dom and Marie. "How could you? How could you?"

Marie was openly sobbing and Dom was doing everything he could to maintain his composure. Mark knew his daughter was hurting, but she was deliberately and maliciously hurting them all and he wouldn't have it.

"That's enough!" Mark got in her face so she could see he wasn't playing around. "I know this sucks large for you, but this is your life. I am your father. You will live with me. And you will let your grandparents off the hook. This is not their fault. Everyone keeps telling me how mature you are… well, start acting like it!"

She jerked and he could see she was thinking about heading for the front door. Thinking of making a run for it, he imagined. It was exactly what he would do if he felt similarly cornered. Fortunately, paranoid former operative that he was, he'd installed a lock that required a key to function on both the inside and outside. And he'd had the foresight to lock it as soon as they walked through the door.

He shook his head. "You can't run—the door's locked and I have the key. However, if you would like to take some time to enjoy your lovely new room—"

The words were barely out of his mouth before

she stormed down the hallway. The slam of a door closing echoed throughout the space.

Mark turned back to a sobbing Marie and a stalwart, but wounded, Dom.

"That went as well as we could have expected, I think."

A crash sounded from inside the bedroom accompanied by a host of discordant electrical noises. Mark had a feeling she would need a new keyboard.

His daughter, it seemed, had a temper.

CHAPTER EIGHTEEN

"HE WANTS TO LIVE with me."

"That's funny. She doesn't want to live with me."

Anna and Mark were sitting in his office eating what constituted a ridiculous amount of Chinese food. To be fair to Mark, most of it was for her.

It had been several weeks since Ben asked the question and she still didn't know the answer. She'd been able to hold him off each time with her standard line that she would think about it. So far all that thinking hadn't gotten her far.

And she realized the debate was starting to become moot. He came over to eat dinner and watch TV with her every night.

Slept with her every night.

The days of telling him she needed space were gone, because the reality was she didn't want space. Not from him. Even now he'd taken possession of closet space and two drawers in her dresser. Not to mention the master bathroom cabinet filled with shaving foam and razors.

Man stuff.

She was fairly certain the only thing Ben didn't

have at her place was his furniture and the tuxedo she knew he owned.

"I take it Sophie hasn't come around yet to her new reality."

"No. She's threatening to petition the court for legal status. Her grandparents are a wreck. I'm a wreck."

"She's a wreck," Anna added.

Mark tossed his chopsticks aside and leaned back in his chair. "Yeah. She's a wreck. And I don't know how to get through to her."

"Don't stop. That's all you can do. If you stop, she'll feel like you've left her all over again."

Mark shrugged. "I wish I could believe persistence and patience will work. Turns out my daughter is very stubborn."

"She and Ben have a lot in common. Are there any dumplings left?"

Mark checked one of the containers. But Anna already knew there would be more. Certain one order of dumplings wasn't going to be enough she had made sure to order three. That should have given them plenty even if Mark was a dumpling man.

"There are, like, a million left."

Anna pushed her paper plate toward him and held up three fingers. She watched as Mark dished out the food and then decided two more weren't going to kill her.

"You're a bottomless pit, you know that?"

"I'm eating for two," she mumbled around the bite of steamed dough and pork meat in her mouth. "Cut me some slack."

"So I know why Sophie doesn't want to live with me. She thinks I abandoned her and now I'm no better than a stranger to her. She's mostly right. What's your deal?"

Anna didn't know what her deal was. At first she'd needed time to think. Her relationship with Ben was changing at a rapid pace and moving in together was a major decision. Now that he was practically already there it seemed a bit silly to tell him she didn't think she was ready for him to move in.

There was the argument for letting him move in completely. Her number-one reason to support that idea? She liked having him there. She really, really liked having him there.

Still, she couldn't get past the fact everything was moving too fast. Her body was growing in leaps and bounds. The baby was mounting an attack from the inside of her body. Anna recalled vividly the doctor telling her she should expect to feel the first fluttering of movement from within.

Not her. The first thing she felt was a swift kick to the ribs. Not too long after that Ben had felt the baby kick, too. He'd spent the entire night with his hand on her stomach waiting for it to happen again. The man was belly crazy. Or at least crazy with what was inside it. One more reason to be cautious before committing to anything.

"We've only been dating for a couple of months," Anna said as she dipped her dumpling in a sauce so perfectly tart and delicious she wanted to drink it. But that might be overkill. "That's too soon."

"You've known each other for six years and you lived with him once already when he was sick. If that isn't seeing someone at their worst, I don't know what is. I think you can safely say you two know what it's like to live together. In good times and in bad."

"This is different."

"Why?"

Anna looked at the man who was her boss, but who had become her friend, too. She wanted to be honest with him. Or, maybe more accurately, she wanted to be honest with herself and she wanted someone else to listen.

"All those years with Ben…I mean, I thought I loved him. I *did* love him. But now I know how easy it was. How simple and uncomplicated it was. The whole time I got to love him I didn't have to worry about his feelings for me. I could simply pretend and it was enough. We worked together. We ate together. We were a team. Even when he got sick that was easy, too. I knew what I had to do. Take care of him. Help him to get better. It didn't start to get hard until—"

"Until you thought you were going to lose him."

She shook her head. "No, I never thought I was going to lose him. I wouldn't let myself form the idea. To me it was unfathomable. It was when I realized *he* thought he would lose his battle. When he decided it was all or nothing...without me, that's when I knew I couldn't pretend anymore."

"So you ran."

Anna winced. "I made a strategic exit. Everything is different now."

Mark laughed. "Yeah, because you're not in an imaginary relationship anymore. You're in a real one."

She hated to hear him verbalize it. But she knew it was true. All those years she thought she'd been in love, but never once had she been scared of it. Now she spent most of her days with a knot in her stomach that no amount of antacid would relieve and it wasn't the baby's fault.

"I was playing at love, wasn't I?"

"I don't think so. If it weren't grounded in something real, you would have ditched him already and fallen in love with me instead. I would be your new fake work husband."

Anna rolled her eyes to mock his cockiness, but it did give her some comfort to know that she wasn't prone to falling in love with every man she worked with. "I don't think so."

"No? I would make an awesome fake husband. Just like I was a fabulous fake father all the way from Afghanistan."

"I'm doing it, aren't I? I'm having an actual relationship with him."

"You are. And how does it make you feel?"

"Like a freaking scaredy cat."

"That's it? All you feel is fear?"

No, it wasn't even remotely close to all she felt. Ben made her feel as though there was another person in the world who knew who she really was. Ben knew she started to get cranky when she was tired or hungry and he either made her sleep or fed her. Ben knew she liked to sleep on the right side of the bed so he slept on the left. Ben knew how she liked to be kissed and touched. Ben knew what her favorite maternity shirt was and that she secretly liked the name Gertrude for a girl, although he refused to allow his daughter to be named that.

Ben made her feel safe when she slept in his arms. Ben made her feel happy when she woke up and he was still there. Ben made love to her as though, even with her round body, she was still the sexiest woman he'd ever laid eyes on.

No wonder she was so scared. For six years he'd been her world and what she felt for him then was a mere fraction of what she felt for him now. Which made the idea of him not feeling the same way about her so much more daunting.

Yes, he cared for her. Yes, he wanted her. But did he need her? Did he get heart palpations at the idea of her not being in his life? It seemed very uncharacteristic of Ben to truly need anyone.

"Has he told you he loves you?"

"Ha!" Anna snorted. "Ben? Feelings? You met him, right? No. Don't get romantic on me, Mark. We're both realists. Ben doesn't want to move in with me because he loves me. He wants to move in with me because he sees it as the next step in his plan to get me to marry him. Because that's what he wants. The kid and me in that order. He thinks moving in will get him to marriage that much faster and he thinks marriage is the most secure way to lock it all up. He's being expedient, that's all. First he gets me to forgive him, then he gets me to date him, then have sex with him, now he wants me to live with him… This must have been how the Germans felt when they knew Patton was on the other side of the battlefield."

"Resistance does sound futile." Mark pinched the last dumpling from the container and popped it in his mouth.

"Was that the last dumpling? Did you seriously eat the last dumpling when there is a pregnant woman in the vicinity?"

"Snooze, lose. Besides, I thought the quart of pork lo mein and the twelve dumplings you already had would have been enough. No?"

Anna patted her stomach. "Well, it does leave me room for dessert."

"Stop changing the subject. What are you going to do about Ben?"

"I'm probably going to lose." Hell, she'd already

lost. The idea of going home tonight and him not being there was unimaginable. He was making her ridiculously happy, and she simply had to find a way to deal with the fear.

"Probably?"

"Definitely. He'll win. I'll cave. It will take a few months, but I'll start to realize he doesn't feel about me the way I feel about him and I'll have my heart crushed."

"Honestly, though, is a lifetime of a one-sided love really that long to endure?"

Anna knew Mark was teasing her, but she wanted to kill him right now. Or at least wipe the smug look off his face.

"Listen, all kidding aside, I think you're not giving Ben enough credit. Forget the fact that the guy bought you a house in case he died. I've known him a long time, too, and I never once saw him lose his control. The night he broke his own rule and knocked you up…that's unprecedented."

Was it? When he thought he might die? The bottom line was that Anna was afraid it no longer mattered. Letting him go, or trying to walk away from him a second time didn't seem humanly possible.

"It doesn't matter. I know what's coming, but I'm not quite willing to surrender the battle yet. If he wants to move in with me, then he's going to have wait until I'm ready. Besides, he's got this really ugly sofa in his home office that I know he'll want to bring with him and I hate it."

Not the memories on it, of course. Those were precious. But the couch looked like an overstuffed piece of beige nothingness.

"There's a reason to put your life in stasis. You don't like his taste in furniture."

She glared at Mark. "If you hadn't eaten the last dumpling, I would have thrown it at you."

"Yeah, right. As if you would waste the food."

"Okay, well, how about we move on to another topic. Have you made any progress finding my birth parents?"

"Absolutely. I've got several leads. I'm tracking them down and making excellent progress."

"Are you lying?"

"Yes. You know that's what I say to all my clients when I've got zilch. I've been tied up with the Anderson case. Because it was a high-profile cold case, the sheriff of Montgomery County was anxious to have my input. I feel like I had to put my energies there first."

"No, of course. You did great work on that case. Based on what you found the coroner confirmed it wasn't a suicide as previously thought. Sally Anderson was murdered and now she has a chance for justice."

"If the sheriff or I can find her killer. The trail is like an iceberg at this point."

"You'll do it."

"Such confidence. But I guess that's what I do… bring justice to the masses."

He was laughing at himself in a self-deprecating way, but Anna didn't discount the importance of Mark's successes. "You know you might consider telling Sophie about some of the work you've done and, more importantly, some of the cases you've solved."

"You think she would listen?"

"I think if I was a girl who didn't know her father—oh, wait, I am that girl—and I learned he was one of the good guys, then, yeah, that might make a difference."

"Is that why you are anxious to find them? Because you're hoping they might be good guys in the end?"

No, Anna couldn't expect that. She knew her father had left before her mother abandoned her so that automatically ruled him out of the good-guy category. Then knowing what her mother was and what her mother did, Anna didn't think there could be a happy ending in any of this. She simply had this need to know what happened. Maybe so she could have certainty that it couldn't happen again. Not to her child anyway.

"Not anxious…only curious I guess. I went so long without thinking about them at all. Now that I've made the decision to do this I can't seem to *stop* thinking about them. Or maybe it's the baby thing."

"I promise I'll let you know when I have something. So, I take it that means Ben hasn't found anything, either? That's surprising considering I've given him a massive head start."

A fact not entirely lost on Anna. "Nope. He says everything has led to dead ends but…"

"What?"

She hesitated in answering. Really, all she had was a gut feeling, and lately her gut was so messed up between Ben and the baby she didn't know if she was coming or going. The other night she'd spent two hours folding and refolding Onesies in different drawers to see which one of them she liked better for the purpose of storing Onesies. It was a little insane.

At one point she'd thought she was losing her mind until Ben came in and showed her the chapter on nesting and explained what she felt was a biological imperative and that her behavior was perfectly natural.

Right. So now biology was running her brain. No doubt she was completely wrong about her suspicions.

"I don't know." She struggled to verbalize what she actually thought. "It's like he's holding back something. I know he was an operative and that should have made him skilled at being sneaky—"

"Ben wasn't trained in sneaky. Not his particular specialty."

"It's just that any time I bring up the subject he gives a terse reply and changes the topic. Maybe *sneaky* is the wrong word but *evasive* fits."

"Well, I can assure you, I am excellent at my job and I haven't turned up anything yet. The names are a dead end. The play on combination of names is a dead end. I'll head out to the hospital where you were born and see what I can find there and let you know how that turns out."

"I appreciate it."

"You're welcome. So should we get back to work?"

Their lunch hour had become more of a lunch afternoon. She probably should accomplish something for him, given that he was tracking down her parents for free.

"There are some payables I can process."

"That's sounds so assistant of you. I love it!"

"But—"

"What?"

Anna's stomach grumbled. "I think I would rather get some dessert first. Ice cream breaks?"

Mark's jaw dropped. "You can't be serious. This kid is going to weigh fifty pounds on the way out."

"It's just that I—"

"Need it. Yes. Ice cream. Go. Then come back and get those payable things…done, filed, whatever."

Anna pushed herself out of her chair belly first. She leaned down and brushed his cheek with a light kiss. "Thanks for everything, boss. I mean it."

"Sure you don't want to ditch Ben and make me the new object of your affections?"

"I'm sure. But you do make an excellent sounding board. Make sure Sophie knows that about you. It could change a lot."

Having stalled on a lead in the Anderson case, Mark decided to make good on his promise to Anna to track her parents more aggressively. The truth was, once he knew Ben was pursuing the matter, he didn't see much point. After all, Ben had more at stake. Finding Anna's parents would be one more way for him to impress her and win the girl.

Except that he hadn't. At least not yet.

Mark went to the Holy Mercy hospital and found the administration floor in the basement. The single person working behind the counter was a girl who appeared as though she was barely out of high school. She put down her nail file as soon as he approached her desk.

"Can I help you?"

"Yes, I'm looking for help with a birth certificate that was filed from this hospital. The names on the certificate were actually falsified and I'm trying to find out how that could have happened."

"I didn't do it. I mean, I'm really careful when I do those things because they are super important."

Mark decided this particular interview would be a struggle. "Yes, of course. I know you weren't involved. I should have been clearer, this certificate was filed more than twenty years ago. Do you have a supervisor or someone who is in charge down here?"

"Yeah. She's getting coffee. I'll let her help you because I wouldn't know about anything more than a week ago. I'm new."

"Go figure."

Mark found a chair in the corner of the office and sat to wait. Not two minutes later a middle-aged woman with a square frame and a matching square face entered the room.

"Natalie, how many times have I told you, I don't want to see you doing your nails behind the desk? It's not professional."

The file was quickly shoved in a drawer. "But there is, like, nothing to do down here."

"Then you find something to do. Go through the filing system. Develop a better system of organization. Clean your desk of the seven different coffee cups you have half filled with cold coffee. That's something."

The girl said nothing but dutifully got out of her chair and started to fuss about her desk. As far as Mark could tell she was simply moving the half-filled coffee cups from one side of the desk to the other.

"Oh, and this guy is here."

The woman turned and immediately Mark knew he was working with a veteran. The woman had the serious expression of someone who knew this basement was her fiefdom and knew how to run it well.

"Can I help you?"

"Yes, I'm here about a birth certificate." Mark gave a brief description of his job and why he was interested in the information.

"I know the names are fake, and I know the hospital typically files the information so I'm interested in discovering how something like that could happen."

The older woman, who had introduced herself as Marge Berry, took the copy of the certificate Mark had brought with him.

"Yes, normally we will handle the filing of the birth certificate. The information for the parents' names comes from their admission paperwork most of the time."

"There is no confirmation with the parents first? An ID check, that sort of thing?"

If Anna's parents had official-looking fake IDs, it would suggest that they had been living underground for some time. Whereas if they decided only at the last minute to change their names, he might be able to find out their real identities here. And that might lead him to locating them now and possibly discovering why they'd lied.

Perhaps they'd been considering leaving Anna at the hospital at birth. They could have left her and disappeared into the city. The fake names would have made it difficult to trace them. Of course, a simpler option would have been to decide to let her be formally adopted, but that required rational thought. And, based on their actions, the couple weren't very rational.

He wondered how young they might have been. Anna didn't have any recollection of how old her mother was. At the age of six all adults probably looked the same. But if the parents had been two scared kids, who also happened to be addicts, it might explain their strange behavior when Anna was born.

Obviously Anna's mother—and possibly her father, too—wanted to keep her and thought they could handle raising her. So why lie about who they were?

Mark considered how different Anna's life might have been had she been adopted by a stable couple who wanted her. Then he considered how different things might be for Ben if that were the case. They might already be married, her abandonment issues nonexistent. Then again, if her life had been altered so radically, maybe she wouldn't have been the person Ben wanted in his life.

It was crazy to think about it.

"I have to say we don't check ID. It's not really needed. After all, we have their insurance cards as ID."

Interesting. "So if someone was admitted without insurance, you wouldn't have any way of validating whatever information they gave for the certificate."

Marge seemed to bristle at that. "Well, I can't say we did, but we should have. If anything, we would require more information from the admitting patient since without insurance we would have to determine alternative methods of payment. Unless it was an emergency—a life-or-death delivery. In those cases the paperwork doesn't get completed until the dust settles."

Mark was grateful to know that if there had been a life-or-death issue, the mother, and more importantly child, would be attended to before the paperwork.

"You know what is odd about this..." She took out a pair of bifocals she kept in the front pocket of her button-down shirt and perched them on the edge of her nose.

"What?"

"These names. They ring a bell. It's funny, too, because the questions you're asking...I feel like I've been down this road before."

Mark silently groaned. Of course she had. Ben had, no doubt, followed the same path and had gotten here first. Typical.

But why hadn't he told Anna what he'd learned?

As far as Mark could see the path was pretty clear. Anna's parents hadn't had insurance. If they'd had legitimate cards, then those names would have been used. All Mark had to do was find the admittance of a non-insured pregnant woman on the particular day and year of Anna's birth. How many could there be?

"Can I ask how recently this was?"

"Recently? No, this didn't happen recently. I would have recalled immediately. Trust me when I tell you we don't get investigators down here every day asking about falsified birth certificates. No, this would have been maybe…a few years ago. But I want to say the circumstances were the same. He was an investigator of sorts and was trying to find some girl's parents."

Mark nodded. Of course he was. He was Ben.

CHAPTER NINETEEN

"RIGHT THERE. OH, YEAH. A little harder. No, no, too hard. Oh, yes. Oh, that's good."

Ben closed his eyes and tried not to listen to the torture that was the sounds Anna made as he rubbed her back. After her thirty-fourth week of pregnancy they had officially crossed the sex-is-no-longer-fun threshold. Her breasts were too tight and achy, her feet were too swollen and he hadn't been able to find a right angle to make her come during intercourse.

He had resorted to using his fingers or his mouth to pleasure her. And while he enjoyed it, he'd learned it didn't give her as intense an orgasm as when he was fully inside of her.

Eventually even those tactics had stopped working and he knew she'd been trying to enjoy the sex for his sake.

The motivation was sweet in a way. But a part of him wondered why she simply hadn't told him to stop. Anna wasn't demure about stating her demands. Hell, in the beginning of their relationship she'd been very clear about saying no to sex until she was ready. So to merely lay back and let him have his way, even though she wasn't getting as much from the experience as he was, really bothered him. She might have continued the ruse, but he'd put an end to it and announced that they were done until after the baby was born.

This was just one of a host of things he didn't understand about her lately. For the life of him he couldn't get her to agree to let him move in with her permanently. He'd managed to sneak in much of his closet, his bathroom stuff, his favorite pillow and several of his books that he'd mingled with hers.

He wondered if she was waiting until they had reached this point where sex could no longer be the glue that held them together. Maybe she thought without the sex he'd grow bored and wouldn't be as interested in staying over every night. Nothing, however, could be further from the truth. In the past two weeks since they had called a halt to their sexual activity, Ben was entirely content to lie down with her at night and rub her back or her shoulders. Anything to bring her a little comfort in a body that was no longer comfortable.

In fact, he loved doing that for her. He just hated the erection he got thanks to the sounds she made—relief was a long way off. Another four weeks or so of pregnancy then another six weeks of healing time—he had already asked the doctor—then the decision to resume sexual activity would be left up to her.

Of course they would have the baby to consider then. They would be up doing feedings. Ben certainly didn't plan for her to take on all the work. The breast pump he'd purchased would allow her to store her milk so they could divide the night feedings.

Still, he'd heard about the perils of sex after the baby from some of the fathers in the Lamaze class they attended. Fathers who were on their second and third child. Some stories he'd heard referenced months…and months before being invited anywhere near their wives. Those men had appeared very stressed-out to Ben.

"Okay, that's enough."

Easing off her side, she rolled toward him. He made room for what they had recently nicknamed The Great Beast—her stomach and their child.

She smiled serenely. "Thank you."

"You're welcome. You want me to do your feet?"

"Nah, I'm good. I'm tired. Even sleep is getting hard for me. I can't seem to get comfortable in any position and then as soon as I do The Great Beast goes ballistic on me."

"You know we're going to have to stop calling it that. What if it can hear us and develops a complex? Because it can hear. It says so in all the books. It hears us calling it *it,* too. Yeah, we're probably well on our way to screwing the kid up."

"*It* will be fine. After all, there was Cousin It in the Addams family and he always seemed very chipper."

"Excellent. Gertrude if it's a girl and Cousin It if it's a boy. Settled."

"Hardeehar. Hey, here's shocking news. I need to pee."

Ben chuckled and watched as Anna rolled off the bed and onto her feet. She reminded him of the girl in the Willy Wonka movie that the Umpa Lumpas had to roll away. He heard her puttering about in the bathroom and he thought this was it. Domestic bliss.

They had really settled into coupledom. He rubbed her back. She made jokes about how often she needed to pee. Their baby was only a few weeks away.

"Anna," he called out to her.

"Yeah?"

"Why won't you let me move in with you?"

There was no response and he knew it had been stupid to ask her while she was in the bathroom and he couldn't see her face. At this very moment she was thinking and retrenching. He should tell her what an amazing operative she would have been—Anna was never without a plan.

She returned and he thought how sweet she looked in the white nightgown that covered her from her neck to her toes. Sweet, but conniving.

And her face looked a little pale. "Are you okay?"

"Fine," she said too quickly. "I noticed there was a little spotting…you know…down there. Is there supposed to be spotting? Now?"

"Should we call the doctor?" Ben instantly reached for his cell phone on the nightstand.

"No, it wasn't like, ah, there's a lot of blood. It was just a little. I'm sure it's related to my cervix stretching or whatever. My appointment is tomorrow. I'll check with her then."

"I can't be with you tomorrow. I have that meeting in D.C. We talked about that."

"I know. It's fine. Geez, Ben, you've been to almost every single doctor's appointment. You see what they are. I hand over my sample, I get poked and prodded then we're done. When they start doing the internal stuff I'm not even letting you in the room."

"Anna, I know what's down there. I spent the past three months becoming quite familiar with it."

She had become quite familiar with what he did, too. Was, in fact, eager to have him there. He believed he made her happy in bed. Happy in bed. Happy in life. So what was her problem? It didn't escape him she still hadn't answered his question about him moving in.

"It's not the same," she said. "Keep your appointment tomorrow. I'll call if the doctor says there is anything to worry about."

Ben had already canceled the appointment mentally. It was a communications company looking to use Greg as their human lie detector for an upcoming hostile takeover. Given the antagonism between the two companies Ben had wanted to be in attendance. But, in truth, Greg could handle any squabble that might occur.

"Are you going to answer my question?"

"Huh?"

"Anna." He felt like growling. "Do not attempt to play dumb with me. Why won't you let me move in here?"

She smiled and climbed into bed, this time plumping the pillows behind her back. "You know I've been thinking about this…"

"Excellent. Although, honestly, I don't see why it required a lot of thought."

"I told you, this is a big decision for me. For us."

Irritation bubbled immediately. "What's to decide? I've been living in this house and sleeping in this bed now for months. We're talking about moving the rest of my things and putting my house up for sale."

"Your house up for sale? No, I don't think you should do that. You might—"

"What?" His temper was slipping away in a manner it never had before. He didn't lose his temper. Ever. He controlled it. But she was making him crazier every day with her need to keep any sort of distance between them. He shot out of bed and paced in front of her.

"What are you thinking? That when this doesn't work out, I'll need some place to go back to?"

She didn't answer. She didn't have to.

"What haven't I done, Anna?"

"I don't know what you mean."

"I mean, what are you waiting for to prove that this is actually happening? *We* are becoming a family. Don't I make you happy?"

If it was possible for a woman of her size to curl in on herself, it's what she did. "You make me very happy."

"Haven't I been attentive? Haven't we connected? We come home to this place together and you put your feet on my lap and I watch you eat more food than I ever thought a human could consume and we laugh and talk. Then we came to this bed and I made love to you and you came. Didn't you?"

"Of course. Ben, you know I love that…with you. It's just now—"

"I'm not talking about now—I know that it's not comfortable, although I'm mad that you didn't tell me sooner." He knew he was sounding ridiculous but suddenly the distance she insisted on, his irritations were all there. She was with him. But not all the way. He was holding on to her, but she was still wiggling to get free.

"Okay, let me get this straight. You're mad at me because I had sex with you."

"I'm mad at you because you wouldn't tell me what you wanted when you wanted it. Or in this case when you wanted it to stop. Since when did you decide to be *polite*…with me?"

"Ben, you're crazy. Maybe the stress of everything is getting to you."

He clenched his jaw and made his hands into fists. He felt like there was this dark monster sitting between her and him and he wanted to fight it. He wanted to take it apart with his bare hands. But stubbornness…or whatever her stubbornness was shielding wasn't an enemy he could take on with his fists.

"It's not the stress. It's you. You're holding back. You think I can't feel it? You think I wouldn't know?"

Her face grew even whiter then. "You—you said you didn't know what love was so how would you know if I'm holding it back. Maybe I'm trying."

Maybe she was. Maybe this was the most she could give him. Then why suddenly did he need more? It was nonsensical. She was right, maybe he was crazy. He couldn't seem to shake this feeling that, as close as they'd grown, he was still losing her.

He couldn't lose her. She had to love him.

"Maybe I don't know what love is supposed to be but I think this is damn close. Isn't it close, Anna?

I mean, here we are living our lives together, enjoying each other and making plans for this new beautiful life that's about to join us. Isn't this what it's supposed to be about?"

"I wouldn't know," she said quietly. "I've never had anything like this before. At least nothing that couldn't be taken away."

"Is that it? Is that what you're afraid of? That I'm going to leave you? That I'm going to die? I can't control that, Anna. That's the chance you have to take. I had cancer. Right now it's gone but I don't know what the hell will happen in five years, or ten. You can't live your life being afraid."

"I'm not afraid!"

Her screech was so loud it made her denial ridiculous. He moved toward her then, trying to calm her with his tone. "Listen to me, Anna. We can do this. We can make this work. I'm an open book. Whatever I need to do for you to trust me I'll do."

He was close to her now. So close he could reach for her hand, but she yanked it away.

"An open book? Really?"

Her low tone confused him. He felt like a witness who had said the wrong thing on the stand and was about to be cross-examined. Then it occurred to him. The one thing he hadn't told her. He knew he should have come clean earlier. Knew it was a risk to keep it from her.

Mark. The man was, unfortunately, too good at his job.

"What do you want to know Anna?"

"Why won't you tell me about my parents?"

Then she didn't know. Not everything. This was a very careful line he had to walk. Especially given how upset she was.

"What do you think I know and aren't telling you?"

A harsh laugh escaped her throat. "And doesn't that answer my question? I gave you that certificate almost four months ago. I've seen you take less time to divert an international crisis. You haven't said a word about it and any time I ask you about it you change the subject."

"Why is it so important for you to find them? Why are you looking to the past when the future is right in front of you?"

"I told you." She looked away from him. "Having a family medical history only makes sense."

"This isn't about our baby's DNA. This is about you, Anna. What do you want? What possible outcome could there be to finding out about whoever these people are? These people who left you. The baby is coming. And I'm here. Let us be your family."

ANNA COULDN'T RESPOND. The fear inside her was suddenly paralyzing. Her stomach felt tight and her mouth was so dry she thought she could drink a pool filled with water. He was asking too many questions. She didn't want to think about why finding her parents was important. She didn't want to say why she was keeping him at bay.

She couldn't believe he sensed something was wrong. How clever she thought she was going through the motions, thinking he was fine with her level of commitment. She actually started to believe that she could make this arrangement work permanently. He could move in and she could have all the comforts and joy of having him here but still hold a little of herself back. As long as she didn't give him everything, as long as there was something that was still hers and not his, then it didn't matter if he left.

Or if in the end he didn't love her the way she loved him. Or whatever it was that she was afraid of.

But now it was Ben who wanted more. Ben… the guy who wasn't supposed to know what real love was all about. She'd gone from despairing that he would ever feel the way she wanted him to feel about her, to being content with what he was willing to give her because it meant she didn't have to give as much to him.

Only now he was changing the game and every instinct she had said to run.

Fast before he catches you.

Except an eight-months-pregnant woman wasn't running anywhere. Which only left her one other option. She needed him to leave. And to accomplish that she needed to start a fight she could win.

"See? There you go again changing the topic. You think I don't know you? You think I can't tell when you're being purposefully vague. The fact that you have to play that game means one of two things. Either you already have the information I want and you're withholding it from me for some reason, or you chose not to go looking for it after I asked you to. And what about Mark? Is he in on this? He told me he was working another case, but maybe that's a lie, too. Maybe you're working together to hide the truth from me."

"It's not a conspiracy, Anna. You're becoming paranoid."

Paranoid. Furious. Righteous. Whatever it took to start the fight. "Oh, so this is in my head? You've had that birth certificate for four months but you're telling me you haven't learned anything? Nothing at all?"

She watched him close his eyes and knew he was deciding how to tell her only what he wanted her to know without actually lying to her.

"I have information, but you're going through a lot right now. I don't know if this is the best time…"

He served up that concession like a softball. How easy this fight was going to be. Part of her felt bad because she knew it wasn't the truth about her parents she was needling him for. It was only the fight she wanted.

She remembered arguing with him the night before taking him to the hospital to have the stem cell transplant. She remembered feeling as though she was fighting for her life as well as his. She remembered with such vivid clarity how her heart felt as if it would burst from her chest when he'd apologized for making love to her.

This was totally different. This time she was in control. This time he was the one who would feel the pain. This time she would be in the driver's seat. She had a reason now. He'd kept something from her. And he had no defense. It would be her best opportunity. Calmly and with a few moments to gather her poise, she eased off the bed so she could stand face-to-face with him.

If she was going to do this, she should at least be on her feet.

"How dare you? How dare you presume to tell me what I can or cannot know about *my* parents? *My past!*"

"Anna, please. I was trying to protect you."

Of course he was. Because that's what Ben did. His natural instinct was to shield and protect. He did it because he cared for her. But that caring was too much. So much it was tearing her apart from the inside. She had only one recourse left.

"Protect me? I've been on my own since I was six years old. I know how to protect myself. I didn't need you then and I don't need you now. You thought we could have a relationship? A committed, serious relationship when all this time you've been lying to me? We have nothing."

She could see he was stunned. Not prepared for the violence of her attack or the anger in her voice.

He held up his hands as if in surrender. "Okay. Okay, if that's what you want, I'll tell you everything I know."

No, that wouldn't do. She didn't want his capitulation. Handing over the information was too easy an out for him. Finding out whatever terrible thing he knew about her parents—because he would have tried to shield her from the knowledge only if it was terrible—was nothing compared to holding on to his deception and heavy-handedness as a weapon she could use to drive him away.

"No, I don't want to hear anything you have to say. If you found them, Mark will find them. I'll get what I need from him. You need to leave now."

"Anna…"

Pain. Real pain. She'd hurt him with her last jab and she could see it in his face. He would learn to live with it. She'd been let go of and abandoned all her life. Eventually a person becomes numb to the agony and the questions. You had to in order to survive. Then a person learned to let go first.

"I'm serious. I can't deal with this. With you."

"Please, let's talk about this. I didn't mean to hurt you or upset you. You've been very emotional—"

"Really? Let's recap. I'm paranoid. I need to be

protected. I can't handle the truth about my past. I'm emotional." She counted the items on her fingers. "Who the hell do you think you are? I asked you for help. I wanted you to tell me where I came from. Who I was. And you know but you won't tell me because you think you know what's better for me? Screw you."

"Anna—"

"Are you going to get out or does this have to get ugly? I mean it. I'm eight months pregnant and I don't think I can handle this kind of stress."

The perfect thrust. He would feel it right through his chest. Because he couldn't stay and fight with her knowing that he might put her or the baby at any risk. He had no choice now. He had to leave. She'd done it.

"Please don't do this. Please."

The trick was not to feel anything. That was the problem. In these past few months he had made her feel too much. What she needed was control over her emotions. Ben would appreciate that. He was a man who understood control.

"I'll text you if there is any information you need to know after my appointment tomorrow. Then after a few days and we've calmed down, we can talk about the plan for the birth. Then discuss custody options for after it's born."

He swallowed. "We shouldn't call it *it*."

He walked into the closet. A few moments later he emerged wearing jeans, a T-shirt and a pair of old sneakers she'd told him needed to be replaced even though he liked the way they fit his feet. Such a wifely thing, she thought, to care about the condition of the sneakers he wore. Yes, ending this relationship now was the right thing. She hadn't realized how close she'd been to completely succumbing.

He grabbed his cell phone from the nightstand and stuffed it in his pocket. He didn't look at her. He simply left without saying another word.

She watched him walk out of the bedroom and waited until she heard the sound of the downstairs door closing. The front door of the house he bought for her because he wanted to make sure if he died, she always had a home of her own.

That's who she had pushed away. That's who she'd forced out of her home. Because she hadn't known until this very moment that she couldn't cope with all of the things he wanted to give her.

A husband. A baby. A family. A life.

Her body started to shake and she reached out for the bed. Sitting on the edge she concentrated on taking slow, deep breaths and tried to gain control of her body.

You'll be okay. You'll be okay.

The words came to her and she thought about what she'd survived before and how much more capable of surviving she was now. Weren't those the exact words she'd thought when she was six, lost in a room with people all around her, bumping into her, not seeing her? Knowing instinctively that the person she needed most was gone.

After a few breaths the spots before her eyes faded and she decided it was safe to stand. She wouldn't risk hurting herself or the baby and, as unsteady as she felt, she knew she had to be extra cautious.

But she needed a glass of water. Her mouth was beyond dry. Then she would try to sleep. Tomorrow would be soon enough to think about what she'd done and start the process of denying to herself why she had done it.

When she stood she felt a warm stickiness between her legs. Turning, she saw the stain of fresh blood on the mint-green duvet she and Ben had picked out together.

Panic immediately surfaced. What was happening? Was she in labor? But she didn't hurt. Did her water break? Was that supposed to be bloody? She didn't think so. And it was too soon. Only thirty-six weeks. She wasn't ready.

Mentally digging deep she locked down the panic and started thinking logically. There was blood, not amniotic fluid. She was not in pain and it was too soon for labor. Something was wrong. Phone.

There was no phone upstairs. Either she or Ben always had a cell phone with them. Ben was gone. She'd sent him away. He'd taken the phone with him. Her phone was downstairs.

Thoughts started to coalesce.

Downstairs. Phone. 911.

Downstairs. Phone. 911.

It became a mantra. When she took a step forward, she could feel more blood rush. She couldn't do this. The baby would fall out. Something was happening and it was coming too early. She couldn't move. She needed to stay still.

Ben!

No. Ben was gone. She'd pushed him away.

Think. Downstairs. Phone. 911.

Wadding up the nightgown between her legs, she tried to press them together and walk at the same time. She reached the top of the stairs and stopped. She felt dizzy and wouldn't risk walking down them until she knew she was under some control mentally.

This happened every time you gave blood at the hospital when Ben was getting his chemo treatment. Heck, you get dizzy on day two of your period if you don't drink enough orange juice. There's not that much blood. There's not that much blood.

She could do this. It would be okay. She would get to the hospital and they could put her on bed rest and give her juice and then she would be fine and the baby would be fine.

The sound of the front door slamming startled her.

"This is horseshit! I don't care what you say. I'm not leaving you. I'm never leaving you. We are going to figure this out so you better accept that and— Anna. Oh, my God!"

He came back. She'd pushed him away but then he came back. That was good. Because she really needed him right now.

How silly she'd been. Of course, he wouldn't leave her. Ben would never leave her.

It was the last thing she thought before she fainted.

CHAPTER TWENTY

MARK STOPPED WHEN HE SAW BEN. This wasn't the first time he'd seen Ben covered in the blood of a fallen comrade. But knowing whose blood it was made Mark tremble inside.

The call had been almost undecipherable. Mark had been jarred awake by the sound of a ringing phone. When he answered he was thinking that it might be Sophie on the other end. What if she was hurt? What if she needed him? He'd been unprepared for the hoarse, nearly raspy voice of Ben saying that Anna was in trouble.

Cautiously, Mark approached Ben who was currently bent over, his head in his hands as his elbows rested on his knees.

The closer Mark got the stronger the smell of Anna's blood became.

"Ben."

Ben startled as if he'd been unaware where he was. Or who he was. Or what had happened. He looked at Mark quizzically as if he didn't remember calling him and didn't remember that he'd asked Mark to come because he didn't know who else to call and he needed someone with him. Someone who would understand.

Mark sat next to Ben and thought of a time when they'd lost three operatives and two special forces agents in what was supposed to have been a routine information gathering assignment across the border of Pakistan into Afghanistan. The party had been ambushed. All of them killed. Mark remembered the way Ben had looked then, as if the responsibility of the world sat on his shoulders... and he'd failed to uphold it. That expression was nothing compared to how he appeared now.

Now, in this moment, he looked as though he'd been ambushed. As though he'd been killed.

Mark thought of Anna and tried to contain the sick feeling in his stomach that something was horribly wrong. Ben hadn't been coherent enough to explain the situation. Had only said that she was in danger. When Mark had checked at the admissions desk, they had told him she was still alive. They couldn't give him any details of her condition, but they could give him a status.

Critical.

"Ben, what happened?"

Dazed, Ben leaned back in the chair. "Placenta abruption? I couldn't understand everything they were saying. It was so fast. Her blood pressure was high, they said, and there was a partial separation. It caused her to bleed. She was bleeding so much. They did an emergency C-section."

Mark swallowed. "The baby?"

Ben looked at him, his eyes unfocused. "I haven't named her yet. I want Anna to do it. The doctor said she's small at four and a half pounds, but her lungs are fully formed. She's in the NICU unit now. But I don't want to see her yet. Not until I can see her with Anna."

He seemed defensive about that. The nurses had probably already asked him if he wanted to see his daughter and he'd felt guilty for refusing. Mark understood though. He knew that if Ben saw his daughter without Anna by his side, he would have to acknowledge she was still in danger.

"Okay."

"She was hemorrhaging so much. They said the blood loss caused her to go into shock. But they're replacing it now. Transfusion." He laughed harshly and held out his blood stained arms. "They wouldn't let me give blood. I couldn't even do that."

Mark took a deep breath. "Downstairs they said her status is critical."

"She's in a coma," Ben said, sounding as if he had to push the word out of his mouth. "The shock was too much. She didn't wake up after the general anesthesia wore off. They don't know— They don't know anything at this point."

The sick feeling that had been in Mark's stomach since he received Ben's call turned to dread.

"She'll wake up," Mark said optimistically. She had to. Because he didn't think Ben would survive if she didn't. The man who had always been so calm under pressure, so cool under fire, was, simply put, unhinged. Like he'd lost his grip on the world. Yeah, he sat here, his jeans stiff with blood, but he wasn't really part of the world around him.

"High blood pressure. We were fighting. I caused this. I can't believe we were fighting this close to—"

Mark grabbed his arm. "Don't. You can't start playing the 'what if' game. This happened. The baby survived. Anna will wake up. You'll get through this. You need to stay focused on what is and not on what might have been."

Ben nodded, but Mark could tell his words weren't penetrating.

They sat for a time and the nonaction was killing Mark. He should be doing something. Helping Ben in some way. Calling family…although he knew neither Ben nor Anna had any. Anna was Ben's family. And Ben was hers. This wasn't supposed to happen. Not to them.

"Did you find her parents?"

The question startled Mark out of his thoughts. He thought about the path he'd followed after Marge had told him about the *other* man who had come in inquiring about fake names on a birth certificate. Like Ben had, he was sure, Mark found the records of those who had been admitted for delivery without insurance on the day Anna was born.

A young girl, no more than eighteen years old,

had experienced complications during delivery and had to have an emergency C-section. Because the child had been sent to the NICU and the mother needed additional care the father had been responsible for giving the hospital all the information needed for payment and, of course, the paperwork for the birth certificate.

Not only had those names been fake, but so had the address he'd listed. The only thing he must not have realized is that when the pregnant girl had first been admitted, she had given her real name: Jennifer James.

From there, tracking down Jennifer hadn't been difficult at all. The story Mark eventually found in the papers six years after Anna was born explained why Ben hadn't wanted to tell Anna anything about her parents. Mark had planned to set up a meeting to confront Ben about it. They couldn't hide the truth from Anna. It wasn't fair.

"You should have told her when *you* found out. Why did you go looking anyway?"

Ben cupped his face in his hands as if trying to support the weight of his heavy head with something besides his neck. He sighed and then finally straightened. "I don't know. We'd been working together for a few years. She never mentioned much of her past but I knew she'd been in foster homes. For some reason I wanted the information. You know me, when I get that idea in my head nothing can stop me. I told myself we were working with the government on several contracted projects and, security clearance issues aside, I should have more intelligence on my staff. It made sense."

Mark shook his head, not believing someone so smart could be so obtuse. "Ben, you wanted to know more about her past because you wanted to know more about *her*. You had been falling for her for years, you just wouldn't admit it to yourself."

He made a harsh sound. "*Falling for her.* What a ridiculous phrase. Something so…powerful…to be described with a euphemism a teenager might use. I wasn't *falling for her*. I was…in need of her. That was what I denied myself. That she was different than any other woman I had ever known and I needed her like I needed to breathe. I thought…I thought if I could give her her past it would change something between us. But the story— It was so awful. I didn't want her to know. You saw?"

Mark nodded.

"Then when I got sick I thought if I could give her security, maybe after I was gone she might figure out the one thing I wouldn't admit to myself while I was alive. It gave me a strange sense of peace."

"Why can't you say it?" Mark asked. "Even now, why can't you just say it?"

Ben turned to him and Mark sucked in his breath. The agony pervading Ben's being was tangible. As if it was so real Mark could smell it and hear it and taste it.

"I wasn't supposed to have her or the baby. I wasn't meant for this life. I've always known that. Always. If I say it now...she'll die."

That's when Mark knew that his thoughts when he first entered the hospital were true. If Ben lost Anna, Ben himself was lost.

"YOU CAN STAY with her now if you would like."

The nurse who had brought Ben to Anna's room left quietly. He'd insisted on a private room and saw that there was a lounge chair that would recline next to the bed where, later, he might be able to sleep. A straight-backed chair was situated on the other side of the bed.

Behind her bed he saw the monitor beeping steadily and the tubes inserted into her arm were connected to pouches that would hydrate her. Earlier an orderly had shown him a staff bathroom equipped with showers. Ben was able to wash off and exchanged his blood-soaked clothes for a pair of blue scrubs.

Two floors above him, the nurses in the NICU reported that his daughter was resting comfortably after a good bottle feeding.

Anna had wanted to breast-feed. But that was impossible right now.

Sitting beside the bed he took her hand in his and thought how pale she looked. She didn't like to sleep on her back. It made it uncomfortable with the pressure of the baby on her lower back and bladder.

Only the baby was gone. Out of her body. Strange, because the thin sheet covering her still showed a predominant bump where her stomach was. But he imagined that was partly from the bandages used to cover her incision.

And partly from the amount of ice cream she had consumed while pregnant.

He smiled as he thought it and imagined the scowl she would give him if he'd said that out loud.

Only she wasn't scowling and her face was like he'd never seen it. Not even when she slept was it this…neutral. It was as though she wasn't inside her body. That the light and the energy and the chaos that was her, was suddenly quiet.

Outside the room Ben could hear the buzz of a hospital. Gurneys being rolled down hallways, people having conversations, both work-related and social, trays of bad food being delivered to each room, the carts moving back and forth along linoleum floors.

But in this room with only the two of them and the sound of the beeping monitor above her head, it seemed so incredibly quiet.

He pressed his eyes shut and squeezed her hand, hoping he might feel a tug from her. But there was nothing. It wasn't possible for him to believe that someone who had brought so much energy into his world, who was the reason he'd survived his battle with death, could be so still.

So utterly...lifeless.

"Anna, I've been told by the doctors I should speak to you. They indicate it's possible you'll be able to identify my voice and this will compel you to wake up. I hope you understand how completely foolish this makes me look as you are not, at present, conscious."

He could only imagine how humorous she would find this. Putting him in any situation where she knew he was uncomfortable was a bonus for her.

"I'm sorry I didn't tell you about your parents. It was selfish, I know. I didn't like that there was this part of your life I didn't know about. Back then you seemed to have no desire to learn about it, either. So I took it upon myself and I found them. Your father wanted to give you up for adoption. That's why the names were faked. I suspect he was thinking he would take your mother to the hospital and then just leave. But he screwed up because your mother gave her name to the admitting nurse, so that was on the paperwork. Her name was Jennifer James and she wanted to keep you. If your father had won that battle, there might have been only one family for you. One life."

Although maybe he wouldn't have met her. Maybe her options would have been different and their paths would have never crossed. That was unthinkable.

"They were addicts. You were right about that. I suppose your mother thought she could stay clean after you were born. And maybe she did for periods of time. But by the time you were six, she was using hard again. That's when your father thought to try to give you up for adoption again. He cared about you, Anna. At least enough to know that you shouldn't be raised the way they were doing it. He called social services himself. Sadly, at that point your mother wasn't stable. She attacked him with a kitchen knife and severed an artery in his neck."

Ben knew she couldn't hear him but, still, the telling of it was difficult. He figured this would be good practice for when she woke up and he had to do this again.

"Anna, your mother didn't leave you. That room you remember being left behind in was a police station. Social services came to get you after they took your mother away. She pled guilty to second degree murder and served eighteen years in prison. Your father's name was Frank Kelly."

He stopped then and thought about what those first six years of her life must have been like. Tumultuous certainly. Yet she had such great capacity for giving and loving. It seemed as though she'd never let any of the darkness infect her soul.

Or maybe that wasn't entirely true. Because as much as he knew she loved him, she still didn't trust deep down that he wouldn't leave her.

Now he knew why she so desperately tried to

protect herself with that ridiculous fight. This separation hurt. It was pain like nothing he'd ever known.

"I hope you're pleased with yourself for putting me through this. You made this happen. You made it happen every day we were together and I didn't even know it was happening. Now I want this, Anna. I want our life together with our baby and you won't wake up! Wake the hell up!"

He stood then, too agitated to sit.

"I love you! Is that what you want to hear? I love you. There, I said it. It's the damn truth and I almost hate it because it's making me feel like I want to explode from the inside out because you're lying there on that bed and you won't wake up! Wake up, damn it!"

He was breathing heavily and no doubt he'd soon have the staff down around his head for shouting at a coma patient. But he needed to get through to her. She needed to hear him.

"Also, just so we're clear. When you do wake up, if you think you can kick me out of your house because I didn't tell you about your parents, think again. I'm not going anywhere. I don't know what the hell was going on in that crazy little head of yours, but we'll work it out and we're going to be together. Forever. Are you listening? I love you! I have always freaking loved you!"

Ben waited for her to stir. This was when it happened, right? In the movies this was always the moment. He'd confessed his heart and her eyes would flutter and she would wake up. Then she would realize how much he loved her. She would feel safe and happy. And she would get better and everything would be all right.

Happily ever after.

He must have seen it that way in the movies and television a million times.

Only her eyes didn't flutter and her hand didn't move. The monitor continued to beep behind the bed and he was still lost without her.

Sitting in the chair he took her hand in both of his and rested his head on the bed. For the first time in his life he wept openly.

This is why I avoided love for so long. This is true sadness.

IT FELT LIKE being underwater. Anna, however, couldn't fathom why she would be underwater. Now certainly wasn't the time to go swimming. Her doctor warned her about her cervix dilating and the chlorine not being good for the baby.

Swimming was out. Had she fallen in the bathtub? Is that why moving seemed like such a struggle?

Wake up, she told herself. She was having a bad dream and she needed to wake up. But it felt like one of those dreams where even when you woke up, somehow you were still in another dream. Eventually if she kept pushing, she would get there. There had to be an end to all this dreaming somewhere.

Forcing her eyes open, Anna blinked and looked at the room around her. She wasn't in a bathtub. She wasn't in her room, either. Her bedroom with the pretty mint-green duvet she and Ben had picked out together.

No, the duvet wasn't pretty anymore. She knew that but couldn't remember why.

The steady beep behind her was annoying. Was it the alarm clock going off? She tried to lift her hand so she could turn it off, but her arm had suddenly gained a hundred pounds overnight.

Her whole body felt heavy and dull.

Because she was pregnant, she reminded herself.

No. Not pregnant anymore. A scene whipped through her memory. Ben holding her, screaming for someone to help. People in blue masks above her, running alongside the gurney she was on. Pushing her through doors, and then a clear mask descended on her face and everything after was a blur.

Until now.

Her baby. Where the hell was her baby? The beep behind her head was speeding up and Anna forced herself to move even though she felt a tight pain across her lower body. She needed help. She needed Ben. She'd lost her baby. He needed to help her find it.

Her mouth was dry and she tried to swallow. He would come. Ben wouldn't leave her. Ben would never leave her. Even when she had thrown him out... Why had she done that?

Because she was scared. Too scared of what she felt for him.

But even when she'd done that he had come back. He wasn't going to leave her. He'd said that, hadn't he? He meant it. Ben always meant what he said.

"Ben." It came out as a whisper. She needed to be louder. Her baby was missing and she had to get it. "Ben. Ben. Ben!"

The sound of something shifting along the floor had her turning her head. Ben was in the lounge chair. Sleeping. How could he be sleeping when their baby was missing?

"Ben!"

He was wearing scrubs but the sound of her voice jerked him awake.

She watched him bow his head. "Thank you, God. Thank you."

Now he was praying? This wasn't the time. She needed him and it was really starting to piss her off that he wasn't paying attention. "Where is it? Where..."

Instantly he was by her side taking her hand. "Anna, calm down. You're awake. You did it. I knew you would do it. Let me go get the doctor—"

"No! Where is it? Where is it?"

"It?" For a second, it was as if he couldn't understand her. Was she making sense? Was she saying the right words? Then a smile broke out on his face and again she thought it was completely inappropriate to be smiling when their baby was missing. "Not *it* anymore. *She.* She is sleeping upstairs. She has already gained five ounces in two days. Apparently she has your appetite."

She. Her baby girl. "Want her."

"Yeah. I'll make that happen. You rest and I'll get the doctor. Then I'll introduce you to your daughter. After that we're going to name her. Finally. *Baby girl* just isn't cutting it anymore."

Weariness was pulling against her, but she fought it. She wouldn't sleep until she saw her baby.

The delay was agonizing. First, the doctors came and flashed lights in her eyes. They pestered her with questions, which, fortunately, she seemed to have all the right answers to.

The words *C-section* and *abruption* and *coma* penetrated her brain, but she didn't want to think about what they meant for her. She only wanted to see her baby. They told her she'd been asleep for two days. Two days! What kind of mother was she that she left her daughter alone for two days?

But she hadn't been alone. She had Ben. Ben wouldn't leave her or their daughter. Anna got that now. There was nothing to be afraid of anymore.

An hour later she was actually sitting up in bed, although her stitches burned across her middle. When she asked to pee the nurse helped her out of bed and told her to walk bent over until she felt more comfortable. The way Anna felt right now, that would be for life.

Slowly, cautiously, she made it back into the bed. After a few bites of gelatin and some sips of orange juice, she felt nearly human. Certainly ready to see her baby.

The door to the room swung open and the sight of the tiny bundle in Ben's strong arms had her weeping immediately.

"Don't be alarmed, baby girl. But you should know in advance your mother is a crier."

Anna could only cry harder. Then Ben was placing her daughter in her arms and the world condensed to only Ben and her baby. "She's so tiny."

"A bit early on arrival, but making up ground. It means she's scrappy."

Anna pulled the blanket back and counted fingers and toes and touched lips and ears, taking in every inch of her little girl as she slept peacefully, only twitching her lips every so often as if she was dreaming about eating.

"So what's it going to be? We need a name. Don't tell me Gertrude because, even knowing what you went through, I still won't cave on that."

A name floated through her mind. Like coming from a dream she'd once had.

"Kelly. I think we should name her Kelly."

"Kelly Summers-Tyler. I like it."

"No," Anna said, even as she brushed a finger against her delicate cheek. "Just Kelly Tyler."

His silence spoke volumes. Anna tore her eyes away from her daughter and saw his deep blue eyes looking at her, wondering.

"Don't ask me today. I'm not ready. I have to do something first. But I promise you, Ben, I'll let you know when I am."

"Okay."

"But I was thinking…it wouldn't be the worst thing in the world if you moved in with us. I mean, I can already see you like her. You'll probably be hanging around all the time anyway. As long as you agree to put your beige man couch in the basement."

"My own man cave with my own man couch. Who could ask for anything more?"

Ben sat on the bed with her, careful not to jostle her or the baby. He put his lips to her shoulder and for a time they simply stared at the miracle they had made together.

Just like any family would.

CHAPTER TWENTY-ONE

"Isn't she cute?" Mark showed his daughter a picture of the recently named Kelly Tyler. Ben had sent him an updated picture. His fifth in, like, three days. The man was clearly baby crazy. At five pounds, two ounces and growing daily, it was decided she could be released from the hospital. Ben and Anna were taking her home today.

Mark had the inspiration that maybe he could break through Sophie's freeze-out with a cute little baby girl. It had worked to an extent. He could see she'd loved picking out pink little dresses and Onesies and all kinds of different baby rattles at the baby store he'd taken her to.

Not that she was actually talking to him, but she wasn't scowling or swearing at him, either, and he figured that was progress. Even now he could see her trying to suppress the need to make cooing noises—because that's what everyone did when they saw pictures of Kelly—just because he was sitting across from her and she didn't want to give him the satisfaction of knowing he'd done something that actually pleased her.

"Look, Sophie, if we're going to get through this, we're going to need to talk."

"I'm here, aren't I?"

Here in body, true. After shopping, he'd taken her to one of his favorite pizza places and they had ordered a couple of slices and some sodas. The plan was to take all the stuff they'd bought to Anna and Ben's place so that Sophie would get to actually squee over Kelly.

That's right. He wasn't opposed to using his friend's child to score points with his intractable daughter.

"Your grandparents said you guys had a long talk."

She lifted a shoulder. "We did."

"You see what kind of shape they are in. You're a highly intelligent girl—you know they can't continue to stay in that house."

"I know it," she said. He knew what the admission cost her. There was no point to rubbing it in. The girl had lost her mother so he didn't need to point out how sickly her grandparents were, too. The fact that she knew she couldn't stay with them in the house was even more progress. Now, he needed her to come around to the alternative.

"I get why this stinks for you. I really do. But I'm not the worst guy in the world. If you're honest with yourself, you can acknowledge at least that. I blew it as a dad. I sent cards and gifts and money instead of being there in person because I was off fighting a war for our country—"

"Oh, please. Don't make it out like you were drafted or something. Mom told me that's why you didn't want to get married. Because you wanted to be some superspy guy like James Bond."

"James Bond is a fictional character. What I did was real. But you're right. I wanted that life."

Mark had to own that. Honesty was the only policy in this case. He couldn't get tripped up in any kind of lie without pushing her away even more. The truth was he had no idea what Helen had told Sophie about him and their decision not to get married. He could only tell Sophie what he knew, without, of course, letting her know what her mom had done to get pregnant.

"You wanted to leave."

"No, that's not fair. From the time I could remember, I knew I wanted to be a CIA agent. But when I found out your mom was pregnant I was willing to let it go for you. Did she tell you that? As soon as we knew about you, I proposed."

Sophie nodded. Then started to shred the paper napkin she was holding. "She said she would have made you miserable. That you would have made each other miserable because she would know the whole time that you had sacrificed your ambition for her. She said you would have resented her and then she would have resented you because she would know we weren't enough for you."

Maybe a little too much information for a teenage girl to know about her father. But it was true, and he had to own that, too. "My whole life I wanted this one thing. Then you came along and I knew I had to let it go. And, truly, I didn't want to leave you. I didn't know what being a dad would be like but part of me was excited. That's the truth. But your mom wasn't wrong. Sometimes I think she knew me better than myself."

"She was really intuitive."

"Yes, she was." Mark thought it was good to hear Sophie talk about Helen. Sophie hadn't done enough of that around him. Probably because she didn't talk much at all around him. "I would like to think I would never have resented my choice. I did love your mom back then. I *know* I wouldn't have resented you. You were totally innocent. But maybe your mom saw something in me that made her think I wasn't the best bet as a father. While that still might be true, I'm the only one you have."

"I don't even, like, know you."

Mark nodded. Again he was pleased. For the first time he actually thought they were communicating. She was talking and, more importantly, she was listening. "Then we get to know each other. You move in with me and we move your grandparents into that assisted living place that's better for them. You'll still see them as much as you want. They're not going anywhere. Certainly not your grandfather, he walks like a snail."

There it was. For one brief second the corner of her lip curled up. The semblance of a smile. Then it was gone.

"It's, like, everything is changing so fast." Her eyes filled with tears.

He reached out to take her wrist. She kept her hand in a fist, balled around another napkin, but she didn't try to pull away. "It is, kid. Because of a stupid freak accident your mom, who should be here, is gone. Your grandparents should have stayed the same forever, but they can't stop age. And I should be in a camp somewhere in southeast Afghanistan, but I'm here."

"Do you miss it?"

"No." This he could tell her truthfully. "I enjoyed working for the government but my time there was done. I was ready for this. I was coming home, Sophie. To you. No matter what."

She seemed to take all that in. Then she tugged her hand away so she could nibble at the tips of her fingernails.

"So…did you, like, kill people and stuff?"

"Classified."

"Did you know where Osama Bin Laden was hiding?"

"Classified."

"Can you tell me anything?"

"George Bush is shorter in person."

"That blows."

No, he thought. It didn't blow at all. In fact, it

had been their first real conversation. "How about another slice? Then we can take all this stuff to the baby who, you know, won't really care about any of it."

"YOU'RE DOING IT WRONG."

"I'm doing it fine."

"It's not snug enough. It's going to fall off."

Mark and Sophie had left an hour ago, and Anna and Ben were getting ready to settle their child, and themselves, down for the night.

Ben looked at his baby girl who was squalling her head off in irritation over being exposed to the cool air as he replaced her diaper. Anna kept making him undo the sticky plastic tab and pull it in even farther across her tiny little body before reattaching it.

"I'm going to cut off her circulation."

"Let me."

He pushed her away with one arm, careful not to jostle her. She was still slightly bent over from where her cesarean stitches pulled on her stomach.

"I will master this. I will not be defeated by the diaper." So declaring it, he finished the task and handed Kelly over to her mother.

Both mother and daughter instantly sighed with contentment.

Anna took the couch and kept their daughter cradled in the nook of her elbow. She was still so tiny, but the doctors had no concerns and, based on her ability to screech to the high heavens when she wasn't one hundred percent happy, Ben knew there was no problem with her lungs.

He sat across from them and thought, for the first time, how tired he was. He hadn't slept much since he'd come back into the house to find Anna bleeding at the top of the stairs. His body, which at its best was still only eighty percent recovered, was letting him know he'd gone as far as he could go. He leaned his head against the recliner.

He'd been able to pick limited pieces of furniture from his home to move here and that one, as agreed, was relegated to the basement. Everything else he planned to sell. He was hoping the potential buyer for the house might want it fully furnished.

"You should go upstairs and get some sleep. We're going to chill down here."

"I'll sleep down here with you."

No stairs was a condition of her release, so she'd been sleeping on the couch with Kelly in the bassinet next to her. Ben figured the recliner would be fine for another few nights.

"Ben, you've been pushing yourself now for days. I don't want you to get sick. It could lead to a setback. Go to bed and we'll be here when you wake up."

He opened one eye because he didn't have the energy to open both. "I'll stay here with you."

He could hear her chuckle. "So, is that the plan? You're never going to leave me alone ever again."

"That's my current working plan, yes. But to clarify, I'm never leaving the two of you alone... ever."

"Kelly, your daddy is a nutcase."

"Kelly," he murmured. "Your mommy almost died and made Daddy a nutcase."

He'd meant it as joke, but not really. He didn't think he would ever forget how it felt in those moments when he was holding her and feeling the damp heat of her blood soak through his clothing. Knowing that their life forces were fundamentally comingled. Did she know? Did she know, even a little bit, how he felt?

He imagined it wasn't fair that she'd been conscious for his confession when he'd been his most vulnerable with her. Of course, he'd told her again what he knew about her parents and when he'd found out. She'd listened and she'd cried. But the anger she'd felt toward him for keeping it a secret was clearly gone. He wanted to ask her why it had meant so much to her on the night they fought but didn't seem to matter to her now.

That fight had nearly cost him everything.

He'd never told her the other stuff he said. About loving her. How much easier would it be to think that she had somehow heard everything and took it all inside? That she just knew what was in his head and his heart?

"Ben?"

"Hmm."

"Do you know where she is?"

"Who?"

"My mother."

He lifted his head and met her gaze. "I do."

"I think I want to go see her."

"Really? Even knowing what you know?"

"She was an addict. An addict who wanted to keep her addiction and her daughter. My father was an addict, too. In his own way he still wanted to try to do right by me. Yes, they both shit the bed when it came to being parents, but I can't claim that they didn't care about me. Didn't love me. Each in their own mixed-up way."

"This is important to you?"

Anna glanced at the baby, the smile she wore practically making her glow from the inside. The light and energy that was Anna was back and even brighter than before. "Yes. I think...I think I need that last piece. Then it will all make sense."

"Okay. In a few weeks when you're up for it, I'll take you to her. She works at a snack shop in one of the Big Foods stores."

"She's clean?"

"Yes. She served fifteen of her eighteen-year sentence. Got sober in prison and was able to get the job through a charitable organization that finds jobs for the formerly incarcerated."

Her eyes narrowed. "And you knew all of this for years?"

"I did."

"Why didn't you tell me?"

Ben thought of the easy answer, that he hadn't wanted to tell her something so awful about her past. But there was more. "I was afraid. I thought if I told you what I had done—looking for them in the first place, even though you never asked me to—that you would know."

"Know what?"

He took a deep breath. The crazy thing was he actually found himself wanting to say it out loud. He didn't want her to just know it. He wanted to say it and know that she heard it. Awake this time.

"That I was obsessed with you. That I thought about you all the time. That I needed every piece of you. Your work, your life, your past and your present. In my head I couldn't reason why, but now it all makes so much sense. I didn't know what love was and yet it was right there. The whole time. Staring me in the face. That boyfriend you thought you dumped five years ago... What was his name? The one who had the nerve to borrow money from me for your date?"

"You mean Kevin?"

"He was going to dump you first. Because I arranged it. I told him if he ever even so much as looked at you again, bad things would happen to him and he could be assured of that because of my background in black ops. At the time I told myself I was only doing it for your own good. He wasn't nearly good enough for you and I was simply helping out a friend who was mixed up with the wrong person."

"Like I said, baby girl. Daddy is a nutcase."

Ben could see she was smiling as she said that. Another fight avoided then. "I told myself a lot of things when it came to you. But the truth is I was lying. Lying about everything. There were times I told myself I hated you for turning me into this irrational creature. I would think about letting you go, cutting all ties so I could go back to my normal life. Then I would laugh at myself because I knew it would never happen. I would never let you go."

He watched as she literally had to work to close her jaw. Then he saw the confusion in her expression and he knew what her next question would be before she asked it. So he gave her the answer.

"I shut you down after we made love that first time because I wasn't prepared to deal with any of those emotions, Anna. Hell, I haven't been dealing with them very well these past nine months or else I would have told you I loved you as soon as I saw you again. I know it's crazy, but that's where my head was then. I had lost control over you, and I was losing control over my body and the two things happening at the same time…messed with my reasoning. It's my only explanation and I know it's not a very good one."

"It's a pretty good one."

"Do you forgive me? For that and your parents? When I learned what happened to them I told myself it was better that you didn't know. Then when you asked me to find them I thought learning about them while you were pregnant wasn't a good idea. I was going to tell you. Eventually. I just wanted to pick a better time. Namely, after you were married to me."

"I should be furious," she said.

She didn't look angry. "You *were* furious. You kicked me out of your home. Remember?"

Anna smiled, then got up and settled the soundly sleeping baby in the bassinet. Slowly she walked over to where he sat and he made room for her on his lap. Gingerly, she settled into his arms and he was careful not to touch her stomach.

"I made up that fight," she whispered, her head against his shoulder, probably so she didn't have to look at him.

"Really?"

"I was scared. I was scared of how I felt about you and I couldn't deal with it. I wanted what you were offering so much. A real family. But it seemed like too much to want. I was afraid that it would end up breaking me apart if anything bad happened. So I used the whole bit about you not telling me your secret as the perfect out. I mean, who wouldn't be furious over something like that? But it wasn't my real reason. Since we're being honest here, I figure it's time to confess. Not going to lie. It was sort of mean of me."

"Although effective," he drawled.

"You *shouldn't* have kept that information from me. That still stands. But it wasn't the reason I told you to go."

"Why are you so scared?"

"Because I didn't think anyone would ever love me. Which is baggage I didn't even know I had. I loved you so much that it completely freaked me out."

"I love you."

She lifted her head and kissed his chin. "Really? Truly?"

"Madly. Deeply."

"I don't know," she said, settling her head back against his shoulder. "If a man really loves a woman who, oh, by the way, happens to be the mother of his only child, you would think he might propose marriage."

Ben could feel his blood pressure elevate until he felt more than heard her laughing against his body. Nothing she loved better than to ruffle him. She would spend the rest of her life trying to do that, and he would love that, too.

"Anna?"

"Yes, Ben."

"Will you do me the great honor of becoming my wife?"

"Geesh. You just moved in with me and already we're talking about marriage?"

"Anna?"

"Yes, Ben."

"You are not funny."

This time he heard her laugh. "Okay. Because I love you. And because you obviously have plans to never leave my side again, I guess I will marry you."

"Hmm."

"Are you falling asleep after we've just declared our love?"

He was. It felt so good, too. As though he'd never truly known what it was to sleep as a man completely satisfied with his life. "Anna. I can feel it now. I'm finally cured."

She brushed his neck with her lips. "Me, too."

EPILOGUE

THE MEETING HAD been arranged. Ben made the call to Jennifer, explained who he was and asked if she would be interested in meeting with her daughter. Anna had listened to the conversation over the speaker phone and, in the silence between when Ben had finally asked if she would like to meet her daughter and Jennifer's answer, Anna thought her heart was going to burst.

Then Jennifer, in a shaky voice clearly filled with emotion, had asked if Anna knew what she'd done.

Ben explained that Anna was aware of the circumstances of her incarceration and that she still wanted to meet. In the interest of keeping the visit short and giving Anna an easy out if she felt she needed it, Ben had suggested they meet at the coffee shop next to the Big Foods store where Jennifer worked. This would define the boundaries of the encounter, ensuring it would last no longer than half an hour, which was the length of Jennifer's lunch break.

Now Anna sat in the coffee shop, Kelly asleep

in her stroller beside her, wondering if she hadn't made a mistake. There was no reason Anna needed to meet this woman. Their family tie had been broken years ago. Given what she'd done to her father, Anna had every reason to go the rest of her life without ever acknowledging the woman who gave birth to her.

"Calm down."

Ben placed two cups of steaming tea on the small table. Winter had hit the East Coast full force this past weekend. Not only was the ground covered with a couple inches of snow, but it also felt as though the temperature had dropped again.

"I shouldn't have brought the baby out. It's too cold. What if it starts snowing? We shouldn't be on the road. We should have rescheduled."

Ben pointed to the sleeping child. "She's wearing fifteen layers of clothing. She would be comfortably warm in the Arctic right now. There is no prediction for snow in the forecast. You're only nervous."

"I'm not nervous," Anna lied, even as her leg jiggled under the table. "I mean, she's probably more nervous to see me than I am her, right? Do you think I'll remember what she looks like?"

"I don't know. Six is young, but maybe not too young."

"Right."

The door to the shop opened, but a man walked in rubbing his hands as if to reinforce Anna's concern that she'd brought her seven-week-old baby out in horrible, freezing conditions. Was this an indication she was a bad mother?

"Do you want me to distract you?"

That probably wouldn't happen, but she liked that he made the offer. "Go for it."

"I've decided it's time for us to consummate our marriage."

That did get her attention. As soon as she'd agreed to his proposal he hadn't wasted any time. Two days later he arranged for a civil ceremony at their home. Having connections helped and Ben had connections everywhere. The mayor of Philadelphia had officiated, with Mark and Greg from the office in attendance. Sophie had also come and offered to hold the baby for the duration of the ceremony. Since it had lasted only ten minutes, the girl had been a little put out. The one thing that seemed to break her out of her perpetually bad mood was Kelly. Mark offered her services as a baby sitter any time Ben and Anna needed her. For his own selfish reasons, he admitted.

So while Ben and Anna had been married now for nearly seven weeks, sex hadn't been an option. Anna was still healing from the C-section. And beyond that, not getting more than two hours of sleep at any given stretch during the night had put a damper on both their sex drives.

It was scary how easily they fell into the routine of living together. Anna remembered at one point thinking that she wasn't cut out for a real relationship, but the reality of living in one hadn't proven to be a challenge at all.

Ben was doing only half days at the office and spending the rest of his time with her and Kelly. They traded off feedings and did their best to let the other get as much prolonged sleep as they could. But their child's lungs were overdeveloped and trying to sleep through her cries when she was in full throttle hungry mode was nearly impossible.

They laughed at their baby bungles. They were in awe of every tiny milestone. Today's had been Kelly pushing her tongue out through her little mouth.

And they loved each other.

"Of course, I mean only if you're up for it. Physically. But you said the doctor gave you the all-clear."

"She did."

"Then I think we need to make it happen. I refuse to be one of those hapless couples who never have sex again because the baby has them up all day and night."

"But we are that hapless couple."

"We can work in ten minutes."

"Ten minutes?" she asked with a wry smile. "You think you can deliver in ten minutes?"

"As hard up as I am, I can deliver in five."

"Deal."

Ben leaned forward and cemented their bargain

with a kiss that promised of things to come that night.

The door to the shop opened again, and this time a woman bundled in a cheap but serviceable winter coat walked in. She wore a hairnet over hair that Anna could see was a dark reddish color.

Instantly Anna stood, and Jennifer, because it had to be her, walked over to greet her.

Yes, Anna thought. *I do recognize her a little.*

"Anna?"

"Yes. Jennifer James?"

The woman placed her gloved hands over her mouth and sobbed. "Yes."

"Jennifer, I would like you to meet my family. This is my husband, Ben, and my baby girl. I named her…Kelly. A family name."

* * * * *

LARGER-PRINT BOOKS!
GET 2 FREE LARGER-PRINT NOVELS PLUS
2 FREE GIFTS!

HARLEQUIN

super romance

Exciting, emotional, unexpected!

ReaderService.com

Manage your account online!
- Review your order history
- Manage your payments
- Update your address

*We've designed
the Harlequin® Reader Service
website just for you.*

Enjoy all the features!
- Reader excerpts from any series
- Respond to mailings and
  special monthly offers
- Discover new series available to you
- Browse the Bonus Bucks catalog
- Share your feedback

Visit us at:
ReaderService.com

RS13